William Peter Blatty, the writer of numerous novels and screenplays, is best known for his internationally bestselling novel *The Exorcist*, deemed by the *New York Times Book Review* to be 'as superior to most books of its kind as an Einstein equation is to an accountant's column of figures'. An Academy Award winner for his screenplay for *The Exorcist*, Blatty is not only the author of one of the most terrifying novels ever written, but, paradoxically, also co-wrote the screenplay for the hilarious Inspector Clouseau film, *A Shot in the Dark*. *New York Times* reviewers of his early comic novels noted, 'Nobody can write funnier lines than William Peter Blatty', describing him as 'a gifted virtuoso who writes like S. J. Perelman.' Blatty lives with his wife and a son in Maryland.

ESSEX CO LIBR
30

D0318688

Also by William Peter Blatty

Which Way to Mecca, Jack?
John Goldfarb, Please Come Home!
Twinkle, Twinkle "Killer" Kane
I, Billy Shakespeare
The Exorcist
I'll Tell Them I Remember You
The Ninth Configuration
Legion
Demons Five, Exorcists Nothing
Elsewhere

THE REDEMPTION

WILLIAM PETER BLATTY

piatkus

PIATKUS

First published in the US as *Dimiter* in 2010 by Forge
First published in Great Britain in 2011 by Piatkus

Copyright © 2010 by William Peter Blatty

The moral right of the author has been asserted.

*All characters and events in this publication, other than those
clearly in the public domain, are fictitious and any resemblance
to real persons, living or dead, is purely coincidental.*

All rights reserved
No part of this publication may be reproduced, stored in a
retrieval system, or transmitted in any form or by any means, without
the prior permission in writing of the publisher, nor be otherwise circulated
in any form of binding or cover other than that in which it is published
and without a similar condition including this condition
being imposed on the subsequent purchaser.

A CIP catalogue record for this book
is available from the British Library.

ISBN 978-0-7499-5373-7

Printed and bound in Great Britain by
Clays Ltd, St Ives plc

Papers used by Piatkus are natural, renewable and
recyclable products sourced from well-managed forests and certified
in accordance with the rules of the Forest Stewardship Council.

Mixed Sources
Product group from well-managed
forests and other controlled sources
www.fsc.org Cert no. SGS-COC-004081
© 1996 Forest Stewardship Council

Piatkus
An imprint of
Little, Brown Book Group
100 Victoria Embankment
London EC4Y 0DY

An Hachette UK Company
www.hachette.co.uk

www.piatkus.co.uk

IN MEMORY OF PETE

PART ONE

ALBANIA

1973

On his way to Damascus . . . suddenly a light from the sky flashed around him . . . And for three days he could not see . . .

Acts 9:9

Ninety three million miles from the sun, in the damp of a windowless concrete room in a maze of other rooms and cells and passageways where grace and hope had never touched, the Interrogator sat behind a tight wooden table with a mind gone blank as the notepad before him. The Prisoner radiated mystery. After seven days of torture he had yet to utter a word. Silent, his head bowed down, hands manacled, he stood beneath the blinding grip of the spotlight in the middle of the room like a barrier to comfort.

"Who are you?"

The Interrogator's voice was straw. All the questions had been asked. None had been answered. Now they all had worn away to this single probe as if locked within the Prisoner's name were his nature.

"Who are you?"

Drained, the Interrogator waited, squinting at the sweat-blurred lines on the pad. In the hush of the chamber he could hear his own breathing and the desultory faint sharp clicks of his pen point tapping at the table's stained dark oak. For a moment his ears twitched up minutely, straining toward a sound heard dimly through the walls: the scuffing of shoes, a body being dragged. He could not tell if the sounds were real or imagined. Here even the dust in the air was heard shrieking. Another odd sound intruded. What was it? The Interrogator rested his pen on the table and lifted a haunted gaze to the Prisoner, silent and motionless yet so vivid that he seemed a disturbance embedded in time. Drops of blood were falling softly to the mottled stone floor from the ends of his fingers, now one, now another, where the nails had been wrenched from their sockets.

The Interrogator shifted his weight uneasily.

He looked down at the quiet pen.

"Who are you?"

The silence held its breath.

The Interrogator's thumb probed under his spectacles, dislodging them a little as he rubbed at the corner of a watery eye. He carefully removed them and polished each small, round gold-rimmed lens with a frayed and faded white cotton handkerchief that faintly smelled of naphtha. Finished, he fitted the glasses back on with slender hands the color of parchment, then nodded a command to a burly torturer.

"Go ahead," he quietly ordered.

The torturer moved to the light, where he paused, gently patted the Prisoner's cheek, then suddenly delivered a thudding blow to the Prisoner's groin with a rubber truncheon. The Prisoner absorbed it, sinking to his knees but emitting no sound. The Interrogator's fingertips touched at a scar that bisected his pale thin lips like a snarl, and under the collar of his olive drab coverall that bore no sign of rank, his neck felt strangely warm and taut. Against all reason the Prisoner frightened him. Like the dark and heavy stars that show no color to the far observer, he blazed with a terrifying inner light.

They had come upon him by chance. On a Sunday, 25 September, near the northern mountain village of Spac, a force of police, trained dogs, and militia had been hunting a suspect in the attempted assassination of Chief of Security Mehmet Shehu. Shots had been fired by unseen marksmen as Shehu, in the city on a tour of inspection, departed from Security Police Headquarters, then housed in the ancient brownstone prison in that section of Shkoder called Rusi i Madh. One man was caught, a peasant from Domni who, under torture, finally implicated a second man from his village, a clothing merchant named Qazim Beg, who was believed to be escaping to Yugoslavia. Hunting parties sped to the routes considered the likely paths of flight: to the west, the mud-brown River Buna and, north, the so-called Shepherd's Pass, a high coil at the crests of the Dukajini

Mountains. Though swollen by unexpected rains, the Buna's roiling, buffeting waters could be crossed at the narrowest pinch of its waist, slightly more than two hundred yards; but because it was known to so few Albanians and was close to the suspect's village, the Pass drew the larger force of searchers, fifty-eight armed volunteers and three dogs. Their climb was daunting, a robber of breath that spiraled through sandstone, marl, and shale to freezing heights of desolation: these were "The Ranges of the Damned." But at the Pass the hunting force found no one and began a return that would have been without incident except for a curl of fate that would later be seen as first contact with the Prisoner. One of the dogs, a ferocious mastiff of enormous muscle and bulk, had been loosed toward a crackling sound in a wood and was later discovered lying still amid gold and orange leaves on the forest floor in autumnal light as if fallen asleep and turned away from all yearning. Its neck had been broken. The leader of the force, a young smith named Rako Bey, felt a shadow pass over him at the sight, for he could not grasp the power of a human capable of killing the dog in this way. His breath a white fire on the darkening air, he scanned the wood with narrowed eyes, sifting hawthorn and hazel in search of his fate and seeing nothing but the cloud that is before men's eyes. The sun was descending. The forest was haunted. Bare branches were icy threats, evil thoughts. Bey thought of his mother. He slung his rifle over his shoulder and urged the force on and away from this place toward a secondary mission in Quelleza: the capture of a murderer, a village baker, and while this objective was not to be gained, at the end of a labyrinthine path another would, for their search would lead the hunting force to the Prisoner, who was a book that had been lovingly written for the Interrogator by Fate.

The hunt for the baker promised danger. The murderer's kin were mountain clansmen and likely to resist the attempted arrest, for the murder, after all, had been part of a blood feud whose tangles were myriad and numbing to the mind. A husband, a reticent man from Micoi, had dragged his unfaithful wife from their house in accordance with the *bessa*, the unwritten code that forbade any vengeful act indoors, and in sunlight he had shot her once in the head. Then the silver bullet in her quiet brain had been given to the husband by the victim's brother as a token that the deed had his prior consent. There it all might have ended. But the woman's lover, in a crime of passion, berserk, found the husband at home and killed him. Because the wife's lover was a rival clansman, the husband's brother, the farmer, took revenge. He, in turn, was sought out by the father of the dead lover, whom he foiled by refusing to venture out of doors from the house where he lived with his wife and one child, a rosy-cheeked, brindle-eyed two-year-old boy, and thus was confident the *bessa* would protect him from harm. Thus, for weeks nothing happened while the farmer and his mounting fear roamed the house like nervous ghosts, one's soft set of footfalls imaging the other's. Strange rappings were heard on those edgy nights, and the farmer and his fear, grown familiar from their lengthy confinement together, were at times heard conversing in quiet tones, and once a hearty laugh rang out between them. Then, on a night when the stars were lost, the farmer bolted from a fitful sleep, awakened by cries from a goat of his herd. It bleated repeatedly, as if injured. Cocking an ear, the farmer listened, confirming that his fear was soundly asleep as its whistling snores rattled dryly through the house, and so he irritably arose from his muttering bed, fumbled into his lamb's wool jacket and trousers, and then sleepily wandered out into the blackness to see to his goat. So are good deeds not always rewarded. He climbed the first mound of a steep double rise jutting up between the house and the urgent bleating, unaware of the trap that had been cunningly set for him by the father of the lover. The avenger, a mild-eyed baker named Grodd, lay hidden in back of the second rise firmly clutching the goat by a leg while repeatedly twisting the animal's ear. But then misfortune struck, things collapsed, for perhaps due to drowsiness or distraction, or a root or a rock where there should have been none, when the farmer had achieved the craggy peak of the first of the hillocks on his way to the goat he lost his footing and was suddenly plunging through space toward the base of the far ravine below. "I am falling," he dismally reflected, and then he murmured aloud, "This should not be," for his behavior all his life had been exemplary, though this record was now in some peril as he muttered clichés about life's caprices, but this looming blot on his reputation was timely avoided when he ended his fall with a definitive emphasis as his head struck a sharp-edged rock. Grodd heard the sickening crack of bone and soon after was shaken by the realization that his quarry might die by other than his hand. When he'd grasped the full horror of the situation; when he stood beside the farmer and then knelt and felt the gouts, the bold gushings of blood, the baker groaned and decried the unfairness of it all. Did he not wear a charm to ward off the evil eye? Had he not with his finger traced a sign of the cross into every loaf of bread he had ever baked? How had the demons taken charge of this night?

Grodd carried the farmer into his home, roused his wife, and then ran to the nearby village where he wakened the doctor and then rushed him back to the house. But it came to no use, the old doctor told him after assessing the nature of the wound, for complex surgery was needed, and quickly, or the farmer would be dead in a matter of hours.

"It's subdural hematoma," the doctor explained.

"It is *demons*!" cried the baker, distraught.

The wife hastily blessed herself.

The old doctor shrugged and left.

With the anguished Grodd breathing curses by his bed, the fallen farmer, still unconscious, very soon contracted a fever, slipped into pneumonia, and within three days was visibly dead.

Inconsolable, Grodd burst into tears.

"It was the demons who killed him!" he shouted at one point.

"Yes, it was only the *appearance* of pneumonia," agreed the wife.

After that no one cared to say anything at all.

The code of the *bessa* could not be satisfied except by the killing of a male. And so one year after the death of the farmer, when wariness and vigilance had relaxed, Grodd the baker returned to the farmer's house where he happened to come upon his two-year-old son as he played alone in a dreamy field, and there, amid the sun-washed, breeze-blown poppies that were bluer and more vivid than Bengal light; among the hazel and cherry trees and the dogwood, the mustard and the parsley and the brabble of larks and the swaying, star-flung Michaelmas daisy petals as white as the Arctic fox, Grodd watched as the boy chased a black-winged butterfly, listened to a cowbell's tinkle in the distance, remembered his youth, heard the little boy laugh, took a breath, and then shot him between his brindled eyes. It was Grodd that the hunting force had been searching for when they happened upon the Prisoner.

Some thought it was not by chance.

FROM THE DE-BRIEFING OF RAKO BEY, LEADER OF THE VOLUNTEER FORCE TO QUELLEZA, TAKEN 10 OCTOBER

Q. And what led you to the house in the first place?
A. Nothing, sir. Grodd was related to the blind man who lived there, but then he is related to most of the village. Nothing led us there, Colonel. It was fate.
Q. Maintain propriety.
A. Sorry, sir.
Q. Our fate is in our hands.
A. Yes, exactly.

Q. About the house, then . . .

A. Oh, it was just another house outside the village. We surrounded it a little after sundown. It was cold. We broke in and found the blind man inside. And the other one.

Q. The other one?

A. Yes. We found the blind man sitting by the fire. The other was at the table. There was food set out, a lot of it: cabbage, bread, cheese, lamb and eggs, onions, some grapes. When I saw the lamb and eggs I knew the other one had to be a guest, an outsider, so I kept my gun leveled at him. He could have been Grodd. Though I was doubtful.

Q. Why?

A. Because Grodd was supposedly blue-eyed and slender.

Q. I don't understand.

A. Well, he didn't fit Grodd's description.

Q. You didn't see the Prisoner as blue-eyed and slender?

A. No, of course not. He is dark-eyed and stocky, a brute. Why are you staring like that?

Q. Never mind. Did the Prisoner resist?

A. No, he didn't.

Q. He did nothing?

A. No, his head was down, he didn't move. He had a small woolen blanket on his lap and his hands were out of view underneath it.

Q. Did he speak to you?

A. No. The blind man did all the talking. He asked us who we were and what was happening. I told him. I demanded their identity cards. But when the oldster stood up I saw his blindness and I told him, "Never mind, Grandfather. Sit." The other fellow dug for his card in his pocket, and then he handed it over and I checked it. It said that his name was Selca Decani and that he was a seller of feta cheese from Theti. But I think he was more than that.

Q. How?

A. I don't know. I can't explain it.

Q. I am handing you the Prisoner's identity card. Did you scrutinize it carefully?

A. Well, no. I mean, he obviously wasn't Grodd so I just glanced at some items, looked at the photograph, and gave the card back.

Q. I invite you to examine the photograph again.

A. He looks slender here. He isn't.

Q. But it's he?

A. Yes, it's he.

Q. And the color of the eyes? What does it say?

A. This is strange.

Q. What does it say?

A. It says blue.

Q. You recall now they were blue?

A. They were black as wet olives in a barrel. I was with him all the way to Shkoder Prison. They are black.

Q. Very well.

A. Are you testing me?

Q. Continue your report.

A. The card is wrong.

Q. I said continue.

A. Well, we were leaving them, almost out the door, when suddenly the blind man spoke very oddly.

Q. Oddly how?

A. Just an odd tone of voice. I can't describe it.

Q. And what did he say?

A. He said, "He is not one of us. He is alien."

Q. What did he mean?

A. I wasn't sure. We came back and trained our guns on the fellow, and I asked the old man to explain. He didn't answer. I said, "Grandfather, hurry, speak up. My daughter will be three years old by the weekend and I promised to be with her. Hurry up, please, give an answer." And the oldster said, "Take him!" I looked into the fellow's eyes and then decided to club him with the butt of my rifle.

Q. Why?

A. I don't know. Just something, some movement in the back of his eyes, some inner struggle. I had the feeling he could kill us if he wished.

Q. You're quite tired, I think.

A. I haven't slept.

Q. We'll come back to this. What happened next?

A. I knocked him out and we chained up his legs, and then we took him to the station house in Quelleza. We asked the police if the man had checked in with them when he first came into the village. That's the law.

Q. So it is.

A. They said no. This was highly suspicious. I explained

things completely to the local commissar and to the commandant of police.

Q. That was well.

A. So then the commandant asked him some questions. Well, the man wouldn't speak, not a word, and we started to wonder about whether he was a mute or some kind of an imbecile, perhaps. But all the wires to Theti were down, there'd been a storm, and we couldn't check out any part of his story. As it happened, though, we ran into wonderful luck. In Quelleza at that moment was a merchant from Theti, a big fellow, bald, very talkative; anyhow, they found him and they brought him to the station and they asked if he'd ever seen the Prisoner before. He said yes, and that he couldn't quite remember his name but that our man was very definitely from Theti. Then the commissar asked if he was Selca Decani, and the merchant said, "Of course he is! Exactly! It's Selca!" and "How in the world could I have possibly forgotten!" Then he started to study our fellow intently and a curious look came over his face and he told us though he didn't know how it could have happened, but he'd somehow made an error, for until that moment it had slipped his mind that Selca Decani had been dead for many years, and that our fellow looked nothing like Decani at all. What made his mistake so amazing, he told us, was that he had known Decani quite well and had been saddened and depressed by his death for many months. It was all very strange.

Q. To say the least. And then?

A. Oh, well, as we were hurrying and still in pursuit of the baker, I suggested that our fellow be kept in Quelleza, but the commandant and commissar quickly said no and they advised me to take our fellow with us to Shkoder, which we finally did and then gave him to your Secret Police, the Sigurimi. They seemed very nervous.

Q. The Secret Police?

A. No, the people at Quelleza. They seemed very anxious to be rid of the fellow.

Q. Did it never occur to you that the Prisoner might be the would-be assassin of Mehmet Shehu you were sent there to find in the first place?

A. Oh, well, of course, but we were told that he'd been captured near the Buna.

Q. And who told you that?

A. The people at Quelleza.

Q. From Quelleza to Shkoder, did the Prisoner speak or in any way give you information?

A. He did not. He didn't speak at any time. Not a word.

Q. And what else did you notice about him that was unusual?

A. Oh, well, one thing, perhaps. While we were marching back to Shkoder we stopped in the middle of the day at Mesi and lunched in a courtyard next to the jail. It was unseasonably warm and humid, so we rested. One of my men played the lute and we sang. We'd chained the Prisoner's legs to an apricot tree and I kept staring at him.

Q. Why?

A. There were swarms of mosquitoes biting. They were biting rather fiercely, in fact.

Q. And what of that?

A. He never slapped at them.

Q. His hands were free?

A. Yes, they were free.

Q. Very well. Now then, earlier you stated that his papers seemed in order.

A. So I thought.

Q. And he never did actually resist arrest?

A. No, not really.

Q. So again I ask, why did you club him with your rifle? I mean some reason besides an odd look in his eyes. Did you think he was holding a gun or a knife beneath the blanket?

A. No, he wasn't holding anything.

Q. Then why did you strike him?

A. I was afraid.

Q. Afraid of what?

A. When I yanked off the blanket I saw blood on his hand. I mean the hand that I hadn't seen before, the right one. It was gashed as if by the teeth of some animal.

Q. And this made you feel afraid?

A. It did.

Q. For what reason?

A. I thought of the dog with the broken neck.

EXCERPT FROM THE QUESTIONING OF THE BLIND MAN, LIGENI SHIRQI, TAKEN AT QUELLEZA 12 OCTOBER

Q. Your door was unlocked?

A. Yes, it was. I heard the knocking and I called out, "Come in, you are welcome."

Q. You didn't think it dangerous?

A. Danger is irrelevant. Things are different here. It's not like below. Had he killed my own children, I had to make him welcome. "I live in the house," goes the saying, "but the house belongs to the guest and to God."

Q. There is no God.

A. No, not in the city, perhaps, Colonel Vlora, but right now we are up in the mountains and our general impression here is that he exists.

Q. Do maintain the proprieties, Uncle.

A. Does that help?

Q. Only facing reality helps.

A. I would face it, *effendum*, but where is it? As you know, in my world I must be turned.

Q. You were saying . . .

A. I called out, "You are welcome," and I heard him come in. A torrent of rain gusted in, a great blow, and as it thundered I could feel the flash of lightning on my skin. It came suddenly, this storm, like an unexpected grief. I got up and I greeted the stranger as I should: I said, "God may have –"

Q. Never mind all that. You said something that triggered his arrest: "He is alien." What did you mean by that statement?

A. Well, he wasn't a mountain man, not a Geg.

Q. That is surely innocuous.

A. Ah, but he'd *told* me that he was a Geg.

Q. You say he *told* you?

A. That's right.

Q. He *spoke*?

A. In the mountains this is common, *effendum*.

Q. Don't be cheeky, old man. Tell me everything he said.

A. From what point?

Q. From the beginning.

A. Well, now, as I told you—or tried to tell you—I greeted him properly. "God may have brought you here," I told him. And "How are you?" "I am happy to find you well," he said. These are formulas of grace that we observe.

Q. Yes, I know. What happened next?

A. Well, I asked him to sit at the table, of course, and I set out some food, a great deal of it. He saw that I was blind, I suppose, for he said not to labor overmuch on his account. I said, "Thanks be to God we have food for the guest. Not to have it is the greatest shame of all." He said nothing to that and I kept putting out the food and the *raki*.

Q. Why so much food?

A. Well, his size. He was big. Or rather, dense. Very powerfully built.

Q. How could you tell that?

A. Just as I knew you're from the north. From his step. He got up and put a log on the fire. That was rude. I thought perhaps he was a city dweller, then.

Q. Just go on.

A. Well, I asked where he was from and he answered, "From Theti," and then he explained he was a seller of cheese. Well, I already knew that, of course, from the aroma.

Q. Which, of course, you promptly told him.

A. What was that?

Q. Never mind. What happened next?

A. Well, then I learned he was a Christian, you see, and I took away the *raki* I'd set out and in its place I gave him wine.

Q. How did you learn that he was Christian?

A. His skull cap. I heard him slip it off and set it down on the table. The hard little button at the top makes a sound. But he wasn't from Theti and he wasn't a Geg. We plant the heel firmly up here, *effendum*. It's from walking up and down the sides of mountains. When he first came in the door, that's how he walked. But then his steps became different. They grew softer, more relaxed. It's when he saw that I was blind, I would guess.

Q. You mean he let down his guard?

A. Yes, that could be.

Q. Where was he from, then, do you think? From the south?

A. I don't know.

Q. From outside?

A. What do you mean?

Q. When he spoke was there an accent? Something foreign?

A. No, no accent. That's what's puzzling: perfect northern, even down to the little inflections that are special just to

Theti.

Q. And what else did he say to you?

A. Not very much. Not in words.

Q. Please explain that.

A. Well, I asked him his name and he told me. After that he—

Q. What name did he give? Do you remember?

A. Yes, he said that his name was Selca Decani. That, too, was odd. Not the name, my reaction. I had once been acquainted with a Selca Decani, and now when he told me that name I thought, "Yes! Yes, of course! How on earth could I have failed to know that voice right away!" So I said, "Please forgive me, old friend, I've grown senile." Then I suddenly remembered.

Q. That Selca Decani had died years before?

A. How did you know that?

Q. Never mind.

A. Yes, he'd died.

Q. Yet the voice was Decani's?

A. No, not really. Not at all. Just at first.

Q. And what then?

A. Well, I urged him to eat. But he didn't. He was quiet and still. Yet I sensed a great turmoil churning within him, some terrible emotions conflicting. At war. But then soon these grew quiet and I felt a new energy flowing from his being, as something comforting and warm, almost loving, washed over me. At first I didn't know what it was. Then he spoke and he asked me a very strange question. He asked if I had ever seen God and, if I had, was it this that had caused my blindness.

Q. This is fanciful.

A. That is what he said.

Q. Well, alright. Did you ask him what he meant by it?

A. No. Nor would I ask you when you came to the city from the mountains. Either question would be rude.

Q. Your ears are dangerous.

A. They hear. They heard your step.

Q. What did you say to him?

A. Nothing at first. I was startled. Then I asked if he was warm enough.

Q. And what was his answer?

A. Silence. But again I was aware of this force he emitted. And then suddenly I realized what it was: it was pity, a pity so thick that you could squeeze it, almost physical. It wasn't the pity you resent, that you hate. It was the other kind: the pity that comforts, that heals. One more thing: for a moment I was sure that I could see him. He was young, a strong face with an archangel's smile. Does this sound like an illusion? Some things aren't.

Q. You are mad. Are you finished?

A. Yes, I'm finished. That was all, that's when your men broke in. They checked his papers. They seemed to be satisfied. As they were leaving, I spoke up and stopped them.

Q. You said you felt pity from him.

A. Yes.

Q. And so why did you betray him?

A. I am loyal to the state.

Q. Try again.

A. I couldn't stand to be near him any longer.

Q. Why was that?

A. It was something that I felt from him.

Q. The pity?

A. Something else: a brutal, terrifying energy. It burned.

Q. That was surely in your mind.

A. No, it was real.

Q. Then what was it?

A. At the time I felt certain it was goodness.

Decani was a dead man roaming the hills seeking momentary life in mistaken recollections. This had been the actual and secret belief of both the commissar and the chief of police at Quelleza (and later of Security people in Shkoder, though none had dared utter so dangerous a view), and the reason they'd disposed of the Prisoner with haste, for who knew what might happen to an ordinary soul when it brushed against the host of a resurrected mist. But then who was the Prisoner?

Some felt unease.

In Shkoder they followed the uses of sense, and so the Prisoner was tested in the scientific way, which pretended that matter was real and could be measured. Their further assumption was far less speculative, namely that their captive was an enemy agent and bent on a mission that was therefore unguessable, for only wide China was Albania's friend, and who could hope to keep track of the shifts and purposes of every other nation on the face of earth? There was simply no time, their hearts complained; but they plodded on listlessly, testing for signs that the stranger had been air-dropped: wax from his ears, a sample of his stool, and dirt scraped from under his fingernails were analyzed minutely in search of traces of food or flora foreign to the land; his clothing was scanned underneath black light, for this would make visible a dry-cleaning mark. But these arcane wisdoms yielded nothing. Further, a check of the Prisoner's teeth showed only an "oversized facial amalgam" fashioned from poorly polished silver, and "two swedged chrome-cobalt alloy crowns" that were "overcontoured and extremely ill-fitting around the edges, resulting in penetration of the gum": Albanian dentistry, without question. Yet how could this be? How could *any* of it be? Every person was known, counted, and followed; every citizen's name was on endless lists that were checked each day at each change of location: to market and work and then back to one's home; to the "cultural" meetings that were held after dinner and the one-hour readings of the news before, where the mind took flight behind etherized eyes. Here no one went anywhere. They were taken. How could the Prisoner be of this land, moving soundless and alone with the papers of a ghost? In a basement of the Shkoder Security Building the Prisoner was stripped naked and then beaten and interrogated in shifts by female security agents from the morning of Friday, 1 October, until just before noon of the following day, by which time the inquisitors' mechanical blows had evoked the emotions that normally cause them, stoking the agents to genuine fury and the shouting of wild imprecations of blood. Even worse was done. And still the Prisoner would not speak. Thus, on the evening of 2 October, entangled in anger and mystification, the agents at Shkoder had shipped him to the capital, Tirana, and the faceless State Security Building, for here there were specialists. Horrors. Means.

Here were answers to questions that no one had asked.

"Who are you?" the Interrogator wearily repeated.

Jerked to his feet amid blows, the Prisoner again stood eerily silent, his gaze a light touch upon the stone floor. The Interrogator stared at the lacework of blood that had dried in a band around his forehead. What did it remind him of, he wondered? And then he remembered: *Christ in Silence.* A miniature print of the Symbolist painting had hung in a cell of the Jesuit seminary close to the center of the city; he had seen it when they'd wrenched the place from the priests, weeks before they decided to shoot its director and replace him with Samia Sabrilu, the notorious fifteen-year-old girl who'd been chosen for her cruelty, arrogance, and cunning, as well as her sexual precocity and hatred of her father. This was almost a year before the time they would throw all the priests into labor camps or their graves and convert the old seminary into a restaurant that specialized in dishes of the north. The Interrogator pursed his lips in thought. No, the painting wasn't all. There was something else. He was certain he had seen this man before. It was somewhere in Tirana, he thought. A state dinner perhaps.

Or in a dream.

"Who are you? If you tell us who you are you can sleep."

Neglect and a cold isolation had preceded, and then afterward the clanging and the ear-bursting Klaxons and the searing white light for the strangling of dreams; then the absolute darkness and fetid waters teeming with particles of unknown matter ominously seeping up into his cell from a thousand grieving, rusted pores, flooding slowly ever higher until inches from the ceiling, where they lapped and waited, stinking and irresolute, and then little by little subsided, a procedure repeated again and again. This phase had a term of three days (if one measured them relative to the observer); and then had come the torturers, all of them with nicknames meant to shield them from possible future retribution. Two were men, one called "Dreamer" for his faraway look and the other, a young one who was always smiling and in fact was the Interrogator's son, was called "Laugher," while the third, a tall and blocky former nun with a heavy step, was known as "Angel." With dirty gray skin, a sunless stare, and a mad, irrepressible tic in one eye that made it seem she was constantly winking slyly, in her dark blue uniform shirt and trousers she was the phantom of the merciless chamber. The Prisoner was resting on his back on a bloodstained narrow wooden table, and

27

when the three had surrounded him "Angel" had lifted a look to the Interrogator, and as soon as he uttered the word "Begin!" her lissome truncheon cleaved the whistling air from on high in a smacking wallop to the Prisoner's kidney with a result that was welcomed by no one in the chamber, for the Prisoner's eyes slid open calmly, as if he had awakened in a hammock of summer. Unsettled, the Interrogator took a step backward, for he felt an unearthliness descending, and soon flurrying fists and truncheons and curses enshrouded the table in a living hot fog made of rage and exuberance and self hate, and he listened to the shouts and grunts of exertion, to the smackings and the infantile bawdy suggestions, the hissed accusations and imprecations, aware that very soon they would thicken and be finally subsumed into a single autonomous living frenzy that would suck up all minds and yet be mindless, gather all souls, but have none of its own, only that of the beast at the center of its whirlwind. "Pig!" "Degenerate!" "Criminal scum!" The flung epithets seethed with a righteous fury that shivered and broke in each voice with every blow. The Interrogator felt himself trembling with excitement, and he gave himself up to the beast for a term, but abruptly withdrew at a glimpse of "Laugher," as the eyes of his son shone madly with pleasure and some nameless emotion not found in sweet air. "Enough! Something else!" the Interrogator ordered, after which "Angel" held the Prisoner's fingers under a door that she slowly pushed shut, at first grinning and crooning a thousand remarkable lascivious suggestions, and then frowning in thickening consternation when the Prisoner's face did not change its expression.

Confounded, it was then they had thought to pull out his fingernails, first placing a helmet on his head that was designed to make him hear his own screams greatly amplified. The helmet failed. He never screamed. But when the last of his fingernails had been drawn, he closed his eyes and slowly sank to the mottled stone floor with a sound like sighs mixed up with bones. Suddenly anxious, the Interrogator jerked his gaze to a withered old man in a cheap brown suit who was standing at the edge of the circle of light. His gaunt and elongated face was in shadow, but he clutched the frayed grip of a black leather medical bag with both his hands in front of him, so that a ring on his index finger caught the light in flashes as a restless thumb kept rubbing irregularly at its flat green stone, made of paste. It glinted like signals from a distant ship.

"Hurry, check him!"

The Interrogator's growl was tense, for he was gripped by the alarming foreboding that the Prisoner would slip away with his secret into the shadowland of death.

"Check him now! Right away! Hurry up!"

The creaking old doctor shuffled forward, spent and bowed by the weight of tedium and the endless repetition of meaningless acts in a purposeless world. He dragged his crumpled soul along behind him like an empty canvas sack.

"*Do not lose him!*" the Interrogator shouted.

Hurriedly, the bloodstained wooden table was wheeled back from darkness into light and as "Laugher" stooped down to haul the Prisoner up off the floor, "Angel" roughly deflected him, scooping up the body with effortless ease and then dumping the

Prisoner onto the table like a crackling bag of sticks. "He is air," she grunted under her breath; and then for a curious instant she hesitated, staring at the Prisoner intently while a curious softness bathed her face: it was as if she had been taken unaware by innocence, by some memory of childhood grace. She stepped backward and out of the light. By then the old doctor had wheezed to the table. He searched for a pulse with fingers that rustled, floppy and dry, as if stuffed with straw, while his other hand opened his medical bag, unsnicking the clasp at the top. In the hush there was a faint sound of clutter being dragged as he groped along the bottom of the bag for his stethoscope. He found it and fished it out. One of the ear tubes slapped at the bag. It made a tiny whipping sound.

"He's alright?" the Interrogator asked worriedly.

The doctor's gaze flicked up, seeing only a tower and a usual grayness, for he was forced to look out at the world through a film of dust that coated his corneas, a chronic and remarkable affliction diagnosed as "disorder of the soul" that had started on the day he stopped believing that the universe had any meaning. Then suddenly things in the chamber grew vivid (he had learned how to "look around" the dust) and he saw the Interrogator standing across from him with a look of intense concern. For a moment the doctor studied him clinically, marking the fatigue in his scarred, rugged face, and the anger, smothered, but always there; then he sank to the work so quiet beneath him. "I need a new stethoscope," he muttered, slipping the hearing tubes into his ears in accordance with the rules of the artificial construct that he knew as time and space.

"Nothing in this world lasts forever," he added.

For that part of the rules he was grateful.

"He's alright?" Vlora prodded him again.

"You must be quiet!"

Fearful of the fist and an empty stomach, the doctor pretended absorption in his work, gravely frowning as he moved the stethoscope sensor around and listened to the unaccustomed sound of someone living. As always, it startled him a little. "Yes, he's fine," he replied. "His heart is very strong. He's just sleeping."

The Interrogator blinked, uncomprehending; and then suddenly a fury overwhelmed him, shaking and ripping him loose from his body; but as swiftly as the spasm had struck, it stilled, overwrestled by the powerful sense of the mysterious that hung above the table like the mists of creation, warm and expectant, waiting for breath.

The Interrogator's thoughts snaked out at paths: Was the Prisoner conditioned against pain by hypnosis? Had his "gates of pain" been sealed so that the signals of torment could not be channeled to his brain? While the doctor tapped and prodded and muttered, the Interrogator stared intensely at the Prisoner as he tried to account for the puzzling variation in how so many witnesses had described him. Even worse, four villagers questioned independently had sworn, when confronted with his photograph, that they had seen him in a shop in Theti at a time when he was known to be in custody in Shkoder. Nor could they be shaken from their reports. The Prisoner's face was so utterly ordinary, the Interrogator

reflected, a slate so blank that the mind might conceivably project its own images upon it from within. His features were
delicate and refined, yet the leader of the hunting force had
described him as "blunt-nosed," "stocky," and "a brute," a perception that invaded the realm of the bizarre. The
Interrogator's gaze roamed the Prisoner's body. It looked quar-
ried from the stuff of Michelangelo's marbles, hard and
chiseled and faintly luminous with an aura of imminent
motion silently awaiting the unlocking of a prayer.

"What is that?"

The doctor's eyes squinted up. "What is what?"

"That scar."

"You mean this dimpling? I would guess a tracheotomy."

"No, not on the throat. On his arm."

The Interrogator pointed.

"Oh."

The doctor's sight found a path through the dust to a crater
on the Prisoner's upper left arm where the skin was depressed
and surrounded by a hairline bloodless circle that measured the
width of a carpenter's thumb. Within the depression the skin
was raised and warty.

"What is it?" the Interrogator asked.

"I don't know."

"A birthmark?"

The words had been blurted, travelers lacking the passport
of thought.

"No, not a birthmark."

"A bullet wound?"

"Maybe. Could be anything at all. I don't know."

The Interrogator's stare remained pinned to the scar. Something made him think it had meaning. The instinct was troubling but vague. He dismissed it.

"If you think it's important," sulked the doctor, "ask the specialists. Mine is a very plain practice." He slipped the stethoscope out of his ears and then folded and returned it to his bag of sharp cures. "As for me, I am finished here now," he grumbled. He picked up the bag and slouched back to his post, turned around, and announced from the gloom, "He is fit."

The torturers regrouped themselves around the table.

"No," the Interrogator ordered. " 'The Cage.' "

His glance caught "Angel's" gleaming gaze and the slight upward curling of her lips. In "The Cage" it was impossible to stretch out a leg or to turn or to stand; one could only squat. Unendurable torment for even one day, "The Cage," when protracted, broke the mind. Was "Angel" merely savoring future delights? Yet her smile seemed discordant with the deadness of her stare. He shifted an expressionless glance to his son, whose smile was less ambiguous. His eyes fairly shone with a pleased anticipation and something disturbingly akin to lust. Vlora turned away, disgusted, and quickly strode out of the room. Outside, two guards saluted him smartly, cracking their rifle butts down on the floor, and then one cupped a hand to his mouth and hissed loudly, signaling to guards posted farther along that an authorized person was approaching as, boxed within the smolder of his thoughts, Vlora moodily moved along the shadowy hall amid the eeriness of echoing cracks and hisses.

Inside the chamber, hell went on.

The Interrogator's secretary heard him approaching. Languid and dark of eye, in her thirties, she puffed at a Turkish cigarette while fanning out a match and then placing it into the crease of a book to mark her place before she closed it.

"Some calls for you, Colonel Vlora."

She handed him the message slips, then appraised him without expression as he quickly and distractedly sorted through the stack. The fever was still in his eyes and she saw that his hands held a touch of tremor. She would like to have him now, she thought. "Nothing urgent," she murmured in a diffident voice. She drew deeply on the cigarette again, held the smoke, and then blew it out gently at a sidewise angle. Vlora handed back the slips without comment, noticing the cigarette butts mounded high in the purple glass ashtray resting on the desk. Stamped on its sides in cracked green letters was a faded inscription: SOUVENIR OF DOBRACI.

"This habit will kill you, Leda," he scolded.

She nodded and cast down her eyes.

"I know," she said, stubbing out the cigarette's glow.

"It is simply a matter of will," he persisted.

The telephone rang. Grateful, Leda answered. "Section Four," she said crisply. Listening, she lifted her eyes to the Interrogator and saw that he was shaking his head. She nodded, understanding. "Colonel Vlora isn't in," she informed the caller in a tone that was vaguely annoyed and chilly, as if in response to some impropriety. It was her tactic for deflecting further questions. "Do you want to leave a message?" she added tersely. The Interrogator turned and walked away. For a moment she stared at his back morosely, then reached to her desk for a fresh cigarette.

As he entered his office Vlora winced, blinded by the unexpected midday sunlight shafting through the small square windows of the room like the fiery blessings of a troublesome saint. He had been in the darkness of the torture chamber for hours. Striding to an old wooden desk he sat down with his back to the clear and relentless light, for in no other way could he protect his delusions, and so briefly he rested, waiting for peace; then, as if wanting to reassure himself, he slid open a drawer of the desk and looked down at his ribbons and decorations: the Partisan Star, the Order of Skanderbeg, the Order of the National Hero. He gave them grudging recognition, pushed the drawer shut, and examined his hands. He saw that they were still, that at least he was calm. He picked up the telephone receiver on his desk, punched into an unlit station and dialed.

In accordance with some arbitrary sense of balance that shifted within him from day to day, he adjusted certain objects on his desk: a paper clip tray; a clutch of fresh-cut flowers propped in a glass half-filled with water; an in-basket stacked with reports on the Prisoner; and an old framed photo of a melancholy woman, his mother, and a five-year-old boy with green eyes. Beneath the layers of tinting and the graceless touch-up strokes, their smiles seemed dreamy and distant, like wan, blurred greetings from a bygone time. On top of the papers that were resting in the basket lay a crudely formed paperweight heart made of clay and, cheerily painted in a swirl of vivid colors, on its back the name "Kiri" engraved in small letters. The flowers and the heart were the room's only life, and already the flowers had the look of coming death. It was something he had noticed always happened in this building. There was something in the air of this place.

The Interrogator's wife came on the line. "Hello?"

Vlora shifted his gaze to the drooping flowers, absorbing the sadness that flowed through the line as he reached out a hand to reposition a violet struggling for breath amid a crush of red poppies. "It is I," he said wearily.

"Yes."

"And how is my little Kiri?"

"She is better."

"And her temperature?"

"Fine. It's just a four-day flu."

"Tell her 'Baba' sends millions of kisses."

"I will."

"And hugs, too, Moricani."

"That, too."

The Interrogator stared at the opposite wall while he waited for the pain to speak again. His wife's voice had grown even more dead and despondent. I must say something kind, he thought. But what? A sudden gloom washed over the wall and he heard a quick spattering of rain on the windows. He reached for the switch on a gooseneck metal lamp that was painted khaki and after a click a bright pool of light spilled onto the desk.

* * *

"That will make her very happy," the wife said damply.

The words had the sound of a rebuke.

The Interrogator twisted the head of the lamp so that it shone on the flowers in the glass like a spotlight. "Good," he said tersely. His guilt was overcome by angry resentment, and he looked on helplessly, surprised, as the comforting words that he had reached for drifted away like shipwreck survivors in a lifeboat, specks at the edge of a chilling sea.

"I must go," he said remotely. He could not control it.

He thought of the artificial rage of the torturers.

"No, wait!" she said quickly.

"Yes, what is it, Moricani?"

She mentioned an errand.

"Elez, the new grocer in the Square," she began.

The Interrogator stared at the papers in the basket. Absorbed in the Prisoner again, he half-listened. "I know that he's lying," she said. "I can tell: when he lies his left shoulder starts twitching." Vlora struggled to focus on the rush of her words. It was something to do with canned beans.

"Did you hear what I'm telling you?" she asked him.

"Beans."

"Yes, the fava beans. He says that he's out, but he's lying. There are cans in the back. He wants a bribe. If you go there he will give them to you gladly, he'll be frightened."

"No, I can't, Moricani."

"You can't?"

"It isn't right. I cannot use my position for personal advantage."

He listened then to silence and the heaviness of nothing.

He could not cut her off now. She had to let him go.

"It's Kiri's favorite," she spoke up mournfully. "The fava beans, cold, with lots of olive oil, lemon juice, and garlic: I was hoping I could fix it for tonight."

He had lost.

"I make no promises," he wearily warned her. "And I'm not about to tell them who I am."

"No, of course not." Suddenly a lilt had come into her voice. "It's just that dealing with a man he'll be different. It's the women who are lied to all the time. That's how it is." She knew that everybody recognized her husband and dreaded him, a fact known to every Albanian but him. How naïve he was in so many ways! she believed: locked deep inside the tower of his ardent ideals he was either a truly good man or just a child. Why, he wanted people treated all alike and to be happy! He should have been a monk in a contemplative order, she thought, glumly smoldering while making perfect cheese. "Keep an eye on his shoulder," she said. "That's the key."

"I'll remember that, Mooki." He had used the affectionate nickname that pleased her. His fond tone of voice had cost him an effort. It was worth it: he was free until her next sad look when he would ask her, "What is wrong?" and she would lower her eyes and murmur wretchedly, "Nothing. No, nothing at all."

"Don't be late," she admonished him blithely.

"I won't."

* * *

Vlora hung up with grateful relief, dimly heard Leda answering a call, and was suddenly assailed by a vivid recollection of a lucid dream of the night before, a chronic nightmare of a terrified infant abandoned in a corner of endless night. Then came a new and more dreadful visitation of which he remembered only disparate images: Russians. Ho Chi Minh. A banquet in Tirana. A death.

What did it mean?

He didn't know.

He turned his gaze to reports in a wire basket and lifted them out. They made an ambiguous rustling sound, the kind in which sometimes in the quiet of dawn one imagines one's name has just been whispered. Carefully, he placed them before him on the desk. The answer was here, he felt, in these papers, though he'd pondered their contents so often before. Staring at the redness of a thing hid its greenness, he knew; he must look from the right point of view. On top of the stack lay a white identity card that was soiled and battered from handling. The emblem of the eagle and the cornstalk on the cover had faded to a bloodless apparition of itself. The Interrogator picked it up gently and unfolded it, then scanned its twin columns of data: . . . father's name . . . mother's name . . . residence . . . profession . . . eyes . . . mouth . . . distinguishing marks. His pensive stare slipped down to the photo glued at the bottom of the left-hand column where the Prisoner's eyes stared back with the trust of a simple heart.

Trussed up in a jacket, shirt, and tie, his head and shoulders were drawn up affectedly in that pleased and prideful bearing

so typical of peasants when posing for this photo, and the too-
tight jacket, buttoned and tugging, had the look of something
borrowed or rented for this day. Was he smiling? Yes, a little
bit, decided the Interrogator. The effect was of a childlike
innocence that he found to be oddly touching. How could the
Prisoner have feigned such a look? He found himself thinking
of *The Brothers Karamazov* and the deathbed speech of little
Rusha: "Father, don't cry, and when I die get a good boy,
another one. Choose one of my friends, a good one, call him
Ilusha and love him instead of me." There were times when
reading it caused him to weep. Why had he thought of it now?
he wondered. What could be the triggering association? He
put the identity card aside and then labored at the papers for
hours in silence, polishing and burnishing each fact, every
riddle, and then turning them end over end and around before
holding them up to the light of sense; but still no insight
gleamed, no hidden fact cried out its secret name, and at the
end was the taunting fog of the beginning.

And that certain touch of fear.

Vlora put away the papers and listened to the reassuring
patter of the rain. Was there nothing amiss after all? he wondered. Were his worries imagined? Danger's dream? From
behind him he heard thunder rumbling faintly high in the
mountains of Selca Decani, and abruptly a keening wind leaped
up, slamming rain against the windows in bursts. Mysterious
flashes danced on his spectacles, far lightning, memory of suns;
then suddenly the wind trailed away to a hush that once again
softly bedded a steady light rain. Vlora listened and for

moments he did not move, his gaze fixed upon a deep bottom drawer of his desk. Then he slid the drawer open, reached in, and lifted out a yellowing cardboard shoebox that he carefully placed atop the desk as if it contained some priceless relic. Thick rubber bands stretched a guard around the box. For a moment Vlora pensively rubbed a thumb back and forth atop a knot where one of the bands had snapped and been retied. Then he slipped off the bands, removed the shoebox lid, and peered down at the items in the whiteness of the box: the stub of a pencil; a packet of matches; a worn brown wallet made of cheap, cracking leather; fifty-seven *leks* in paper and coins; a small frayed ledger logging sales of cheese in a cramped and tiny hand; a snapshot of a woman; and a personal letter that seemed written in a hurried but stately script: these were the contents of the Prisoner's pockets that were found by his captors in the village of Quelleza.

Vlora stared at the photo of the woman. Worn and faded, its borders were ragged, as if it had been scissored from a larger scene. The woman looked young, in her twenties, though her features were clouded from the softness of the focus. Through a veil, from a place where the air was all tears, glowed great dark chestnut eyes filled with anger. Vlora put down the photo, resting it close to the paperweight heart; and then his hand dipped gingerly into the box, pinched a corner of the letter with his thumb and forefinger, and then slowly and soundlessly lifted it out like a miniature crane in a penny arcade. Folded over several times, it was a single small sheet found tucked between the pages of the ledger. With the back of his hand Vlora nudged the box aside and bent the lamp head lower, adjusted its beam, very carefully unfolded the letter, and read it.

> *My universe! Who knows if this letter will reach you? Enver has died. May God be good to him, for always he treated me kindly. But now you must come to me, my heart! Oh, Selca, my morning light, my angel! Have you any idea how much I have missed you? Oh, come to me! Come now, sweetest boy! My love, my youth, my very soul! I must hold you. Come quickly. I am free but I am not.*
>
> *Morna*

At Theti every villager had told the same story: that Selca Decani and Morna Altamori had dangerously and recklessly loved one another since the earliest days of their youth, and that nothing—no parental threat, no punishment—could keep their laughter apart. But when the girl had reached seventeen years of age her parents married her off to another, a quiet and stolid-eyed irrigation expert in comfortable employ of the State. His soul snatched out of his body, torn open and robbed of day, the young Selca Decani abandoned the village and settled far away near the marshes of the south, and soon time lost track of the lovers' names. But then Death spoke. First, Morna's husband was killed by a lightning bolt when surprised in the field by a storm. Almost a year before that stroke, however, the mournful, hollow-eyed Morna had herself begun to languish in the arms of an illness that, while nameless and undiagnosed, was quietly and steadily eating her breath. On her husband's passing she sent for Decani, who arrived back in Theti to find her dead, and after grief too immense for human thought to contain, Decani resumed his life in the village where soon he, too, was stricken dead by an illness for which no doctor had a name, but which anyone in Theti, when asked, could tell you was surely nothing other than a broken heart.

I am free but I am not.

Vlora stared at the words. What was their meaning? Amid the tumble of his thoughts the now-hesitant raindrops tapped at the windows like a blind man's cane. Complex analysis had shown that the letter had been folded and unfolded again and again; in fact, innumerable times. Who would cherish and reread such a letter repeatedly other than the man to whom the letter was addressed?

The dead man. The phantom. Selca Decani.

Vlora's eyes flicked up. An eerie whipping wind had arisen behind him, softly moaning and thumping at the windowpanes. Uneasy, feeling watched, the Interrogator swiveled his chair around and looked through the windows to the flickering north where thick black clouds were scudding toward the city from the mountains like the angry belief of fanatical hordes, and in a moment they would darken the Square below and its anonymous granite government buildings, the broad streets drearily leading nowhere, and the rain-slick statue of Lenin commanding the empty storefront windows crammed with the ghosts of a million longings, dust, and the dim recollection of hope. Clanking and aimless, two dilapidated automobiles crawled wetly amid whirring streams of grim-lipped bicyclists glumly churning their way on plodding errands, damp, drab souls underneath their bright slickers, while pedestrians trudged in shabby dress beneath wall posters shrieking at "enemies" and "traitors" in huge block letters that rain and the cheapness of the ink had caused to run in moody red and black streaks. The Interrogator singled out a column of children, two by two in their collarless tunics, as they trooped to the Palace of Culture or some other of the Square's monolithic museums. They were passing in front of the Dajti Hotel, and for a moment the Interrogator wished that it were June and he were sitting at the Dajti's sidewalk cafe tasting beer and the plentiful assortment of snacks that went well with a tango or *The Blue Danube* rasping thinly through the cafe's outdoor speakers into the tired evening air.

Vlora furrowed his brow. The children had stopped. What were they gaping at? Something below and out of view. And now other pedestrians stood and stared. Silent and motionless in the drizzle, they sprouted from the curbs like dead gray souls. The Interrogator's knee joints cracked as he rose to scan the streets below. And then he saw it: in the middle of a sopping intersection, drenched in blood and dirty rain, lay the crumpled body of a Jesuit priest with pewter skin and sightless eyes still searching for the answer to an interrupted prayer. While confined in a labor camp he had baptized a newborn infant, and, tried and found guilty of this offense, he'd been shot by a firing squad that morning. Now his corpse, wrapped in clerical robes and trussed like butcher's meat, had been dumped into the street where it would lie for three days to teach the people God's reach was shorter than a bullet's.

The Interrogator's eye caught a blur of motion, a tight, quick, furtive signing with the hand. Someone in the crowd had blessed himself. Blood pounded at the scar slashing Vlora's lips and, furious, he wheeled and rushed from his office down to the sodden streets below without hat, without coat, and without companion except for his rage and the scar's bright ache, but once outside the Security Building he found only lifeless streets and the rain and, beneath the reckless, teeming sky, the body of the man who had purchased death on the cheap with a few sprinkled droplets of water. Two Chinese men in Mao-style uniforms emerged from the Dajti Hotel beneath the shelter of glistening black umbrellas that were hemmed with tiny yellow dragons. They ambled to the curb and gawked at the dead man, at first, and then they turned and stared at Vlora as his booted feet sloshed forward until he was standing by the body of the priest. But for the two unblinking Chinese, the streets were deserted, nothing stirred; but Vlora knew that they were there. The watchers. They were hiding. He could feel their wounded stares like burning sins upon his back. "Do you think this pig was a hero?" he bellowed. The words echoed damply in the concrete emptiness. "Do you think that he loved you at all? Don't you know that his lies are what have kept you so poor and your children so ignorant and sick? Do you believe in the Devil still? Well, *there* is your Devil! He is *there*!" He had flung up his arm in accusation at the corpse and he wheeled around pointing and shouting *"He is there!"* until at last a great weariness weighted his legs and he faltered, his arm limply sagging to his side. The two Chinese turned their gaze to him incuriously, then grinned as he met their stares. Aware of nothing but the largeness of their top front teeth, Vlora slowly turned away and bowed his head, and, with his clothes soaked through, his throat raw, he stood and listened to the rain's soft stitching of despair into the hardness of the stubborn, unwon streets.

On the following morning, 20 March, Vlora ordered the Prisoner moved to a cell that was crowded and cramped and yet dimensionless, a haunted, lightless sea infested by moans and ceaseless whispers eerily drifting above the sounds of restless shifting on straw-filled pallets, of sobbing and litanies of better times lost. Here a lightbulb dangled by a wire from the ceiling, painting the blackness with an amber haze, while food was scraped and pushed through slots—cold poppyseed noodles and moldy bread—and at random a tap would gasp and bleed water. With the Prisoner's arrival the cell contained thirteen men and six women, but guards would come often to drag someone away and by 22 March only five were left, among them the Prisoner and a seemingly half-mad one-eyed priest who apparently remembered that it was Sunday. "Before the Big Bang," he started preaching to the cell, "the entire universe was a point of zero size and infinite weight. Then the point exploded, creating space and, with it, time and its twin, disorder. And yet for the cosmos to come into existence the force of that primal outward explosion needed to match the force of gravity with the accuracy you would need for a bullet to hit a one-inch target on the opposite side of the observable universe thirteen billion light-years away."

A fist lashed out from the darkness, striking the priest on his cheekbone with the crunching sound of gristle and flesh. "I told you I wanted to *sleep!*" snarled an angry, deep male voice. The priest listened to the ringing and the rushing in his ears and the pad-pad-pad of hands slapping at stone as the priest's assailant crawled away, a brawny and extremely irritable Muslim who had announced to the cell upon his arrival that although he had "murdered many others" he was "totally innocent" of the "outrage" that had brought him to this horrible place, the brutal and ultimately fatal beating of a bicycle repairman in Shkoder Square.

"Then along came the living cell," dared the priest with stubborn defiance, although prudently lowering his voice. "But how? Ah, yes, there was a chemical soup, we are told, wherein by the usual and much-loved 'chance' a virus finally happened to form. And then another and another. Need I go on? But never mind that this soup, we've since learned, did not exist, or that the odds against even *one* such virus appearing in as much as a billion years is more than the odds against flipping a coin and having 'eagles' turn up six million times in a row. The beloved reply is, 'A unique event.' Is it rude to suggest that at such magnitudes the distinction between the unique and the supernatural would appear to have lost its utility, if not its *insouciant je ne sais quoi?*"

From somewhere came the gasps of a couple making love. The priest glanced toward the sound.

"Coition brings the keenest of pleasures," he noted. "And why? To ensure continuation of the species. That is purpose. But purpose is the business of a *mind*! And so we see that—"

The blow struck the side of his head. The priest swayed, fought to hold himself erect, then fell, and for moments he lay on his back, unmoving, his breath flowing labored and spattery with blood. "I have made this a Mass upon the Universe," at last he murmured dazedly, "and my preaching this Sunday—Is it Sunday? No matter. In any case, we haven't any wine." And then feeling the light being squeezed from his eye, he lifted a quavering hand into the air as if about to give a blessing to an infant or a barn and with blood trickling down from the side of his mouth he murmured, just before losing consciousness: "Go! The Mass is ended."

Minutes later—or perhaps several hours or days, who can tell, for the arms of pain crush time as they will—it was the silence that awakened the priest with a start. He sat up and looked around. "So they're gone, the other lunatics," he exhaled into the dimness, "hauled off to asylums, no doubt. Just a joke. Without a doubt they're all dead." He looked over at the Prisoner, who was sitting on the ground close beside him with his head bent low and his forearms braced upon propped-up knees so that his hands hung loosely with spatulate grace. He had yet to utter a word. "You there, hello," said the priest. "What's your name? What's your crime, your unspeakable offense? I mean, besides going mad, which is definitely criminal, especially if caused by recollections of Eden. Tell me, what have you done?"

The Prisoner made no reply. He did not move.

The priest appraised him dismally.

"Please don't pay me any mind," he said dryly. "After all, I'm just a poor old reactionary cleric, adjunct and running dog of the Vatican and all-around enemy of the people. Please don't work yourself up over anything I say." The priest waited for an answer, then looked away. "It's the babies," he murmured cryptically. "I am sorry. I am not Stephen Kurti. Stephen Kurti fought the soldiers with his hands, with his fists, when they came to destroy his church in Drin. They sent him to prison and then to a labor camp where he secretly baptized a child, and for this he was executed by firing squad. Did any saint fear God as much as these villains?" He lowered his head to his chest. "No, I am not Kurti," he continued softly: "My body is a house of pain, I am in torment, I am hopelessly insane and a river of grief; and yet I cannot extinguish my yearning to live. I live for the cold, slimy noodles that they give us." The priest jerked his head up and looked to the door as in the hall steely footsteps crunched, implacable, approaching the cell with deadly intent. Then they passed and their echoes lost their way into death. The priest lowered his head again.

"Father Lazar Shantoja, the famous man of letters, he was another," he mournfully recalled. "After years at hard labor, they released him. Do you know what his mother did when she saw him, her only son, her beloved boy, when he first came walking up to her door after all those years of unbroken separation?" He turned and looked at the Prisoner again. "She danced. Yes, she found she couldn't speak so she danced; she danced uncontrollably, on and on. Months later Shantoja was rearrested. His hands were sawn off, and his forearms and his leg bones were broken, and only then was his mother allowed to come visit him. When he entered the room where she was waiting he was walking in the only way that he could, by supporting his weight on his elbows and knees, and she screamed at the jailers to be merciful and kill him. They obliged. I saw him dragged by his feet down flights of stairs, and by the time they had reached the second floor his skull was ripped open. When they saw that I had witnessed this, I was put in isolation for a month. They let me out early so I could play in a volleyball game."

He lifted his head, looking off.

"Oh, once I was brave, I suppose. When I was first captured they started to question me: Wasn't it true I was a Vatican spy? Would I recant? Pledge allegiance to the new Albania, the first official atheist state in all the world? I said no. And then the torture came, the electrodes. Blue-white lightning filled my skull; I thought the top of my head was about to come off. I was screaming and my teeth would slam shut on my tongue. Then I felt a warm liquid pouring down on my face. I thought it was water to spread the current, but I heard the men laughing and opened my eyes and saw that one of them was pissing on my face. Soon after, when maddened by thirst one day, I suddenly plunged my burning head into the fouled and stinking bowl of a toilet, my parched tongue lapping like a maddened dog's, and then in vain were the shouts and the threats and the kicks, the rifle butt blows to my head and my back; no, nothing, no power, no pleading angel, could stay me from my frenzy of lapping and slurping until many strong men at last wrenched me away. And that's where it began, I think, my revulsion at my own humanity. Until that moment I hadn't been broken. There had even been a day when a guard brought me news that my elderly mother, grievously ill, had been put in an ambulance, and that the driver and his very young helper, on their way to a hospital, because they were running so late and it soon would be dark and they would miss their dinner, decided that the whole thing was too much trouble and they stopped and dumped my mother down the side of a mountain. By the way, the driver's helper was Vlora's son. Yes, the torturer. The very same one. The guard told me he was sorry and as a consolation he gave me an apricot. An apricot in place of my mother.

"And yet that night, while grieving alone in my freezing cell and suddenly doubting the existence of God in the face of the suffering of the innocent, I heard God's voice. Oh, yes, really and actually—*his voice*! 'James, when did I ask you to solve the Problem of Evil?' he chided. 'That is *my* problem,' he told me. 'What I ask is that you be the best priest that you can be.' He sounded rather cross, like the God of Job, perhaps because he saw me surreptitiously glancing all around the cell in search of hidden microphones and loudspeakers. Then 'Trust me,' he said, 'and leave the brooding and theology to me.' Oh, well, this was God, alright, no doubt about it, and apparently lonely for those days in the desert when he'd make his appearance in the form of a cloud, or, at night, as a burning pillar of evasions.

I had a few caveats to offer but prudently said nothing as I wanted no insufferable blasts about my whereabouts when he was laying the foundations of the world. Talk about torture! Never mind, though, it all ended well. Oh, I confess I'd grown nervous when I heard him say, 'Trust me,' but mostly his words had a wonderful effect and from that moment I determined to become a great priest, consoling and caring for my fellow prisoners, encouraging and giving as much as I could. 'I will go to the altar of God,' my heart sang, 'unto God who gives joy to my youth.' And then I saw the warm piss pouring down on my face. It was after this incident, I think, that it finally dawned upon me that even if God existed it was simply not possible that he could love me.

"Oh, I did say Mass after that in the labor camp at Mali, where we worked in swamps, an interminable army of men in rags sinking down into mud slopping up to our chests. I even heard some confessions, such as they were. Can you imagine the paucity of sins in such a place? But don't think I was brave. They just didn't care about these things. Only baptism. That's what they hated and feared. But I baptized no one; no, no infant that was born in the camp." The priest lowered his head and his voice. "I am here because I failed to fulfill my work quota." For a time he fell silent. Then abruptly he burst into tears, sobbing wrenchingly and beating his chest with a fist. "*Mea culpa, mea culpa!*" he kept repeating. When he'd recovered, he leaned back against the wall of the cell and turned his head to look over at the Prisoner.

"Are you a priest?" he asked softly in the darkness.

He waited, and then went on. "Yes, I think so. I can smell the holy oils on your hands. Would you hear my confession, please, Father?"

No response. The only sound was a single drip of the faucet.

"They'll be coming to get us soon. That's alright, all of life is preparation for death. Yet I'd hoped to face God with— well—it's just all of those babies that I've kept from his sight . . ." His voice trailed off, and as tears coursed down his cheeks he crumpled to the merciless stone of the floor with a muffled groan made of all the unanswered prayers of his life. "*Meme, meme,*" he murmured, calling softly for his mother again and again until in time his quiet sobs and pleas had all dwindled, enfolded in the steady sure river of his breath.

The Prisoner lifted his head and stared at him.

And then slowly reached out his hand.

Moments later, heavy steps in the hall were heard approaching. The priest bolted upright and, gripping the Prisoner's shoulders, he shook him, shouting frenziedly, "They're coming! They're coming to get us! For the love of Christ, give me absolution! I am sorry for all of my sins! Absolve me!" Then the door to the cell was thrown open and the lightbulb flared to a shocking brilliance as the priest, still screaming "Absolve me! Absolve me!" was dragged from the cell by cursing guards.

N o, he isn't a priest."

"Are you sure of that?"

"Yes. Absolutely."

They were seated at a thirty-foot T-shaped table in a massive room with lofty ceilings, Vlora at the center and head of the T, the Muslim and the one-eyed priest at the bottom. Clean-shaven and wearing an eyepatch now, the one-eyed priest was neatly dressed in brown tweed pants and a bright green lamb's wool turtleneck sweater. Dragging on a loosely packed cheap cigarette, he looked aside and then blew out a ragged cone of smoke.

"Any priest," he finished saying, "would have heard my confession."

He angled a disapproving glance to the Muslim.

"You might have pulled your punches just a bit," he said coolly.

He picked a bitter shred of tobacco from his lip.

The Muslim gave a diffident shrug and looked away.

"It's my method," said the Muslim.

"Some method."

It had all been staged.

The cell had been populated by actors.

"Don't complain, you have your freedom for it," Vlora told the priest. "Now what else? Any other impressions? Either one of you?"

"My pain," the priest uttered remotely.

His faraway stare was fixed on a scratch mark vivid on the dark stained pine of the table. It resembled a tiny omega sign.

Vlora frowned. "Your pain?"

The priest looked up.

"Well, after all of these powerful blows I'd received I had

this terrible pain in my head. It was constant. I couldn't shake it. The fellow put his hand on my forehead and it vanished." For a moment Vlora's stare was blank; and then a corner of his lip sickled up in derision. "Do you still believe in magic, priest?" he spat. "You're exhausted. Go home to your wife."

Vlora's words hid his bafflement, fear, and frustration. On the night before he'd thought of the ruse in the cell, he had dreamed once again of the banquet in Tirana, of Ho Chi Minh, and of a death, but now added to the scene was a spectral servant, a worker in the kitchen whose face was a blank. And then Vlora was back in the interrogation chamber, where the Prisoner was chained to a wall with his arms in the T of crucifixion, and "Angel," the torturer, was in front of him, tilting a cup of cold water to his lips. "Elena," the Interrogator called out to her, using her actual given name. She turned to him, smiled, and walked over to join him, and they quietly conversed, discussing the Prisoner in pleasant, easy tones. "Who is he?" the Interrogator asked her warmly, and she amiably answered, "Your rescuer." The next instant Vlora found himself standing in the street staring down at his drenched and deluded oppressor in the rain, the executed priest, and when the dead man's eyes opened wide to stare balefully back up at Vlora, he awakened with an inchoate new suspicion: Was the Prisoner another of those tiresome martyrs whose courage was inhuman enough to be hateful? Was the man who carried Selca Decani's papers a priest who'd been trudging through the mountains of the north hawking Masses and forgiveness and a bread that was God while in the guise of a peddler of a crumbly white cheese? But then apart from the failure of the ruse in the cell, the theory that the tactic had been founded upon was soon utterly blasted, demolished, by receipt of a report from Security pathologists dealing with the scar on the Prisoner's arm:

> The area in question is thought to be the site of an operation that appears to have been logical, and therefore, most probably performed by plastic surgeons. The most obvious feature is the absence of structures, such as follicles of hair and sebaceous glands. As there seems to be a likely donor site with attendant slight scarring and depigmentation high on the Subject's inner right thigh, the procedure is deemed to be a graft, a finding consistent with the grossly discernible scar where the grafted skin joins the pre-existing skin, and with the difference in texture between the skin at the site of the graft and the skin that surrounds it. Beneath the graft there is noticeable thinning of the superficial skin as well as scarring of the underlying tissues, with a few aggregations of inflammatory cells. In evaluating these data, there is probable cause, we conclude, to presume that the graft was meant to hide a vaccination.

Sitting in the chill of his office at daybreak, the Interrogator blinked at the final sentence. Hide a vaccination? Who would do such a thing? To what end? Frowning, he put the report aside, and while the pink and blue flowers in a glass on his desk breathed death, his mind made a puzzling, angry leap to his people's old backwardness, to their illiteracy, to the blood feuds and infant betrothals and the terrified, shrieking children penned up in dark corners for the first twelve months of their lives lest the demons should see them and do them harm, this but one of the numberless crippling superstitions made to seem almost credible, almost sane, by belief in a suffering, bleeding God. Vlora glanced down at his hand atop the desk. It had curled itself tightly into a fist. He unclenched his fingers. They continued to tremble. He had been one of those children of the dark.

Vlora turned to look out at the morning street and the pewtery light of dawn seeping in, glowing softly on the fog enshrouding the city so that portions of buildings protruded here and there like gleams of ghostly rubble. Why had he thought of such things? he wondered. Vexed, he looked down at the pathology report: ". . . meant to hide a vaccination." What could it mean? He didn't know. But as he shifted his gaze to the photograph of his time-lost wife and child, he caught his breath at the sudden and disturbing recollection that it was not until after a scourge of smallpox had scythed through the land more than thirty-five years ago that the practice of infant vaccination had made its appearance in Albania. The Prisoner, a man in his forties, was born a few years before that time, and, if a native Albanian, could not have been vaccinated!

Vlora shuddered. The room seemed colder. Who would have the need or even *think* of the need to conceal the telltale vaccination other than a formidable enemy agent on a mission of power and unthinkable menace? Vlora brooded on the blind man's eerie report and the perfectly flawed Albanian dentistry; on the strangled dog in the wood and the spectral, unsettling Selca Decani. If the Prisoner wasn't a foreign agent, Vlora concluded, then he must be a devil.

"Or both," he murmured.

He'd once heard of such a legendary agent from Hell.

That night Vlora slept with the demons.

Then events took a turn that was wholly confounding. Early on the morning of 3 April, cutting short his visit to an ailing father, there returned to Tirana from Beijing at Vlora's urgent and imperative summons, a tall, gaunt Chinese Army medical officer, Major Liu Ng Tsu, a drug-hypnosis interrogation expert assigned as an adviser to Central Security. On the third and the fourth, Vlora briefed him and allowed him to study the written record. On the fifth there was action. The Prisoner, kept sleepless for thirty-six hours and deprived of water for twenty-four, was placed on his back atop a gurney cart, strapped down with leather restraints, and wheeled to a narrow, white-tiled room. Immaculately clean and brightly lit by surgical spotlights affixed to the ceiling, this was the so-called Magic Room. Here tricks could be played on top of tricks. First Sodium Pentothal was injected. After that the hypnosis began and the illusions: "Your hand is beginning to feel very warm," recalcitrant subjects had often been told; this to convince them they had entered the hypnotic state and that further attempts at resistance were useless, when in fact the subject's hand was responding to the current from a hidden diathermy machine. Or concealed holographic projectors were invoked: "Do you see the solid wall there in front of you?" "Yes." "Look through it. You'll see roses that are floating in midair." These were the games. When they were done, methamphetamine was injected to create an irresistible, driving urge to pour out speech, ideas, and memories, giving the subject no time to think; and then there sometimes came forth, at the end of it all, a bruised and slurry thing called truth.

"Come, begin! What's the problem?"

Exhausted and driven, impatient, consumed, Vlora glared in consternation at Tsu, who was standing across from him at the gurney. Leaning down to inject the Pentothal, he had inexplicably hesitated: the syringe held poised in midair, he stood motionless, studying the Prisoner's face.

Vlora looked worried. "What is it? What's wrong?"

Tsu shook his head, remained still, then said, "Nothing."

He bent lower and administered the injection.

"For a moment I thought I might have seen this man before."

A polygraph expert shuffled into the room. Short and middle-aged with close-set eyes, he wore a threadbare suit several sizes too large so that the trousers bagged in folds at his feet. "I'm here," he muttered sourly in greeting. Pulled away from his breakfast, sullen and begrudging, he noisily unfolded a metal table and chair and banged each of them down near the head of the gurney. After setting his polygraph machine on the table, he wired the Prisoner to the device, then settled into the chair looking wounded and abused. Snuffling, he slipped on his earphones and nodded as he murmured in a tone of patient suffering, "I'm ready."

"If you will help us just a little, you may drink this."

Tsu held a frost-covered glass of iced water to the Prisoner's cheek. "Fresh water from a spring," he told the Prisoner amiably. "If you obey my next command you may drink it. All right? Nothing onerous. Just open your eyes."

Vlora shook his head. "This will not work," he said. "It won't work." Staring intently at the Prisoner's face, an incredible and chilling suspicion had just occurred to him concerning the enigma's identity.

The Prisoner opened his eyes.

Vlora took a quick step back from the gurney.

Propping up the Prisoner's head with his hand, Tsu held the water to his lips with the other. "Just a sip or two for now," he cautioned gently. Then he made a quiet promise: "More later."

The Prisoner spoke. He said, "Thank you."

Startled, Vlora flinched while Tsu met his look of amazement with a smile. And so began the series of steps and events that would lead to the belief that the Prisoner had weakened, an impression that would finally come to be viewed, when the annals of the "Magic Room" were completed, as surely its most incredible and lethal illusion.

All of the early moves were routine: the lights were dimmed down to a ghostly murk, the usual "road hypnosis" begun: the application of a steady, repetitive rhythm, in this instance an illuminated metronome blade that the Prisoner watched as it tocked back and forth. Such had always been shown to be highly effective against the desire not to be hypnotized and to retain one's alertness of will. Then the favorite tricks of the room were invoked, and when persuaded that the spell had at last taken hold, Tsu followed by injecting the methamphetamine in a larger than usual dosage—6.4 milligrams per kilogram of body weight—needed for introverted neurotics. And then, in an ordinary, nondescript voice, and with flawless inflection of the language of the north, the Prisoner not only spoke but also answered all queries.

It might have been better for his captors had he not.

Under questioning, the Prisoner repeated his claim to be Selca Decani, the peddler of cheese and the lover of Morna Altamori, explaining that, in fact, he had never died but had simply vanished, fled away to the West, the reports of his death a deliberate fiction contrived to protect Decani's family from certain harassment by the State. His return to Albania had been prompted by his fear of the imminent death of his ailing mother. This, fundamentally, was Story Number One.

There were others.

Enemy agents of the deadlier class had been known to use drugs and hypnosis defensively with nefarious "Pentothal blocks" so that the subject, under torture or if questioned by this method, would repeat a hypnotically programmed recitation. In the event that his questioners probed even deeper by attacking the block with more drugs and hypnosis, underneath the first story they might turn up a second, which, just as the first, had been scripted and implanted. A third such block had been found, it was rumored, in a rare if not mythical number of cases. Thus everything seemed to be running to form, every paranoid fear and suspicion confirmed when, under much deeper interrogation, the Prisoner's story drastically changed. While retaining the carpentry of the first it differed in subtle but significant ways. This time the Prisoner admitted that Selca Decani indeed was dead, and that he himself was named Sabri Melcani and had years ago fled to Yugoslavia, and from there moved on to Greece, to escape a murder charge that had arisen from his actions in the course of pursuing a blood feud: hearing that the man he thought he'd killed had recovered and was happily walking the earth, Melcani felt compelled—"by the sting of conscience," he said—to return and try again. This, in essence, was Story Number Two which, if left at that, might not have proved so upsetting, except that there were also Story Three, Story Four, and Story Five, while Story Six, to the fury and utter consternation of all, was a faithful repetition of Story Number One, thus announcing—provided the Prisoner could live through the added injections of the dangerous drugs—the prospect of an endless and fruitless cycle. Which was not, as it happened, the most appalling thing at all. This honor was reserved for the polygraph machine.

It corroborated *all* of the Prisoner's stories.

At this juncture it was difficult to know where to turn, and so the natural direction, by default, and to the immense relief of anyone harboring a longing for the familiar, was directly and immediately into chaos as, desperate, Vlora embraced a new tactic that was neither in his nature nor his power to control. From beginning to end the scenario was Tsu's.

It began very calmly. In fact, rather pleasantly. The Prisoner was taken to comfortable quarters where, after receiving medical attention, for seven days he was able to bathe, given food and drink and clean clothes, and was permitted to sleep in a downy bed undisturbed until he naturally awakened. In the meantime, Major Tsu had given strict instructions that no one in contact with the Prisoner was ever to speak while in his presence, either to him or to anyone else. On day eight, a Monday, action resumed. The Prisoner was escorted by four armed guards to the room with the T-shaped table where Vlora alone sat waiting for him. The black velvet drapes had been drawn aside from the great high windows along the east wall so that sunlight shattered down in smoky columns, trapping particles of dust and fear in their swirl. The Prisoner was placed near the bottom of the table by two of the guards, all of whom then exited the room and left him standing alone at the bottom of the T with his head bowed down and his hands held clasped in front of him as if gripped by invisible manacles. Music played softly through speakers in the walls and all the windows stood open so that one could hear traffic from the street far below. Now and then a child's shout or silly laugh floated up.

"So here we are," began Vlora in an ordinary way. "New surroundings are refreshing at times, a great tonic; they can pry us from our ruts, our fixed habits of thinking. By the way, do sit down if you like. Please be comfortable. Really. Never mind, then. Just as you wish. Incidentally, is the music to your liking?

We can change it. Should I change it? It is Strauss. Very well, then, we shall leave it. In the meantime, let me tell you what is happening here. First, we thank you for those fascinating stories that you told us. I myself am a lover and avid admirer of any great work of the imagination. I've translated many of them into Albanian: Shakespeare's *Macbeth*, and his *Hamlet* and *Othello*. Also *Lady Inger of Ostrat* by Ibsen. *Don Quixote*. Do you find that surprising? Yes, I did the work personally, it was when I was a teacher at college. They awarded me the 'Partisan Star.' Well, never mind. I've been garrulous. Why is it that we always feel this gnawing necessity to justify ourselves to every stranger that we meet? Do you know what I'm talking about? Perhaps not. Well, that's enough of that now. Back to business. Listen here, I want to tell you what we've come to. Alright? We want to have a new relationship with you. The old one, you'll admit, was unrewarding." Vlora gestured down the length of the table to a tan wicker basket that was crammed with fresh fruit. "Incidentally, try an apricot," he offered. "They're in season."

Into the room now strode three torturers, all brutes of powerful build, including "Laugher," who led them in. He was gripping a briefcase made of shining blue leather and the arm of a club-footed ten-year-old boy who was dressed in the olive drab denim of a prisoner. The boy's hands had been tied in front of him and his arms were trussed to his sides. Arriving at a point that was midway along the table, Vlora's son pushed the boy forward until he was captured, wincing and blinking, in a column of sunlight.

"Well now, yes, we're all here," began Vlora. "Very well,

then, let's not waste any time. This boy is a Gypsy, deformed from birth. In addition to the problem with his foot he has a paralyzed arm, the left, which is numb and completely insensitive to pain. He is also retarded, a mental defective, as well as being dumb and unable to speak. He murdered his parents in their sleep, an understandable action but not his prerogative. One could argue he is better off dead. But we aren't going to kill him. No, not for us to judge. We may not do anything at all to him, in fact. It's really all up to you."

At a signal from Vlora, "Laugher" lifted the briefcase onto the table, snapped its locks, and withdrew from it a clear and colorless plastic bag at whose bottom was a drawstring made of leather. The boy's eyes widened with fear and bewilderment as the bag was slipped over his head. Vlora glanced at his watch as if checking the time until his next appointment. "Suffocation is a horrible death," he said casually. "Worse yet is to die in this manner many times; in fact over and over again without limit. Until you reveal your true name and your mission, plus the data that is needed to verify both, we intend to repeatedly bring this boy to the brink of death by suffocation. His fate is in your hands. But do not feel any pressure. By all means, take your time. As I said to you before, you have suffered enough." One torturer tightened the drawstring and knotted it. Another put his arms around the boy and held him still, so that he stayed within the compass of the column of light as he wildly thrashed, his eyes bulging in terror and his mouth gaping open in a soundless shriek while through the speakers rasped the lilts of *The Blue Danube*.

"This is truly regrettable," Vlora uttered sadly. "Yes, it is. It truly is. But the danger to thousands outweighs the pain of one." He stood up, walked over to a door, and pulled it open. "Come!" he commanded into the shadows of a dimly lit ante-room, summoning Tsu and the creaking old doctor with the black valise. The doctor moved quickly to the nearest corner, while Tsu took Vlora's seat at the table. "Major Tsu will take my place from here out," announced Vlora. He was staring at the Prisoner with fatherly patience. "You have grown too used to me. Yes. Much too comfortable. That's very clear. Major Tsu will resharpen your interest. In the meantime, do not think that this boy is an actor. He is not. Should you doubt that, I now give you proof."

With a lift of his chin Vlora gestured toward the boy, and instantly "Laugher" plucked a knife from his pocket, unclasped it, and sliced off the screaming boy's little finger, lazily tossing it onto the table in front of the Prisoner. It landed by the basket of fruit.

The Interrogator glared at his son with fury.

"*Damn* you!" he flung at him, seething. "*Damn* you!"

Against his orders that the finger be cut from the boy's numb hand, Vlora's son had cut the finger from the hand that had feeling. Vlora turned and strode angrily out of the cham-ber, fleetingly assailed, as he was from time to time, by a stabbing flash of doubt that surcease from pain for thousands could ever be purchased with the torment of one.

Vlora's habit was to bludgeon and strangle such thoughts.

This time he did not.

What happened after that would be carefully analyzed but never quite understood; after all, the incontestable facts were so few. As he exited, Vlora had been hastily saluted by the two armed guards who were posted at the door. From there he had proceeded directly to his office, passing many other guards in the halls along the way. But after thirty-seven minutes Vlora suddenly decided to terminate Tsu's experiment and, bursting from his office like the search for a quarrel, he strode rapidly back to the questioning room. The two armed guards were not at their posts. Vlora found them inside, both of them stripped of their uniform and weapons. They were unconscious, concussed and drugged with hypnotics that had come from the doctor's medical bag, while the old man himself, although not touched, had apparently suffered a fatal heart attack, and inasmuch as the boy was discovered alive, this meant that the number of those who had been killed totaled only four, not five as originally thought, and included a torturer who had died from a powerful blow with the heel of a hand that had instantaneously crushed his windpipe, and another whose spine had been broken by a single smash to the nape of his neck, while the back of Tsu's skull had cracked wide open from the force of his body being slammed against a wall. The other torturer, "Laugher," Vlora's son, greeted death without a noticeable change of expression except for his eyes, in which frozen forever was a faint odd glimmer of something that no one could properly identify, but more than anything resembled surprise.

His neck had been broken.

The two guards who survived could tell their questioners

little. On hearing a "scratching sound" on the door, one said, he had entered the chamber alone, caught a glimpse of the Prisoner for "only a flash" before feeling his hands around his throat and being rendered immediately unconscious by "something, some pressure that he put on my nerves." The other guard, who'd gone into the chamber moments later, related an identical encounter, as did four other guards on other floors. As to why the Prisoner had spared their lives, they could offer no opinion, nor could anyone else. There were searches, questionings, crime team reports, but in the end they illuminated nothing, and as night and whispers and paranoid terrors filled the mazes of the State Security Building, no heart there beat regularly.

The Prisoner had escaped.

T hree days later, on the evening of Sunday, 17 May, and beginning at precisely forty minutes after sundown, seven young men came together in a straw-strewn barn in the high craggy village of Domni, just as they had gathered every Sunday before at precisely this time for hopeless months. Rough-hewn peasants in their early twenties, they spoke little and in guarded whispers lest the dreaded Sigurimi discover their presence. When they first began to meet they were excited by their mission, at their breath-holding peril in these secret watches, but the hammer of time had blunted their edge and they felt only tedium now, the grip of habit, as they huddled in darkness on the earthen barn floor and waited for a man who never came.

"And so what do you think?"

The husky whisper pierced the silence.

"Do you think he's been captured?" continued the speaker, a brawny smith from the village of Drishti. "Is he dead?"

"I am happy to find you all well."

The men were startled. The voice was unfamiliar. Not one of theirs. They scrambled to their feet with sudden fear. This someone in the darkness, this stranger: Who was he? Where had he come from? They had seen and heard nothing: No creak of a door. No movement. No step.

The young smith from Drishti recovered his poise.

"God may have brought you here," he ventured in a quietly probing, hopeful voice. He felt the pulsing of a vein in his temple as he added the words that could trigger the password:

"Tell us, did you come by the road less traveled?"

The Prisoner stepped forward and uttered the countersign:

" 'All of creation waits with longing.' "

The smith took in a quick little breath of realization.

"The Bishop! It's you! You have come!"

The next moment the young men were kneeling all in a row on the earthen barn floor with their heads bowed down while the Prisoner moved swiftly and silently forward and, cupping his hands atop the head of the smith, began to recite with urgent speed a Catholic formula of prayer:

" 'We ask you, All-Powerful Father . . .'," he began.

The ritual completed in less than a minute, the Prisoner moved to the next of the men, laying on his hands and repeating the prayer until, by the end of the seventh repetition, his rich, firm voice had begun to quaver and his hands, lacking fingernails, to tremble, as he sank to his knees and wept convulsively.

The newly made priests looked on.

S tanding, breathing above his desk in the haunted darkness of his office, Vlora inhaled the ghosts of flowers, withered and dry and dead in their glass; heard the crisp, rough click of the metal switch as he turned on the crooknecked khaki lamp and held under its beam the puzzling object, the mysterious token, whole and unmarked, found crammed into the mouth of his murdered son.

It was a golden-skinned apricot.

"Dimiter," Vlora murmured numbly.

It was the name of the agent from Hell.

PART TWO

JERUSALEM

1974

Doctor Moses Mayo began each day as if expecting the world would end that night. He could find no other way to endure its griefs, the quiet terror of living in a human body. Waking at dawn's cool touch each day, by seven he was hunkered down at his desk munching poppy-seed bagels and sipping sweet tea as he greeted *The Jerusalem Post*'s grim headlines with a murmured, "Who cares? The world is ending tonight." But this early March morning found a different path. In his narrow staff quarters at Hadassah Hospital's medical school, the neurologist awakened in the tunnels of night with a quietly pulsing sense of dread. Wide awake, he lay still, staring up into darkness while he listened to the whirring and the flurry of his thoughts. He had dreamed. Something strange. But what? He sat up, turned on a bedside tensor lamp, and squinted down at the tiny brass moonfaced clock ticking loudly in the hush of a circle of light. Mayo groaned. It was minutes after 2 A.M. The neurologist sighed, swung his feet to the floor, and was cradling his lowered head in his hands when an overwhelming sadness, a depression, fell upon him. What was it? he wondered. The dream? Dully staring at his curled-up bony white toes, Mayo moodily wriggled them up and down. One of his patients had died the night before. Despondency and guilt always followed, he knew. Was that it? Or was it still the mad horror in the Psychiatric Ward, the shocking murder that no one could comprehend? Mayo scratched at his scrawny chest through the flannel of a red and white striped pajama top. No, he decided: neither one. He stood up and his feet made fleshy padding sounds as he entered a white tiled bathroom where he turned on the light, gripped and twisted a spigot, and splashed cold water onto his face. In the pipes, wakened air clanged and rattled, then abated. *Yes, shut up*, Mayo thought, *there are sick people here who are sleeping*. "Not me, though," he murmured aloud. "Not me."

Drying off with a threadbare, faded blue towel, Mayo paused in his tentative dabbing and rubbing to meet his own gaze in the cabinet mirror where grieving green eyes in an angular face beneath a bristling of iron gray hair stared back

with the sting of recrimination. "Incompetent!" Mayo murmured bitterly. "Fraud!" He was brooding about the patient
who had died. Flopping the towel back onto a hook, he stared
into the mirror at a quiet birthmark, a milk white oval inden-
tation palely nestled near the corner of his drooping right eye.
"Come on, what did I dream?" once again he asked himself.
Nothing came and he turned away.

And then suddenly the dream opened up its heart to him,
beginning with a Christ Child aged about five. Wearing only
a dhoti and brown leather sandals in addition to a stethoscope
dangling from his neck, he was solemnly conducting grand
rounds through the Neurology Ward as he led a procession of
note-taking medical students to the bed of the blind man he
had famously cured at the Pool of Bethesda. The Child's
expression was mild and sweet and his body was shrouded in
a faint white glow. He nodded at the blind man reassuringly.
"We meet again," he told him with a smile. His head propped
on pillows, the miracle's recipient did not respond but lay
rigidly still, his eyes wide with suspicion and apprehension.
The Child unhooked his chart from the bedstead, scanned it,
replaced it, and then turned to the students who lifted their
clipboards and pens to take notes.

"What we have here is a genuine miracle," announced the
Child. He pointed to the patient with an index finger at the
top of which an inch-high Band-Aid was wrapped. "This man
was blind from birth," he recounted, "so I applied a bit of
spittle to his eyes with my fingers and then asked him if he saw
anything. He said, 'Yes. I can see. I see people. But they look

like trees that are walking around.' " At this the formerly blind man appeared to relax, as if at last understanding that the group had not come to accuse him of some crime or perhaps a lack of adequate appreciation, and the miracle of sight was not about to be reversed. He shut his eyes peacefully and nodded as if in confirmation of what he was hearing. "So I gave him a second application," said the Child; "but no spittle this time, just my fingertips touching his eyes. And right away he saw everything without distortion. And *that*, please observe, was the actual miracle: it was that *second* laying on of my hands." The Child glanced around at the students who were rapidly scribbling on their clipboards and pads. "Now can someone tell me why?" he asked them benignly. A young woman with violet hair raised a tattooed hand that was clenched in a fist, and when it opened a pure white dove fluttered out. "Yes?" the Child said to her, his eyebrows curving upward expectantly.

"Oh, well, even if the blindness was psychosomatic . . ." she began, but the formerly blind man's eyes flared open and he cut her off.

"Are you calling me a liar?" he angrily challenged. Above the group the white dove was now circling and diving, making random, quick pecking attacks that drew blood.

"No," the student responded, "I'm just saying that the cause wouldn't matter. After many years of blindness, you still wouldn't have had any depth perception or be able to synthesize shape or form. Remember how it hurt when you opened your eyes? How all you saw was just a spinning mass of lights and bright colors? Sure, your eyes were repaired but your brain still hadn't learned how to process their data. It takes a month of hard work just to be able to distinguish a few simple objects." Here the blind man looked mollified, lowering his gaze and mutely nodding in agreement. "No, of *course* you're not lying," the student summed up. "It's *only* if you'd really had your sight restored in that first attempt at a cure that you would have seen men who looked like trees. If the whole thing was a lie you'd have said you saw perfectly the *first* time you were cured."

Here suddenly the dove swooped down with stunning speed and bit the Christ Child's pale soft cheek. A gout of blood gushed out of the puncture, splashing on the whiteness of the blind man's bed and from there to the floor in pumping streams as the dove became a bloodstained winged hypodermic syringe flapping swiftly away to the end of the hall, where it sharply turned a corner and, gleaming, vanished. Then abruptly, and ending the dream, the violet-haired student was standing in front of Mayo dressed in Victorian widow's weeds. She raised her arm and her hand unclasped to reveal three bright green dew-glistened fruits while her other hand held out a folded-up newspaper. "Cousin Harriet," she mournfully intoned, "here is the *Boston Evening Transcript* and some lovely poisoned figs."

Mayo put a finger to his lips and nodded, thinking that he knew what might have triggered the dream. He'd recently pondered this very episode in the gospel of St. Mark in which the blind man cured at the Pool of Bethesda could at first see only men who looked like "trees that are walking around," and saw perfectly and clearly only after Christ had repeated the healing action. An avowed agnostic—though the mystery of design in the human body had nagged him to belief in an amorphous intelligence at large in the world, which he would sometimes refer to as "Maurice"—Mayo found the gospel passage baffling. And unnerving. In the time of Christ, cures for blindness were medically unknown. So if the healing at Bethesda hadn't actually happened, how could Mark have known the symptoms of post-blind syndrome? Mayo lifted a hand and looked at his fingernails as he nodded his head a little. Yes, the dream had regurgitated his musings.

But the winged syringe? The blood? Poisoned figs?

The neurologist finished his waking ablutions, dressed, and boiled water on a single-burner hot plate for the brewing of a heavily sugared tea in an oversized thick white porcelain mug which he carried with him out into the dimly lit hall where, for a time, he stood silent and still, irresolute, his head bowed down in thought and a hand in the pocket of a medical jacket that, just as with his rumpled baggy trousers, was much too large for his sticklike frame. He seemed not to wear his clothes but to inhabit them. "Miracles," he muttered. They'd been suddenly as common in these antiseptic halls as the moans of the soldiers in the Burn Ward late at night. On Monday a nurse named Samia Maroon had reported to him breathlessly that she had seen some sort of apparition. And then there was that two-year-old boy in the Children's Ward with rabdomial sarcoma, a rapid-spreading, always fatal cancer. For weeks the boy's X-rays had turned up a mass in his chest growing steadily and ominously larger. Overnight the mass vanished. Examining the X-ray, "It's that damned elusive Pimpernel," the confounded neurologist had murmured. The boy had also suffered from dysautonomia, a mysterious crippling of the nervous system that afflicted only the Ashkenazim, the descendants of Eastern European Jews, and whose victims were unable to cry or feel pain. Like the cancer, the disease and its symptoms had vanished. *Maurice!* Mayo thought. *The crazy goniff doesn't play by his own damned rules!* As for the nurse's apparition: *Couldn't be!*

Staring down into his tea, the neurologist sighed and looked wistful; no poppy-seed bagels to be found at this hour. *They don't drop from the sky anymore*, he mourned. He lurched ahead, disconsolately slouching through the open double doors beside the barred and shuttered counters of a Bank Leumi branch, thus exiting the medical school to cross the dark stone squares of a courtyard and enter the hospital's main reception. Two heavyset women were mopping the floor, sloshing water and suds back and forth hypnotically on the beige and black speckle of the tiles. The cavernous and echoing hall that by day was filled with bustle and the chatter of life was now still and deserted except for the charwomen. And one other person, Mayo saw with dismay. His gaunt face gray with a stubble of beard, a shriveled old Arab in a threadbare dark blue pinstriped suit was seated on one of the cedar benches where the outpatients waited their turn to see a doctor. His spindly frame drawn tightly erect, the old Arab was staring at Mayo intently with an air of hope and expectation. *Meshugge*, thought Mayo;

in the Arabic velterrein, *completely lost in space*. Softly groaning, Mayo sidled to the bench and sat down.

"Good morning," he quietly greeted in Arabic.

"Morning of roses."

"Morning of gold. Tell me, why are you here again so early, my brother? We've gone through this once before, friend, have we not?" Mayo had recently encountered the Arab while returning from a late-night call on a patient complaining of excruciating "phantom limb" pain. The old fellow had been adamant in his conviction that because he was an Arab he might not be treated unless he was clearly the first in line.

"Uncle, didn't you get to see the doctor last week?"

"Yes, I did."

"And he treated you?"

"Yes."

"So then why are we here now, Uncle?"

"Why not?"

Mayo pursed his lips and looked blocked "Why not?" served a function in colloquial Arabic closely akin to the Yiddish "*nu*," a vague and multifaceted response with innumerable shades and twists of meaning including no meaning whatsoever. But before the neurologist could narrow the question, the Arab touched his fingers to the side of his head, declaring woefully, "Please. This is new. I have headaches."

"There's no need to come so early, though. Really. Arab or Jew, it makes no difference. Have we still not discovered this, Uncle?"

"Well, the war."

Mayo's gaze flicked down to the patient application form rolled up in the Arab's left hand. At Mayo's glance a faint papery crinkling sound could be heard as the apprehensive Arab tightened his grip.

Mayo looked up at him again without expression.

"Did you fill out the form?" he asked quietly.

"Yes."

"And did you tell them again that you are Puerto Rican?"

The Arab's eyes shimmered with guilt and defiance.

"Why not?"

Mayo lowered his head for a moment, then looked up.

"You're a farmer, Uncle?"

"Shopkeeper."

"Shopkeeper. What do you sell?"

"Souvenirs."

"Ah, I see. And now business is bad?"

"Yes, bad. Very bad. It's the war."

Mayo's gaze ran a scan of the Arab's face. And then abruptly he stood up. "Upstairs they will probably X-ray your skull," he pronounced, "but I am guessing your headaches are due to stress. When the tourists come back you'll be fine. In the meantime, eat fried green bananas. Doctor's orders. They're rich in potassium, Uncle. Your people all love them. They're a Puerto Rican specialty. Eat them."

Mayo turned and strode away.

"God be with you," the Arab called out.

"*Fried bananas!*"

Mayo stepped around a charwoman's flailing mop and then

81

made his way slowly to a bank of elevators. Finding one open and waiting, he stepped into it and pushed a round black button marked "3." The doors closed. A slight lurch and then soundless ascension. But on arriving at "3," Mayo did not get off. He impulsively pushed the black button marked "Mem," rode down to that floor, and then again pushed the button marked "3." Because the hospital's elevators during normal hours were crammed to asphyxiating fullness, Mayo's sense of untrammeled space was luxurious. At one point, he murmured, "Toyland, please." He left the elevator glutted with satisfaction.

Headed for his office, Mayo stopped as he came to a nurse's station where behind the high counter, head bent low, a pretty, dark-haired nurse in her thirties was entering notes into a patient ledger.

"Good morning, Samia."

"Good morning."

Still writing, the nurse had not looked up and her tone of voice was flat and cool. With a sigh, Mayo lowered his head and shook it. He had recently injured the nurse's feelings by scoffing at the story she'd excitedly told him concerning a patient named Isabell Lakhme, an elderly woman with mild dementia who'd been recently crippled by a fracture of the hip. "I was checking on the burn case in 304 about one in the morning," the nurse had recounted, "when I hear someone *shnuffling* around in the hall. I look up through the doorway and who do I see walk by? Swear to God? No lie? Mrs. Lakhme!"

"You're not serious."

"I swear. Absolutely. It was her. Except she looked—
well . . ."

"How, Samia? How did she look?"

"Well, like rosy. You know? Sort of youthful. And she
turns and looks me straight in the eye and she smiles. Well,
my jaw drops a foot. I mean, I can't believe she's walking!
Right? So I blurted out, 'Hey! Mrs. Lakhme!' I was shocked.
She walks on and out of sight, so I go after her, okay? But
by the time I'm in the hallway she's gone. There's no one
there. She's disappeared!"

"Samia? . . ."

"No, no, wait a minute! Wait until I tell you! I went straight
to her room, and . . ."

"She wasn't in her bed, you're going to tell me?"

"No, she was. She was there. She was asleep."

"Tell me, what is the point of this, Samia?"

"It's this: The next day, I'm in her room when her daughter
comes to visit and—"

"You told them that you saw her?"

"Can you stop interrupting? No, Moses. No, I didn't say a
word. So now the daughter takes her hand and she gives it a
kiss. I can see she's kind of shaky. You know? About to cry.
And then she says to her mother how she wishes that she
weren't always 'stuck in this bed.' And then Lakhme—swear to
God, Moses! God's honest truth!—Lakhme says to her, 'Don't
worry. I'm not stuck here at all. I go traveling with young
people all of the time.' Then she turns to me smiling a little,
and she says to me, 'And *you* know I'm telling the truth because

you saw me last night, Nurse, didn't you?' Oh, my God, I almost fainted, Moses! Can you believe it?"

"No," the neurologist had answered. "Moreover, you haven't any right to be delusional, Samia. That's a privilege reserved for the chief physician and higher ranking hospital staff." That had done it, Mayo ruefully reflected. He listened to the scratching of the ink-fed pen as the nurse kept writing, head low to her task. She had told him she had seen something else that night. Mayo's gaze fixed dubiously on the crimson Star of David stitched into her oversized starched white cap. His quest for unwavering faith in her accounts had been less than heroically advanced by the fact that he knew her to be a neurotic as well as a courageously innovative tester of the outermost limits of paranoia. Once she had bitterly and memorably complained that the clerks at a grocer's near Jerusalem Hills, the inexpensive neighborhood where she lived, had refused to carry her bags to her car because "that whole creepy staff there is anti-Arab," whereas in fact the store's owners were Palestinians. Mayo stood patiently, waiting and hoping for the nurse to stop writing, until at last he gave up with a sigh and moved on. Instantly, the scratching of the pen behind him ceased.

Mayo shook his head and kept walking, trudging down a corridor lined with narrow cots and restless sleepers. A breakdown of the hospital's main computer had delayed the release of dozens of patients who had only come in for routine tests. Mayo shook his head at that, too. At the door to his office he fumbled in a pocket of his jacket for a key and whisked it out, but then as he was slipping it into the lock he turned his head to stare pensively down the length of a dimly lit hallway at whose shadowy end some beckoning mystery faintly glowed. *There*, Mayo thought. *It had happened there.* "Samia, you're a lunatic," he murmured. He extracted the key, slipped it into his pocket, and in moments was scuffing through the long win-dowed hall past idle oxygen tanks and gurneys until he had neared a dead-end wall filled with brightly colored painted car-toon figures that marked the beginning of the Children's Ward. Mayo stopped. There was something on the floor just ahead of him. He reached down and picked it up. It was a white chef's cap, very narrow in size. Mayo judged it to be part of a child's Purim costume and a fond, sad smile warmed his eyes as he carefully placed it on a parked medication cart silently awaiting the squeak of its rounds. He heard a faint *click* behind him, like a sewing needle falling to the ground. He turned around but saw nothing. The hall was empty. What had he expected to see? he asked himself. "Mrs. Lakhme?" he said aloud dryly. He walked on to an observation window, where he stopped and looked in at the ward's tall gray metal cribs, in each one a sleeping child. Mayo stared broodingly at the dark-haired boy in whom the cancer and dysautonomia had vanished. The double remission was but part of the puzzle. There was yet that other mystery hovering here, that second tale of the improbable as told by Samia.

Mayo thought he detected movement and, shifting his gaze, saw that one of the children was awake, a two-year-old girl with rosy, plump cheeks who was lying on her side with a thumb in her mouth. She was staring at Mayo with a mischievous smile most resembling amused anticipation. The moment the neurologist met her gaze she sat up with a giggly laugh of delight and clapped both hands together in front of her. After that, for a time she sat motionless, squinting at Mayo with an air of expectancy until the smile in her eyes slowly faded and, slipping her thumb back into her mouth, she gave a sigh, lay back down, and turned away her head. The neurologist continued to study her, puzzled, then at last turned around and shuffled away still gripping the mug half-filled with tea now cooler than his search for the meaning of his life.

At the door to his office Mayo paused. He'd caught an odd flash of motion at the end of the hall, something black and quick, but when he turned to look directly he saw nothing. Mayo sighed, and with a rueful shake of his head he unlocked the door and entered his office. *The deadly Samia Virus is spreading*, he thought. *We must notify the World Health people!* Mayo shuffled morosely to the dark oaken swivel chair faithfully waiting behind his desk, sat down, and briefly scanned the accumulated chaos of the room. When he'd served as chief physician, a post he had mysteriously abandoned at around the time when his weight had begun to so dramatically drop, Mayo's tight little office was a match for his mind: a silent temple of neatness and organization. But since his resignation the cubbyhole sanctuary had gradually become a mad warren where books and medical reports on shelves jostled humorous trivia and mementos, while the once-bare walls were now gasping for breath under framed citations, photos, and oddities such as the faded printed label from a jar of a plum-colored liquid substance evocatively identified as "Nosferatu Beet Juice"—just below the name appeared the word "Imported"—and a pair of quotations from Israeli humorist Ephraim Kishon. One was headed "Advice to Patients":

> DON'T BE TOO FUSSY. IF YOU ASK FOR CLEAR SOUP
> AND GET NOODLE SOUP, THE NURSE WILL TELL
> YOU: "SO EAT THE SOUP AND LEAVE THE NOODLES."

The other Kishon quotation was beside it:

> **WHAT CAN YOU GET FOR A POUND THESE DAYS?**
> **A CURSE FROM A BEGGAR!**

Prominently centered between a travel poster of Carmel, California, and a photo of the fog-shrouded lovers' farewell at the end of the film *Casablanca*, the advisories steadied Mayo's walk through the world.

Mayo stared bleakly at the desktop's clutter: Letters. Reports. Memoranda. Scribbled notes. With the tips of his fingers he pushed a few papers apart until the desktop's bare stained pine was revealed like a patch of pale sea amid a jumble of floes. He set the mug down on the cleared-out space and gave some thought to his upcoming 10 A.M. lecture. He knew he needed sleep. But his mind was too agitated, still shadowed by a vague foreboding. He thought of the Band-Aid in his dream. What did it mean? As was his custom he had left his office door wide open, still another quirk in his habits that had started at the time of his dramatic loss of weight, and now he lifted his head and looked out into the hall with a curiously sad and wistful expression, as if hoping that a long lost love might pass by. But the hall remained empty of life. Mayo sighed. He longed for the distraction of the morning paper, for the balm of immersion in routine, and, grown desperate, he reached into a wastepaper basket that was underneath his desk and hauled out the prior day's *Jerusalem Post*, spread it out on his desk, and began to reread it, his eye skimming rapidly across the headlines: "SYRIA MIGHT RENEW THE SIX-DAY WAR;" "WATERGATE GRAND JURY INDICTS 7;" "U.S. COLLEGE STREAKING CRAZE SPREADS TO EUROPE;" "22 CHILDREN DIE IN VIET CONG ATTACK;" and "PYTHON SWALLOWS BANGLADESHI WOMAN."

At the last two reports Mayo groaned but said nothing.

He had used up all the worlds he could end that day.

Seeking sunnier fare, Mayo turned to an ad for "CHUTZPAH," a perfume created by Aviva Dayan, the daughter of the celebrated Army chief of staff, and with this Mayo found the wry smile he'd been seeking. Her lips puckered in a sultry and provocative O, Dayan's photo stared back smolderingly at the neurologist over copy that declared the scent's virtues:

ARROGANT! DIRECT! PROVOKING!
BUT AT THE SAME TIME REFRESHINGLY
NATURAL LIKE THE SABRAS IN WHOSE
IMAGE IT WAS CREATED!

Near the bottom of the ad another perfume was touted:

MAZELTOV—THE PERFUME THAT BRINGS
LUCK!

The rustling of newspaper merged with a chuckle as Mayo turned the page to a daily feature that was headed "What's on in Jerusalem Today":

> Thursday Daily Walk: Fourteen Stations to Church of the Holy Sepulcher. Free snacks to follow at Mandarin Chinese Restaurant. Meeting Place: Convent of the Flagellation.

A smile. Then Mayo turned to even deeper and richer heart's ease in two items on the paper's back page:

LONDON POLICE IN MANHUNT FOR UNAPOLOGETIC FLATULENT OFFICER

LONDON (REUTERS)—British police sought a flatulent officer Wednesday after a family complained that a policeman broke wind in their London home during a drug raid and failed to apologize. A Scotland Yard spokesman confirmed tonight that the Department of Professional Standards was investigating the charge.

The other item's solemn report:

A sex-starved moose in Norway mistook a small bright yellow Italian car for a would-be partner, but apparently defecated on it after it failed to receive a response.

"And so here we have the answer," Mayo murmured expressionlessly, "to the problem of the frigid wife's headaches." His gaze drifted down to two quieter headings that had also caught his eye on the day before, although not for any reason that he could name. One reported that units from the Soviet Union had arrived to replace the Albanian troops who were rotating out of the U.N. peacekeeping force now patrolling the Golan Heights. The other item had to do with the body of a man found dead at the base of the Russian Church Tower. Though the autopsy hadn't been completed as yet, he was thought to have fallen down the Tower's steep steps, "this consistent," the article went on to report, "with the trauma to the dead man's body," although "a homicide had yet to be ruled out."

The cause of death was a broken neck.

Mayo looked up from his reading. He had heard an odd creak. He stared at a corner of the room where a dust-covered black violin case rested, propped on its end at a woozy angle. Mayo's inner child regarded it askance: with this reported recent rash of the benignly supernatural, might there also be a darkness prowling the halls? *No, you twit! The violin case slipped and it made a little noise!* It could also be a warning from Maurice, Mayo thought, that having failed to play a note in several weeks he needed to practice more conscientiously; and thus reminded of duty and its obligations, he folded up his copy of *The Jerusalem Post*, dropped it back into the trash, and groped through the litter of papers on his desk until he found the articles he had been studying in preparation for the morning's lecture.

One dealt with peduncular hallucinosis, a rare and bizarre neurological condition in which people who were totally sane saw small and familiar cartoon characters like Porky Pig or Daffy Duck dressed in military uniform, frequently that of the Nazi S.S., while the second of the studies had to do with pain and a remarkable experiment recently conducted at the UCLA Pain Control Center involving a "white-haired man" in his sixties and a very thin board, three feet by three feet, through which had been hammered a hundred nails with their thin sharp points sticking up an inch above the surface. To make sure that no trickery was involved, just beforehand several members of the UCLA medical school faculty had placed the palms of their hands on the upright nails and agreed it would take only minimal pressure to drive them into human flesh. After this, the white-haired subject removed his shirt and undershirt, lay down beside the board, and then rolled onto it so that his back lay atop the sharp protruding nails. Exhibiting not the slightest sign of pain or even discomfort he remained on the board for several minutes, then "rolled off with a sickening sound of popping as his flesh came off the nails." Except for one site on his shoulder there was no bleeding on his back, and when the bleeding on the shoulder was called to his attention it immediately stopped. There existed individuals born with "congenital insensitivity to pain," a most rare neurological disorder in which for reasons still unknown the connection between the nerves that sense pain and the brain's recognition of pain was missing. But the white-haired man was not one of them. "You're an interesting person, Maurice," Mayo muttered, his lips barely moving as he stared at the report. "Some of your creatures cannot shed tears while others were made so as not to feel pain. Did you mean these as a blessing or a terrible curse?"

"Is there anything you need, Doctor Mayo?"

Startled, Mayo looked up.

Looking down at him benignly from in front of his desk stood a tall, bearded, rugged-featured, blond-haired man dressed in hospital whites, a sometime volunteer attendant who did basic tasks but spent most of his time reading books aloud to patients.

"Oh, Wilson. Didn't hear you come in."

"I was passing and just wondered if you needed something done."

"Yes, I would like you to teach me teleportation."

"Beg pardon?"

From the hall, approaching footsteps could be heard.

Wilson's eyes slanted subtly toward the sound.

"Haven't seen you around for weeks," Mayo told him, a wry mischievous smile in his eyes. "Been on vacation or something, Wilson? Floating around on your back jaunty-jolly on the surface of our scenic Dead Sea smearing hummus all over your face and drinking vintage Manischevitz thinking, 'Wow! This is life! This is living!' " Mayo's gaze flicked out to the hallway as a red-bearded, brown-robed Franciscan priest hurried by with a rattling of olivewood rosary beads that dangled from a belt made of rope: Dennis Mooney, the cigar-chomping, jovial, storytelling priest was in charge of the Church of Shepherd's Fields a short distance from Bethlehem in a town named Beit Sahour. On his occasional visits to Jerusalem, he made chaplain calls at Hadassah. Mayo found him tiresome and felt a deep relief he hadn't stopped for a chat.

Mayo's glance shifted back to the attendant.

"What did you do to your hand? Is that a burn?"

"Hot stove."

"Stove shmove! Understand something, Wilson: you can't build a fire for a marshmallow roast by pouring kerosene on matzohs and then striking a match. Matzohs treated in this way will invariably attack. And stop biting your fingernails for heaven's sakes. What are you doing prowling around at this hour? Who are you reading to, Wilson? Bats?"

"Oh, well, the Burn Ward. Sometimes they can't sleep."

Mayo lowered his eyes and nodded.

"Yes, I know," he murmured glumly.

"I'm going down to the lab. Did you need something?"

"No. No, not a thing, Wilson. Thank you for asking."

Mayo's mood had again turned somber, his bright shield of humor now too heavy to lift into place. Wilson stood studying him intently for a moment, and then mutely turned around and left. Mayo lifted his head and stared after him. Once a month Mayo would drive to Ramallah, volunteering his help at a leprosarium run by an order of Austrian nuns. Once or twice he'd found Wilson there, reading books or bits of news to those lepers who were either illiterate or blind. It reminded the neurologist of yet another "miracle," this one concerning one of the lepers, an older and heavyset peasant woman who, little by little, had lost her sight. Sitting silent and alone in her darkened cell, she would wince and give a low sharp cry of pain if ever suddenly exposed to bright light. Two months ago her sight had returned. The leprosy was still with her but much of her loneliness was not.

"I need a nose job!"

Samia had exploded into the room, her arms swinging and brushing against her sides making starched cotton swishing sounds. She plopped down into a torn green Naugahyde chair. "There, you see?" She had turned her head to the side, pushing up on the end of her nose with a fingertip. "I need somebody good, really good." Mayo stared in quiet disbelief as the nurse slumped all the way down into the chair with her legs a few inches above the floor and her size ten shoes thrust out in front of her. "I've got Americans coming for dinner next week," she said. "What do I do? What kind of food do I serve them? Give them Jewish food? Arabic? What?" Hands rapidly gesticulating while her large and dark moody eyes flashed, she then launched into a rapid-fire, breathless soliloquy that bounded from subject to random subject: from the upcoming dinner, to the Golan Heights, to the right amount of lemon juice to use when making hummus, until finally, her box of non sequiturs emptied, she leaped up out of her chair to browse and scrutinize the photos and sayings on the walls.

"I see there's lots of new stuff here," she observed.

"Why not?"

"Was that Wilson I saw coming out of here?"

"Yes."

"It's always so peaceful around him. Ever notice that, Moses?"

"No."

"You're a stone. He's a little bit slow. But, oh, that smile! It's a killer! But why he doesn't shave off that beard I haven't a clue. You know, he lives across the street from me. I see him all the time."

"Geographically desirable, Samia."

"Yeah, I know. And he's cute. But too young for me, Moses."

Mayo looked puzzled.

"Too young?" he said. "He's *older* than you."

"No way. Plus he hangs out with lowlifes at the Club 2000."

"And so how would you know that? Are you stalking him, Samia?"

"Don't be smart. You know, sometimes when I'd look across the street I could see there's this guy there in Wilson's apartment. He's got the curtains pinched aside and looking down out a window at a fruit peddler clanging his bell. And I see that this guy's in pajamas. You think Wilson could be light in the loafers?"

"I doubt it."

"Wouldn't hurt if he'd shave off that beard. It covers too much of his face. Oh, what's this? Does this mean something? What? Is it a line from the movie?" She was pointing to a caption in bold block letters that Mayo had inscribed beneath the *Casablanca* photo:

I NEVER MAKE PLANS THAT FAR AHEAD

"Yes, it means something."

"What?"

"Never mind."

"You are such a curmudgeon. And what about this?" the nurse asked. "This one here next to Meral when he made that big arrest." She had moved from a newspaper photo of a uniformed sergeant of police to another of two smiling teenaged boys with their arms around each other's shoulders. She pointed. "This is you here, right? On the left?"

"Yes, that's me."

"And who's the other one?"

"Meral."

"I never would have guessed it."

"Why?"

"He's smiling."

Mayo stared at the photo with a distant sadness in his eyes as he remembered how three months after it was taken the last of Meral's family, his mother, had died, and the twelve-year-old Meral had to make all the necessary funeral arrangements.

"What a quiet man," remarked the nurse. "Is he seeing anybody?"

"What do you mean? A psychiatrist?"

"A woman."

"I don't think so."

"Too bad," said the nurse.

Then she wheeled around to Mayo with shining eyes.

"Oh, but wasn't he great with that maniac in Psycho!"

Nesting in solitude on Floor 7, the hospital's Psychiatric Ward had once harbored two docile schizophrenic inmates, each of whom believed he was Jesus Christ. Six weeks ago one of them had murdered the other. The killer, a captured seventeen-year-old Syrian soldier who had lost his genitalia in combat, had unexpectedly, blithely and without provocation slit his victim's throat with a twelve-inch kitchen knife, which he afterward held against his own throat while threatening suicide at the approach of hospital security. Locked in this impasse, someone had thought to call Meral, waking the policeman in the dead of night. At the sight of him entering the ward, the young black-bearded killer, at that moment in the midst of a raving preachment he was offering as proof of his divine identity, fell instantly silent, and when Meral walked up to him with his hands held out, palms upward, and in Arabic softly uttered, "*Ibni*—my son," the knife slipped from the soldier's grasp to the floor and, bursting into wrenching, wracking sobs, he fell forward into Meral's arms, reaching around him and gripping him tightly while Meral placed both his hands on the young soldier's head and said over and over again in Arabic, "Yes, my poor son. I know. I know."

"He was only amazing," Samia rattled on as she turned to the wall again. "I mean, there's something about him that gets you. I don't know what it is, but you trust him. Okay? You just trust him. So what's this?"

She was pointing to a plaque reading "CUBA, SÍ, MASADA, NO!"

"I don't get it," she said. "What's—"

The neurologist cut her off brusquely.

"Alright, stop it, Samia! Just stop it! Come on, sit down here and tell me the whole thing again!"

The nurse turned to him with a look of incomprehension.

"Tell? Tell you what?"

"You know very well what."

"No, I don't."

"That whole thing about the clown."

"Oh, that." With a limp, dismissive flip of her hand the nurse turned to examine the photos again. "You know I'm really not too sure I can—"

"Stop it, I said! I surrender! All quiet on the paranoid front! Look, I've thought it all over, and I want to hear the whole thing again, every detail, every scrap you can recall. This time I'll listen, Samia. I swear it!"

The nurse's mask of indifference fell away, and looking touched and grateful, she moved quickly to the Naugahyde chair and sat, this time not slumping down but instead leaning forward with a breathless eagerness to recite once again her story of how on her break at 3 A.M. two days before, Monday, 11 March, she had sauntered into the Children's Ward for a visit with Tzipi Tam, a good friend and the charge nurse on duty at the time, and on the way momentarily paused in wonder on observing that behind the glass partition of the ward a clown in full circus costume and makeup was adroitly juggling three orange-colored vinyl balls for an audience of the only two children in the ward who were awake: a rosy-cheeked two-year-old girl and the rabdomial cancer "miracle" child. Her recitation ended, the nurse leaned back and folded her arms across her chest. Mayo asked if she was sure of the date this had happened. She was.

It was the day that the cancer and dysautonomia had vanished.

"Could you tell who it was?" Mayo asked.

The nurse shrugged.

"You couldn't?"

"All that makeup and stuff. The red wig. Long and bushy and frizzy," she said. "Frizzy curls."

"Surely had to be staff," Mayo mulled.

"I don't know."

"Or someone hired by a parent?"

The nurse's eyebrows knitted inward.

"What do you mean?"

"Well, did any of those children have a birthday?"

"When?"

"That day." Mayo was remembering his time in California and how parents on a child's birthday would sometimes send greetings to the place of celebration by way of a clown on roller skates.

But in the middle of the night? he immediately questioned himself.

"I don't know, Mayo. Why?"

"Never mind. And how tall was this person?"

"Pretty tall, I think. Big. A big person."

"Strongly built you mean? Husky?"

"Yeah, both."

"So then you're sure it was a man."

"I don't know."

"You don't know?"

"I can't be sure is all I'm saying."

"But you think so."

"Have you ever seen a female clown?"

"I've dated them, Samia. Did you talk to him?"

"No. I was only passing by."

"Did he see you?"

"I don't know. I don't think so."

"He kept juggling, though?"

"Yes. He kept juggling."

"Did the children seem bothered by this?"

"They seemed happy. The little girl put her hands out in front of her and clapped them together and giggled."

Mayo stared at the nurse without expression. Then he lowered his gaze to his desktop and nodded. "Yes," he said, staring abstractedly. "I believe you. It's all as you've said."

Mayo glanced back up.

"You called Security, Samia?"

"No. I thought maybe it was authorized and I'd ask her first, ask Tzipi. When I got to her station, though, she wasn't there. So I walked back to find out what was going on but when I looked into the ward again he was gone."

"You mean the clown?"

"Yeah, the clown."

"The two children. Still awake?"

"Just the boy."

"Did he seem somehow different to you?"

"Different? Like what?"

"Well, like healthier, perhaps."

She shook her head. "I wouldn't know."

"More alert?"

"I wouldn't know. Not my ward."

"Yes, of course."

"I was reading: there's this drug now in Europe, a hypnotic, men are slipping it to women and then raping them, Mayo."

Mayo nodded. "Yes. Rohypnol."

"Does it actually work?"

"Why, Samia? Want to slip it to yourself?"

The nurse emitted a chuckling snort and then stared at the neurologist fondly. "You're so funny," she said.

Mayo lowered his gaze.

"Yes, funny is forever," he uttered distantly.

"You want to hear about Lakhme again?"

Mayo looked up with a frozen expression, then leaned forward, shuffling papers around on his desk.

"No, not now, Samia. Thanks. I've got a lecture to prepare."

"Oh, well, I've got to get going myself."

Samia stood up.

"Let me know if you've got some more questions."

"I will."

"Thank you, Moses."

"For what?"

"Oh, you know."

The nurse turned and walked out of the office, and even after she had vanished from his sight, Mayo's gaze remained fixed on the empty hall until the squishing of her footsteps faded away. He remembered reading in a medical journal that in London there was once a Sleep Disorder Clinic located directly across the street from Big Ben. After that, Mayo thought, could there be any tale mad enough to doubt? An elevator door sighed open somewhere, waited, and then slowly and quietly closed. *Maurice making his getaway*, Mayo reflected, *before the "Crazy God Police" come to pick him up. Can we ever have a rational, dependable universe with this kind of crazy hocus-pocus going on?*

"Never mind," he then murmured. "Just so long as the magic is white."

A faraway melancholy painted Mayo's eyes as for a moment he stared at the *Casablanca* photo, and from there he turned his gaze to the Europa cigarette butts bent and mounded in an ash-tray on his desk, and from there to the blackness outside his window, wishing it were dawn when the U.N. Headquarters building could be seen high on a hilltop to the east in Ein Kerem where John the Baptist had been born, thus permitting the neurologist his customary smile upon reflecting that the rise on which the building now stood was the biblical Hill of Evil Counsel. Then he quietly lowered his head to his work, desultorily studying the paper on pain and scribbling notes on a blue-lined yellow pad. Twenty minutes later he tossed down his pen. Racing thoughts. The foreboding. The dream. Restless, he got up and left his office to wander, prowling the quiet pre-dawn halls with their regularly posted SPEAK SOFTLY signs. In the Burn Ward he chatted with a sleepless young soldier who had carried his own severed arm from the battlefield of October's Yom Kippur War in the hope that surgeons could reattach it: *"That's what I remember, that I took my arm by the hand."* Then Mayo drifted up to the fourth floor Neurology Ward where, on stepping out of the elevator, he saw Father Mooney approaching. Seeing Mayo, the fortyish and handsome Franciscan paused in his stride for a moment, looking hesitant and somehow blocked; and then, smiling broadly, he resumed his approach with his hand outstretched to shake Mayo's. The neurologist inwardly grimaced: a relentlessly hearty raconteur, the Franciscan would batter any cornered listener with tiresome and seemingly endless recitals meant to illustrate his daringly mad sense of humor, such as posing as a pregnant nun in a wheelchair when meeting a fellow priest at an airport and loudly and joyously exclaiming with his arms thrust out to the mortified arrival, "Oh, Jim! I'm so glad it was you!"

"Hey, Mayo! Good to see you!" Mooney exclaimed.

Mayo put an index finger to his lips.

"Oh, yes, sorry," said Mooney in a lowered tone. "Forgot the time." As the elevator door began to close, Mooney's hand stabbed out to hold it back. "How've you been, Mayo?"

"Still on this side of the grass. Saw you passing by earlier."

"Yes, I know. Couldn't stop. I was taking communion to someone. Emergency. One of those things." Mooney raised an arm for a glance at his watch. It was a chunky gold Rolex. "Oh, well, got to get back," he sighed. "Lots of tourists due early at the chapel today." The rounded walls of the priest's little church were filled with mosaics of heralding angels chorusing "*Gloria in Excelsis Deo*," and no matter the season, December or July, tourists gathered underneath its glass-domed nave to sing Christmas carols, often with an unexpected stirring in their hearts. As Mooney stepped into the elevator, Mayo glimpsed a scar at the base of his neck. The priest turned, pressed the ground floor button, and then lifted his hand in farewell so that Mayo saw the wide white Band-Aid that was wrapped around the top of a middle finger.

"Got some new stories for you, Mayo. Come and see us."

"Yes, I will," Mayo murmured absently.

"Oh, well, good! Make it soon, then! Okay? Make it soon!"

The elevator door whined shut.

Hands tucked into the pockets of his medical jacket, the neurologist lowered his head in thought, and as he listened to the elevator's lurch at the start of its descent, he tried to fathom why an icy tingling in his bloodstream was raising up hairs on the back of his neck.

A thump of the elevator stopping below.

Mayo looked up and stared abstractedly down a long hall and its rows of numbered patient rooms. What was wrong with him? he wondered. Which among the colorful and crowded palette of bizarre disorders of the mind had left the ghost of a brushstroke on his brain? A flash of white as a nurse appeared abruptly, emerging from an intersecting hall in the distance, and then an attendant, possibly Wilson, Mayo guessed. He waited until they had walked out of view, and then again began shuffling down the hall until he arrived at Room 406, where he stopped and stared sadly through the door's observation port into darkness and a night light's feeble glow. The room's last occupant was a man named Ricardo Rey. He'd been Mayo's patient. The one who had died. With a soul of patient kindness and the face of a white-haired elderly cherub, Rey was an official of the Spanish consulate who had come under Mayo's care after suffering a devastating stroke. As the nurturing weeks of convalescence slipped by, Mayo's outlook had grown cautiously optimistic, this in spite of a problem with the patient's eyesight: he could not see anything beyond two feet. Then the matter turned somehow vaguely sinister, as Rey began reporting seeing people in his room who weren't there. This included an incident in which the Spaniard, while sitting up in bed conversing with Mayo, interrupted himself in midsentence to turn and look up and a little to his left to inquire with aplomb and exquisite courtliness, even in the face of an apparition, "I'm so terribly sorry. Do I know you?" Mayo had at first not been overly concerned, attributing the visions to probable damage to the ocular portions of Rey's brain, but things changed when Mayo asked what the apparitions said to him.

"Nothing," Rey had answered.

"Nothing? What about to each other? Do they talk to one another?"

"No, they don't."

"Well, then, what do they do?"

Here Rey had looked down in thought for some moments as he seemed to be weighing the question judiciously. He then looked up and answered simply, "They witness." For some reason that he couldn't precisely grasp, this response had caused Mayo to worry.

Five weeks later Rey was dead.

Mayo brushed at the bottom of his nose with a knuckle. Rey's death. Was that the problem after all? he brooded. He recalled being haunted very early in his practice by the dying words of a motion picture star who was barely into his sixties, the plaintively whispered words, "I just got here." But in time Mayo grew to be inured to such loss. *And besides*, *this isn't grief*, he thought; *grief I would damn well know*. From afar, the muffled clatter of dishware and clinking glass. Mayo glanced at his watch. Almost four. Preparation of patient breakfasts had begun. *And soon the dawn will render visible the U.N. building*, Mayo thought with gratification. *Not every conceivable event is to be feared*.

Mayo continued his amble down the hall, turning right at an intersecting corridor, and when he saw that light was spilling out of a window in the door to patient room 422, his spirits immediately began to pick up. The room's patient was Eddie Shore, the legendary 1940s "Big Band" leader who, at the brassiest peak of his fame, had inexplicably decided to give up music and retire to a farm in northern Virginia to begin a career as a writer of novels. In Jerusalem to research a historical novel that was to be set in the time of Christ, he was here in Hadassah not because of any neurologic disorder but rather with the symptoms of salmonella poisoning. He had been given a bed in the Neurology Ward because of its superior rooms. Mayo picked up his pace. In his youth an avid fan of Shore's music, Mayo had boldly introduced himself and had already had long conversations with his idol in which he discovered him to be a completely unexpected human being: at once genial and warm and yet brusquely curmudgeonly; keenly insightful and brutally candid. Though at times there was an air of evasiveness about him, when he would seem to deflect or evade a question and sometimes pretending, Mayo thought, not to hear it, and it was on these occasions that a veil of mystery seemed to enshroud him.

Almost totally bald, yet with high jutting cheekbones and a riveting stare that made him strikingly handsome even now in his sixties, Shore had been briefly and serially married to a number of Hollywood's most glamorous starlets, once explaining to Mayo, who had asked how he could possibly have cast them aside, "Are you kidding? It was *hard*! I mean, how do you turn to this naked goddess lying in bed with you that every other guy in the world wants to jump and just tell her straight out, 'You bore me!' You really think that was easy? For God's sakes, *think*, Mayo, will you? *Think!*"

He had also confided what had caused him to abandon his career in music. "So one time I'd decided I'd do a very special tour," he began to explain. "I mean, a tour with a really great band. The top musicians in the country. The *best*! And we were going to do original, innovative stuff, not that tired dumb *drek* that we played at the Paramount on Times Square, right after 'Don Dickhead at the Mighty Wurlitzer' was done, and at colleges and high school proms. So I came up with some classy compositions, really wild, really wonderful stuff, and I put this terrific band together and we toured. And guess what? People hated it, Mayo! They booed! Yeah, every gig that we played they'd start booing and yelling we should play my big hits, all the popular faves, until finally I said, 'Fuck it!' and I cut the tour short and went back to my penthouse apartment in Manhattan where I stewed and I grumped and I farted around. And then I got really pissed off, really ticked, and I went to my booker and I told him to round up some hands, I was doing another tour, but I didn't want to pay any more than minimum, I told him. 'Minimum?' he yelps at me. 'Eddie, are you crazy? You can't get good musicians for that! You'll get stiffs! You'll get trumpet players with emphysema!' But I said to him, 'Stiffs are exactly what I want! I don't care if they can barely read music! I mean it! Make it happen!'

"So he gets me these guys, these bums who think sheet music's some kind of Rorschach test, and we go out on this tour and it's sounding really putrid, just awful — The Romantic

Mantovani's Greatest Stock Car Racing Hits'—but we're playing all my biggies, my most popular numbers, all that Viennese pastry Mozart's wife used to throw in his face, and all the troglodytes, they're cheering and applauding and stamping their feet. I can't believe it! I'm sick! I'm disgusted! So one night when we're playing and I hold up my hand to show the boys with my fingers what stanza comes next—see, like this—I held my hand up *sideways* so they couldn't really tell how many fingers were up, they had to guess, so they all wound up playing different stanzas and it's sounding like galaxies in collision. Just cacophony. Sawmill sounds. Total garbage. So what happens? *They give us a standing ovation!*" Here Shore had stared glumly into space. "That's what did it," he said. "That was it. I called off the rest of the tour that night, bought a farm, took up writing, and I've never looked back."

"Well, now, Maestro, up so late? Or so early, I should say."

Peering through the door's observation window and seeing Shore awake and sitting up in bed with pen in hand and a notepad and a facedown open book on his lap, the neurologist had breezed into the room and now was standing at the bottom of Shore's bed with his hands in the pockets of his medical jacket.

"Oh, hi ya there, kid! What's happening, huh? What's up?"

Shore had slipped off his reading glasses and smiled as he recognized Mayo. Then he frowned a little, looking aside in thought. "Oh, yeah, something got me up, I guess. Something. Don't know what."

"Feeling better?"

"Oh, yeah, better, much better, Mayo. Thanks. At least the headaches and the stomach cramps are gone. And how are you? You okay? You look weird." Shore had craned his neck forward, squinting, as he studied Mayo's face intently. "You look like a guy who's just lost his best friend."

Mayo's smile was thin and wan. "Oh, I did that a very long time ago."

"Well, you look like you're fixing to do it again. Here, come on. Come sit down. Pull up a chair."

"No, I can see you're working. I won't keep you."

"No, no, no, kid! I really want to talk to you! Really!"

Mayo loved it that Shore always called him "Kid."

Shore picked up the book from his lap and held it up. "You know, as part of my research I've been reading New Testament scripture and I think I've found something interesting here in this gospel. It's the gospel of John. Come on, sit, kid! Sit! You should hear this!"

Mayo nodded and said, "Okay," and then slowly sat down in a chair by the bed. "So what is it, then, Maestro? Tell me."

Shore slid his glasses back into place. "You know, this part here in John," he said, pointing to the open pages of the book. "Oh, well, maybe you don't. It's where they're stoning this woman for adultery. You know, I used to think all these stories were probably bull. But guess what? There's this passage"—he was pointing to a page of the book—"it's got a giveaway in it, a 'tell' that lets you know that this story here wasn't made up! Any fiction writer sees it right away!" Shore then avidly recounted that passage in John in which the Pharisees, hoping to embarrass Christ, brought before him an adulterous woman and asked him what he thought about the law of Moses that commanded such a woman be stoned to death. Christ "bent over and wrote on the ground with his finger," then stood up and said to those who had confronted him, "Let he who is without sin cast the first stone."

"Then he bends to the ground and writes something more," Shore went on, "and then these *momzers*, these Pharisees, they all took a hike." His eyes bright with the thrill of discovery, Shore hunched his body forward toward Mayo. "Now if that's in a novel," he said with intensity, "if it's fiction, let me tell you something, Mayo; in fact, let me damn well *guarantee* you, in some chapter down the line we're going to end all this pain-in-the-ass suspense and find out what exactly it was that Christ wrote. But these gospels don't do it! No! We don't *ever* find out what he wrote! Down the line there's not a word of explanation, *none*, which has to be because the guy who wrote that gospel didn't know, and not knowing, didn't make something up!"

Mayo gently nodded his head, his thoughts adrift.

"Very nice," he said.

" 'Very *nice*'? That's really all you have to say? 'Very *nice*'? I, the Jewish Sherlock Holmes of the Judean Desert have just proved that the gospels aren't all made up stories and to you it's like I just played a riff on the cello. Are you deaf or just a putz of interplanetary standing?"

Mayo looked up with a speculative air. "This is something rather new for you, isn't it?"

"What?"

His eyes narrowed, Shore's evasive persona had appeared.

"Aren't you Jewish?" Mayo clarified.

"Huh?"

For a moment Shore stared blankly. Then he softly uttered, "Oh," and put his head back on a pillow. The guarding veil and the tension in his face had disappeared. "Yeah, I'm Jewish to the core," he said, staring up the ceiling pensively. "Still in all, you've got to wonder, don't you think? Here are these guys, pretty young. Some barely literate. Fishermen. Whatever. One minute they're all totally depressed and crapping their pants behind locked doors because they're terrified of guilt by association and that they're going to be rounded up and crucified next, and then all of a sudden they're these death-defying maniacs climbing onto rooftops yelling, 'Come and get me, copper!' and they go out on the road breathing fire and doing real fun stuff like getting beaten and tortured and thrown into jail; getting killed and even crucified upside down for preaching big-time winning ideas like 'you've got to love your enemy' and 'no more divorces,' plus incidentally 'our dead guy isn't dead anymore and you've got to eat his flesh and drink his blood,' all winners, all popular notions, easy sells. But these frightened guys *do* it, they actually *do* it, and in less than twenty years they're recruiting in Rome and are practically taking it over. What do you call that, Mayo? You've got to wonder. Something happened to these guys. Something big. Like a resurrection, maybe. I dunno. But *they* sure must have thought they'd seen him walking around. Getting killed is an awful lot of trouble to go to just because you're feeling bored and the fish aren't biting."

For a moment Shore paused, and then he cryptically added in a pensive tone, "You know, sometimes you get into situations and you have to start thinking about these things." A long silence ensued, causing Shore to turn his head to scrutinize Mayo, who was staring at an empty Band-Aid wrapping on the floor near the top of the bandleader's bed. It had triggered recollection of the Band-Aid in his dream. Shore frowned. "You know, you've still got this zombied-out look," he told Mayo, "like this temp fill-in drummer that I picked up in Phoenix one time. He'd heard that pandas get high on eucalyptus leaves, so they wound up his drug of choice, and he'd be doing these lazy, slow-mo brush sweeps, slack-jawed and staring straight out at the crowd with that same spacey look that's on your face right now, just without the purple teeth. You been listening to anything at all I've been saying?"

"Yes, everything, Maestro. Everything."

Mayo stood up.

"I'd better go," he said, "I'm not feeling too well myself."

"That's too bad. Take care of yourself, kid."

"You, too."

Smiling wanly, Mayo turned and left the room to continue his drift through the hospital's halls, stalked by specters of light and of darkness, of miracles and murders and the need to find an answer to an overwhelming question that no one had asked, or could even formulate, until finally, just before dawn, and without any notion of how he had gotten there, he found himself standing in front of the gray metal entry door to the Psychiatric Ward on Floor 7. Pasted onto it, random bright thoughts from some elsewhere, were a large crayoned drawing of a rainbow and another of a clutch of blue and yellow daisies. There was also a photo of a staff clinician, a smiling young woman in a medical jacket. "Sarah," Mayo murmured fondly. The door was never locked. Beyond it were patients who were thought to be harmless: a woman addicted to plastic surgery, elderly victims of dementia, and odd assorted others, such as a professor of deconstructed English whose daily attire while teaching class had included knee-high paratrooper boots and a sinister shiny black leather jacket. He had once been ejected from the Club 2000 for allegedly "emitting threatening vibrations" while standing at a pinball machine. *And so why am I here?* wondered Mayo. The Child in his dream? The murdered Christ? At this Mayo thought of Meral, recollecting the haunting thing he had told him after shepherding the murderous Christ to Kfar Shaul, an asylum for the criminally insane just outside of Jerusalem's walls. On returning to Hadassah to brief the Sub-District police on what had happened, he said, *"He was silent all through the ride until, trying to give him some comfort, I told him he was now the only Christ in the city. And then for the very first time he spoke to me. He said, 'No. There is another.'"*

Mayo stared at the colorful drawing of the daisies. What had that tormented young soldier meant? Then while shifting his weight as he once again sifted his dream for connections, suddenly one flashed into view as Mayo realized that in both his dream and on Father Mooney's finger there hadn't been one Band-Aid, there had been two, one wrapped atop the other. His fingertips absently brushing at his chin, Mayo felt that icy mist of foreboding settling lightly once again on the back of his neck as he pondered what, if anything, the Band-Aids could mean. Then abruptly, with a grunt and loose flip of the hand, Mayo turned and shuffled toward the elevator bank. *So what of it?* the neurologist mentally harrumphed. *This is all a Middle Eastern Marley's ghost*, he scoffed, *a bit of undigested lamb*. But as also occurs in the subatomic world where electrons, like saints with bleeding hands, are reportedly seen in two places at once, Mayo soon would abandon the uses of sense and come to radically change his mind.

It was morning.

And then would come night.

CHAPTER 2

7 MARCH, 3:20 A.M.

Dearest Jean,
Meral is the saddest of men. I saw him again at the Tomb
of Lazarus this morning. It touched my heart. All the
tourists had clambered up the jagged stone steps of the dark-
ened crypt into terrifying light, the stunning last of them a
tall black woman from Texas, her hair in tin curlers that
danced in the sun as she emerged crying, "Praise be to
God!", her face a glory. When she'd ambled to the others

picking over remembrances in the Lazarus Tomb Souvenir Shop, I boarded the dilapidated dusty old tour bus, sat alone amid its empty rows of seats and thought about dead men walking out of their graves. A storm was blowing in. Whipping gusts set up a moan at the yellowed windowpanes and the air in the bus turned gray. On a slope above the tomb there's a shabby little house, a poor family of seven or eight, perhaps more; and it was when I glanced over at their brightly colored laundry flapping billowed on a line above a tether of goats that I spotted him. Meral. He was just as I had seen him there once before. A tall and imposing, strongly built man, yet looking somehow crumpled in his blue winter uniform, he was seated at the wheel of his police car wistfully staring at the entrance to the tomb. For as long as I watched him he was utterly motionless, his head slightly tilted to the side as if pondering some hopeless expectation. Poor Meral. His parents, all his brethren, are dead, as are his wife and only child, a beloved young son. Coming home at noon on the five-year-old's birthday at a time when they lived in the country's north, Meral thought to surprise him, the story is told, and had parked his jeep out of sight behind a hill and then hurried toward his house with a blaze of bright sunflowers clutched in front of him—they were the little boy's favorite flower—and a stuffed toy dinosaur tucked behind his back. The little boy, who had spied him through a kitchen window, raced out of their house with a radiant smile, his slender bare arms outstretched to greet him, when a whim-launched rocket from across the border fell upon his life with a sound he never heard. Soon afterward, cancer took Meral's wife. That was four years ago. Meral still mourns. He is a man who seems to ache at the slightest parting, always turning, when he leaves you, for a long glance back as if against the possibility he might never see you again. When we were ready for departure and the engine of the bus roared to life, a mist of rain began to fall on that quickening dust and as we left him, forlorn amid the dead white stones, Meral's gaze was still fixed upon the tomb.

Quiet Meral. Honest Meral. One day I must touch him.

I was glad to get back to Old Jerusalem and its bustling vaulted bazaars, the pungent scent of ground cardamom and new leather and the tumble of countless church bells ringing; to its jostling hurly-burly and the women with trays of warm bread on their heads and the blue-and-white uniformed, dreamy-eyed children singing as they march in neat columns to school, their little voices made hollow by the high stone walls on narrow dark streets that abruptly burst out into sunlight like an unexpected glimpse of joy; to where the blind always travel in pairs, hand in hand.

It is here that I will find him, the one that I am hunting.

He is here in this city of crumbling stone.

I must stop. My mind is on Meral.

Your Paul

CHAPTER 3

Abooming thunderbolt rattled the windowpanes of
the Old City's local police post, a hulking former
Crusader castle stolidly crouched by the Jaffa Gate.
The young lance corporal behind the reception desk lifted a
sullen stare to the sound and then slowly let it settle back
down to a ledger bristling with notations in black and red ink:
black for a log of arrivals and departures and red for the
recording of citizen complaints. The corporal's gaze was on an
item in red: the charge of a weeping, frail old man that his
burly young son had beaten him severely in a fury at the

father's habitual drunkenness. The corporal noticed something. Leaning over, he picked up the pen that was infused with red ink and very slowly and carefully corrected a misspelling, leaned back to review what he had done, and then set the pen down and looked through a window at the rough stone cobbles outside the post where a gust-driven rain spattered back and forth in hesitant, indecisive sweeps like a wispy gray soul just arrived on the empty streets of some afterworld, lost and forlorn. The sounds were muted by the station's thick block walls so that except for the soft dull clacking of a typewriter floating down from an upper floor, the damp yellow-walled reception room was quiet. The corporal shifted his gaze to the portable police radio on his desk. It had suddenly emitted a feeble sputter, but when nothing more came, he looked up at a sign on the wall beside the entry to the jail, a reminder that guns were to be checked in and out. The corporal's stare was one of quiet incredulity, for almost never was the ledger's red ink spent on matters warranting the use of a gun.

With its district encompassing all of the Christian Quarter and its bustling bazaars, the Old City's Kishla Police Post dealt largely with crimes that were commonplace, if not trivial: pickpockets, children missing in the markets, family troubles, a knife fight late at night involving boys, or the need to detain and interrogate tourists who had bought either opium or hashish from the locals. There was also the problem of female tourists' frequent complaints of "indecent touching" by shopkeepers fitting them with clothing, which was currently a widespread cause of neurosis among many of the merchants in the bazaars who had been encouraged in their practice of "touching" by the favorable reactions of some women who had liked it, thus creating the belief it would bring them more business. This was the level of crime in the Old City precinct. Once in three years there was a murder.

His thoughts grown dreamy, the bored corporal was absently rubbing his arm below the single chevron on his sleeve when the blustery wind and rain turned his gaze to the station's high front door. A tall and brooding yet commanding presence in a rain-slick poncho had entered the post. Quietly closing the door behind him, the stoic and strongly featured policeman somberly nodded at the corporal, his wide-set eyes resting fleetingly upon him with a faraway look of unutterable sadness and something very close to compassion, the unchanging expression that he gave to the world, before turning away and striding past with raindrops dripping from his glistening poncho onto the beige and orange tiles of the floor. The corporal nodded and smiled faintly. In the tall man's presence he always felt comforted. And safe. He picked up the pen with black ink and inscribed into the ledger:

Sgt. Major Peter V. Meral.

The silvery metal Star of David at the front of the policeman's black beret made a muted thudding sound on the soft pine wood of the desk where Meral had tossed it upon entering his office. A white-walled cubicle, its only furnishings were the desk, a desk lamp and chair and, up against the wall beneath a large round window looking out to the station's vehicle yard and its rows of blue and white police cars, a narrow cot with a dark gray blanket that was smooth and tightly tucked. Meral paused, staring out at the rain for a moment, then looked down at the heading on the cover of the folder he had just retrieved from the File Room: REMLE INCIDENT OF 14 JANUARY 1974. Meral placed it on the desk, sat down and, frowning, once again reviewed his notes.

They baffled to the edge of a taunt. No evidence existed that a crime had been committed. Yet the facts of the case, like the dream of some darkness one cannot remember, vaguely hinted at some hidden and deep transgression. At approximately 3:25 A.M., the time that a call had come into the Fire Department, a 1971 Land Rover fitted with a cowcatcher at its front and moving at extremely high speed crashed into the single-pump Paz gasoline station located on Remle Street where it intersected Jerusalem Brigade Road just below and outside the Jaffa Gate. An explosion and a fire followed. When police and firemen arrived at the scene, they found the burning and badly damaged Land Rover there, but not its driver or possible other occupants, nor any trace of the driver's identity. The two witnesses, a husband and wife who lived in the modest two-story apartment just above the Paz station office, had given puzzling and conflicting accounts. The couple's third floor bedroom looked out onto the street, and as the husband had a prosthetic leg, it was the wife who, after hearing the crash and the explosion, had looked down at the scene through a bedroom window and then raced to the opposite end of their apartment to dial 1-0-2 for the Fire Department, and then 1-0-0 to the Kishla Police Station situated just a few minutes away. The wife then returned to the bedroom window and, looking out once more, saw nothing but the burning Land Rover and gas pump. The vehicle was empty, she reported, and its driver was nowhere in sight. But the husband told a slightly different story.

A. There was a second man.

Q. Are you sure?

A. Absolutely. I didn't see him, understand. I never got out of bed. The leg. But I heard it.

Q. Heard what?

A. Oh, well, at first a car door opening, and then someone getting out of it and moving very quickly. After that another car door opened and I heard something heavy being dragged across the gravel.

Q. Some*thing* or some*one*?

A. I couldn't tell. Then after that, small noises. I couldn't really make them out. Then a car door closing again. It was a sound just like the first. But much softer. And then one more opening and closing sound, and then the sound of the car driving off.

Q. At great speed?

A. Not particularly. No. It was a very small car, by the way.

Q. How could you tell?

A. Oh, I see and hear them all. Thirty years. At night early when we're closed I sometimes hear them pulling up to use the tire inflator. We also leave out cans of water for cars that might have overheated. Cans of gas. The taxi drivers, the ones down by the Damascus Gate: they all know that.

Q. That's kind of you.

A. Only God is kind. It could have been a VW.

Q. What?

A. The second car. Or more likely a Topolino. It made that little puttering sound they always make.

M eral had just returned from re-examining the scene of the crash. He had also reinterviewed the husband and wife. This time he challenged the wife's account by presenting her with that of the husband, but she remained insistent that neither had she seen nor heard a second vehicle or seen any "second man," although she did at last admit that her first look out the window had been just "a quick glance"; and then she yielded even further, admitting that as she was somewhat in shock, her gaze riveted to the burning Land Rover and the gas pump, perhaps there was indeed another vehicle after all. She couldn't be sure. As for the husband, this time around he recalled a detail that he said had slipped his mind. He said he had heard someone's voice.

Q. When?

A. Just before I heard the dragging.

Q. Right after hearing the second car door being opened?

A. Yes, that's right. A man's voice. It was low. Very angry. I'd say horrified.

Q. Horrified?

A. Yes. That I'm sure of. And pleading.

Q. And what was being said? Do you recall?

A. He said, "Anyone but you! No, not you!"

Q. Nothing more?

A. No, no more talking. Just the dragging and the footsteps.

T he husband was unable to explain how he could have forgotten this when first questioned. He'd looked down, his eyes vague, and said simply, "I don't know." He seemed troubled about it. Afterward Meral reinterviewed the two other witnesses in the case. No paperwork, no clues of any kind that would identify the driver had been found in the charred and battered hulk of the vehicle. However, the license plate had survived and led Meral to the Eldan car rental agency clerk who had processed the rental to a man who had paid in cash and presented an international driver's license in the name of Joseph Temescu, while a supplier of farm equipment in the area was found to have a recent invoice of a sale to him of a cowcatcher, and it was this, Meral thought, that not only pointed most strongly to a crime but to one carried out by a professional killer, for if the driver's intention was homicide, he would want to assure himself that his vehicle still would be drivable after the hit.

While the salesman who had sold the device to Temescu

could not remember the transaction very clearly, the mechanic at the firm did remember affixing it onto Temescu's car. But as for a description of Temescu, though the Eldan clerk had made a copy of his driver's license, Temescu had apparently moved as his photo for the license was being taken so that the focus was blurred and indistinct, and neither the mechanic nor the car rental agent were able to provide very much that was helpful: "in his forties" with a "soldierly bearing" and a "very strong face." That was all. Both also reported that Temescu spoke English, but that it was clear it was not his native tongue inasmuch as he spoke with a heavy accent that was neither Israeli nor Arab. "Maybe Eastern European," the clerk had ventured. But even here he seemed uncertain. There had been one tantalizing lead. Meral had gone to the Arab Government Hospital to ask if they had any record of a serious burn case admitted on 14 January. And as it happened, there was. It was a male about fifty years of age with third degree burns, in particular on his face and both his hands. He was accompanied by another man of indeterminate age who said the burned man's name was Thomas Hulda, while his own was Martin Kerr. Fluids were given to Hulda intravenously and antibiotic creams applied. Kerr insisted on staying in the burned man's hospital room for the six days that he was there. According to a hospital nurse in attendance, he would sit on the floor near the bed with his back against the wall and his hands clasped around his knees, never speaking, just staring at the man in the bed and his thickly bandaged hands. On the seventh day he helped the burned man into a taxicab. It drove away with Kerr following after. Kerr had given the hospital the same address for both of them, an apartment in the Jewish Quarter, but when Meral had gone there to question them he found that no such persons were living, or ever had lived, at that address.

Meral took a long look at Temescu's driver's license. There was something about it. While the photo generally agreed with the description by the car rental salesman and the mechanic, it was so blurry and indistinct that if one were to stare at it long enough it would seem to somehow change. Meral checked the time, put the driver's license back into the case folder, closed it, returned it to its place in the File Room, then went out again into the hall where he walked past a kitchen and the station's Sleep Room with its multiple cots for weary patrolmen, and then turned in his Webley-Smith revolver at the Gun Room for it now was the end of his duty day. On his way to check out at reception and leave, as he passed the open door to the office of Ari Zev, the fortyish but white-haired Station Commander, Zev called out to him loudly, "Meral!"

The Arab policeman stopped and took a step inside a blue-walled office. Zev was at his desk. Behind him on the wall was a large detailed map of the Old City's quarters, plus a trophy case containing, among other things, an arm patch of the Maplewood, New Jersey, police force, the gift of a visiting American policeman in Israel to study Israeli methods. Zev had been writing on a notepad and still gripped a sharpened yellow pencil in his hand.

"Couple of things," he began. "The Albanians keep calling

about that chap of theirs who's gone missing. Next time I'm putting them straight through to you. They're a pain. Any news on this guy?"

"No, none at all. We need a photo. I've now asked for one three times. When it comes perhaps we'll have some better luck."

"*If* it comes."

"Yes, 'if.' "

Zev's eyebrows rose.

"And Remle Street, Meral?"

"Nothing new."

"As I pretty much expected. So I'm thinking that maybe you should drop it. It could be nothing but a whole lot of smoke."

"No, something's there. I feel sure of it."

Zev turned to look thoughtfully out a window for a moment, the point of the pencil still in his hand lightly tapping on the desktop in desultory spurts.

He turned back to Meral.

"Okay, Sergeant, keep on it. Your instincts have always been terrific."

Meral nodded, turned and exited the office. As he walked down the hall Zev watched him through the open door. "Poor bastard," he murmured. Then he grasped the pencil firmly and returned to his work, making summarizing notes of the inconclusive coroner's report on Yusef Tamal, a Yemeni immigrant who lived in Beit Sahour and was suspected of various criminal activities. He was the man found dead with a broken neck at the bottom of the Russian Church Tower.

. . . fractured skull and neck, as well as numerous lacerations, abrasions, and contusions; shearing of platysma, splenius, trapezius, and various smaller muscles of the neck, with fracture of the spine and of the vertebrae . . .

Broken in the fall, Zev wrote, *or before?*

Outside the station Meral stood with his back to its creamy beige dolomite walls. The gusting wind and drizzling rain had stopped and he stared at its glisten on the cobbles of the street with his thoughts still entangled in the Remle Street case: the sound of something heavy being dragged. What was it? Who was Joseph Temescu? And then the strangest thing of all: discovered in the Land Rover after the crash were the charred remains of a large black owl and that of another much smaller bird that could not be identified, perhaps a finch or a common house sparrow, both the favorite prey of the Southern Little Owl that frequented the city and hunted at night. Meral couldn't fathom it. He shook his head and moved his thoughts to a matter more prosaic. The Walk. Every Kishla policeman was required by the Commandant to make walks through the Christian Quarter for five after-duty hours each week for the purpose of "keeping in touch," as Zev had explained, "to bond with the people and hear their complaints." Three more hours, Meral mused, would fill his quota for the week and still put him at the Casa Nova, the ninety-room hostel where he lived, just in time for the communal evening meal.

Now decided, he adjusted the tilt of his black beret and stepped into the street, the Orthodox Armenian Patriarch Road, on which he took a quick left and then later a right on David Street to its teeming covered bazaars drenched in sights and sounds that always made Meral feel that he had just left the flatness of a colorless dream and awakened into real and vivid life, into a place where he was jostled by slender old porters bent by enormous loads on their backs, and by pedestrians in every conceivable dress—Arab workmen on donkeys and tourists with shopping bags; Kurdish women with trays on their heads filled with freshly baked sesame crusted bagels, pita bread, and cooked spotted breakfast eggs; ultra-orthodox Jews with long beards and curled side locks wearing black caftans and black fur hats; Muslim women and dignified Christian prelates—all bustling past souvenir stalls and shops, past huge wheels of baklava moist with honey and stood up on end in metal pans, past spice bins brimming with khaki-colored cumin, almonds, walnuts and powdered red pepper, dried apricot paste and figs, shredded coconut and bright yellow-orange lentils; past the younger male shopkeepers hawking their wares with loud voices and cajolements while their fathers, wearing tasseled fezzes or keffiyehs, sat in chairs mutely watching with placid faces while the Arabic music blaring out from their shops shouted up to the vaulted roof of the bazaar where it mingled in a strange and haunting counterpoint with the Angelus bells from Gethsemane and a muezzin's call to prayer.

Everywhere Meral was greeted warmly, very often with affection and always with trust, so that at times he was asked for personal advice. On this walk it was an eighteen-year-old girl who approached him complaining of a marriage arranged by her parents with a man whom she neither loved nor even liked, and then later, on The Street of the Chain where the air was thick with the smell of new leather and of stagnant water, coffee, and smoke, and beneath the baleful watch of a goat staring down through the black iron bars of a window in a second-floor apartment, Meral's counsel was sought by an elderly unofficial mayor, a *mukhtar*, expressing worry about the raucous behavior and "repugnant" blue-jean attire of the long-haired teenaged Arab "Teddy Boys" copying the latest British fad. Farther along, on the Via Dolorosa, Meral stopped and gave a coin to a beggar, a middle-aged, stubble-bearded man who was crouched against a wall with a transistor radio pressed to his ear raptly listening to the latest pop tunes of Greece underneath a Station of the Cross. Meral looked up at a plaque on the wall that marked it.

JESUS FALLS FOR THE SECOND TIME.

Abruptly the music stopped for an announcement. Meral guessed it was the weather and time. He glanced at his watch. Yes, time to head back, he decided. On his way, like a withered old Valkyrie late for the battle, an elderly nun on a motorized bicycle, a wraith in white garments wildly flapping up behind her, came suddenly varooming out of an aqabat, narrowly missing him as she passed. Behind her chugged a dusty and battered blue Fiat that was hauling a flatcar with a donkey aboard, sitting up on its haunches and facing backward, in its eyes a look of mild incomprehension.

Even at this Meral could not smile.

As he strode toward the Casa Nova and his dinner, Meral paused for a moment as he rounded a corner of the Via Dolorosa and entered the street called Khan el Zeit. He had seen something odd. A youngish, blond-haired and fair-complected woman wearing oversized sunglasses and a colorful "Souvenir of Jericho" babushka was standing in the doorway of a seedy hostel called The Shalom in what seemed a heated argument with a tall and stocky Franciscan priest, when suddenly the woman turned her head and looked at Meral, said something to the priest, who then also quickly turned his head and looked. The woman then clutched the Franciscan's arm and pulled him quickly out of sight and into the hostel. For some moments before moving on, Meral stared at the hostel door as he sifted for the meaning of the strange vignette. How very curious, he thought.

Not curious, actually.

Lethal.

CHAPTER 4

8 MARCH, 2:11 A.M.

Dearest Jean,
Last night an odd dream. It was vivid. I had died and now
a bright red light was confronting me. It was painful and
I tried to turn away. I was aware that the light was com-
pletely responsible for the government of the universe. Two
of its ministers had been put in charge of space and of see-
ing it was kept in good working order. But these creatures
had failed, and space was like a badly fitting jigsaw puz-

zle. *I wanted to extinguish this piercing red light that was trying to tell me that space was all awry when I suddenly realized with dismay that I had been chosen to put things aright, all the jarringly chaotic, inconsistent laws of nature.*

And some mysterious mission beyond.

What could it mean?

Now, something I've been hesitant to tell you. While my once-deadly "visitor" is healing, it would seem that someone other than he has tried to kill me. Several days ago, a Sunday, in the soft air of dawn, I made the puttering drive in my little Topolino to the Russian Church Tower, a spiraling column of Jerusalem stone jutting up from a hill above the Garden of Gethsemane. I go regularly to the top of the Tower, where I'm able to travel backward in time. To the west, behind Herod's block stone walls glowing faintly rose in the waking light, you see the Old City's clustered jumble of churches, minarets, courtyards, steeples, and spires squeezing breath from the cluttered sprawl of its homes with their white domed roofs huddled tightly together and still shivering in fear of the God of Job. But then circle to the opposite side of the tower and abruptly you're in another dimension, stunned and engulfed by the hushed immensity of the burnished Judean Desert; by the Mountains of Moab and, beyond, the Dead Sea and the River Jordan's mud-brown torrent whispering remembrances of the Baptist: all as they have looked for thousands of years.

On this Sunday I had made the twisting climb to the top

and then ambled around to the eastern side where the sun was slipping up from behind the dry mountains to dapple the beige and barren land with that incredible light of the earth's first day when, barely before I could take a breath of the sweet sharp scent of Jerusalem pine, from out of nowhere a wind arose with such force that it pushed me back hard against the brittle stone wall. I was pinned. I couldn't move. I could hardly breathe. Then the shockingly powerful gust subsided with the suddenness with which it had arisen, and I thought about ghosts and Christ walking on the water: that recounting in the gospel of St. Mark of a violent squall that rose up out of nowhere only to just as suddenly fade and die. Afterward I lingered, as I always do, for an hour-long session of my "special thinking," this time placing myself in Galilee when the wild wheat swayed on the slopes in shining stands in cloudless May. But my thoughts were soon shattered by the rumbling of nearby diesel-fueled buses that were starting up their engines. The spell broken, it was useless to go on and so I turned away to leave, walking slowly to the opposite side of the tower and the top of those winding slippery steps plunging down to the rock-strewn road below. But as I started my descent I glimpsed a sudden flash of light. I stopped and looked closely. It was a "wire." It was strung above the seventh step down from the top and as I bent to remove it I was suddenly aware of someone rapidly approaching me from behind.

And then the problem was solved.

Now I find myself anxious to say, "Please don't worry, I

am always on my guard, always watchful." What is this need that I have to protect you, to hold you in my care even though you are dead?

There is no parting.

Your Paul

CHAPTER 5

The genial and diminutive Armenian prelate's wily little eyes held a mischievous glitter. "Yes, water from the Jordan River, Mister Parker! Little bottles of it! Blessed! Do you think it would go over in the States? Would it sell? And, oh, Sergeant, would you pass the risotto?"

The high vaulted ceiling of the Casa Nova dining room magnified the chatter of the Catholic pilgrims and the scrape of metal cutlery on plates as they fed at communal refectory tables joined tightly together on both sides of the room. It gave Meral almost all of the little comfort he was capable of

receiving: a vivid human contact that could ease his inner loneliness without the need for him to fully engage, to grow fond,
to attach and risk pain. And there were sometimes those
momentary leaps of the heart when emanations of the confident joy and excitement of so many believers crowded together
would float up from their tables to create a penumbra of faith
that would sometimes descend upon Meral and, if only for the
briefest of moments, enfold him. But more enduringly helpful at these nightly dinners, like the breadcrumbs on the table
the Italian Franciscan serving nuns swept into their hands at
the end of the meal, were those stray bits of hope that Meral
sometimes gleaned from the comments of the priests who
led the pilgrims on their tours, though their balm was always
brief. Over coffee during Easter week the year before, a former
United States Army chaplain, after noting how so many of
Christ's disciples had chosen to die rather than to deny that
they had really seen the risen Christ, ended wryly, "Call me
nuts, but I tend to believe a man's deathbed confession." On
hearing this, Meral had felt a slight warming elation, but by
the time the osso bucco and the salad had been served, he had
lapsed back into the dryness of doubt and that night, as he did
on every other, he knelt down in the hostel's chapel to pray to
a God he wasn't sure existed that his little boy somehow, somewhere, did.

"Some more San Salvatore? Shall I fill it?"

A freckle-faced young Italian nun, a black apron worn over
her all-white garb, stood holding up an empty decanter of the
pure and strong red wine.

"Oh, yes, please," the Armenian bishop answered avidly. He then turned back to the American couple sitting opposite him. "And so what do you think?" he asked. "Tell me really."

"To be honest, I don't know," said the husband. He looked doubtful.

"Oh, well, I think it would do very well," said the wife. "I mean, come on! Holy water from the River Jordan? I think it would do *wonderfully* well!"

Waiting for his first course plate to be cleared, Meral lowered a dull and disappointed gaze to the table's little decorative clutch of pink cyclamen. This was not to be a night of uplifting insights. Although later, when the oranges and bananas had arrived at the table for dessert, for a moment Meral thought that events might turn.

"What do you think about the Shroud?" someone sitting to the right of the bishop asked him, a young engineer with crewcut blond hair and a delicate German accent. He was speaking of the burial cloth of Christ. "I have heard that two American physicists are saying that this image of the crucified man could be only produced by something that is having to do with nuclear fission. What do you think about this, Father Youkemian?" At this, Meral's mind made a leap to that enigmatic statement in the gospel of John by the risen Christ to Mary Magdalene outside the empty tomb when she fell to the ground and clutched at his feet: "*Noli me tangere*": "Do not touch me for I have not yet been to the Father." What did it mean? No one really knew. And now this mention of a nuclear event. But Youkemian told the German, "I don't think that would sell," and attempted to rekindle a discussion of the prospects for his bottled Jordan water scheme, although the man named Parker did return to the theme of Christ's tomb with a comment whose seriousness no one could accurately gauge: "Oh, well, why don't they go in there with a Geiger counter, fellas?"

Over coffee a visiting priest stood up and clinked a spoon against his water glass for attention. Meral stared at him, riveted. It was the priest he'd seen quarreling with the blond young woman in front of The Shalom. "Hello, I'm Father Dennis Mooney," he said, and then after a string of quips that drew a few chuckles, he announced an impromptu entertainment that consisted of a "singing contest" between himself and Father Mino Mancini, the chubby bald director of the hostel whose constant expression was a kindly smile and who reminded almost everyone of Friar Tuck. Meral lowered his head for a moment, as his mind replayed the scene in front of the hostel. Was the handsome priest involved in a secret dalliance? Meral lifted his head and stared as Mooney led off the singing contest with "The Rose of Tralee" in a pleasing and emotionally tinged tenor voice. Mancini then countered with "Non Dimentica." A few popular ballads by each of them followed, including a reversal of roles when Mooney spoofed the rotund Italian by singing "That's Amore" with a mock-drunk Dean Martin imitation, while Mancini's riposte of "My Wild Irish Rose" proved equally amusing due to his heavy Italian accent.

The contest ended with no winner declared and soon

afterward the room had almost emptied of life, its vibrant sounds dwindled down to a few scattered voices, the clearing of dishes, and a pair of continuously ringing tones as a playful Rumanian count and countess sitting near the opposite end of the room were each rubbing the tip of a moistened forefinger around the rims of their empty wineglasses. Alone, and with his head bent deep in thought about the eerie find of the two charred birds, Meral finally noticed the sound and looked up. And then inwardly groaned. Seated at the head of the Rumanians' table was Scobie, once a British clandestine agent now retired from the SIS, the British Secret Intelligence Service, and, like Meral, a longtime Casa Nova resident. He was also a notorious windbag and a bore with apparently not even the slightest regard for the "Top Secret" stamp on the record of his exploits, which, after two Pimm's Cups he would freely divulge to any guest at the hostel or, in desperation, to luckless staff. He was staring intently at Meral down the length of the nearly empty tables with his eyebrows raised and a speculative look in his eyes. Meral made a show of glancing at his wristwatch and shaking his head with a troubled frown, and then quickly stood up and walked out of the dining room without meeting Scobie's gaze.

Suddenly fatigued, Meral started toward his room, but then remembering a promise to Sister Angelica, the wrinkled and tiny Casa Nova head nun, he reversed his course and went to the reception lobby to mildly reprimand Patience, the tall, willowy Abyssinian concierge who tended bar both before and after dinner and had a fondness for quoting from the works of

Shakespeare and randomly dosing the hostel guests' drinks with Mickey Finns.

"Why do you do it, Patience? Tell me. I want to understand."

"I don't know."

"Are they people you don't like, the ones you do this to?"

"No. No, I like them very much. I truly do."

"Then why, Patience? Why?"

"I don't know."

With a pious promise of reform in hand, although still without a clue as to the concierge's motive, Meral left the reception area and was wearily walking toward his room when, at the intersection of a hallway leading to the sleeping quarters of the nuns, he stopped for some moments to stare down the hall to its very end where a strongly built man wearing khaki pants and shirt and a belt of workmen's tools with a dangle of room keys attached was standing with his back to him close to the door of the head nun's room. Motionless, his head inclined toward the door, he appeared to be listening to violin music issuing softly from a phonograph within. Meral's stare was distantly fond. The man was Wilson, whom he knew to be a likeable and seemingly simple-hearted American, with the radiant and transparent smile of either the innocent or the retarded, who did handyman work for the nuns free of charge. Meral recognized the music as well, Bruch's soul-catching *Violin Concerto #1*, and for no more than the moment that it takes the heart to break, Meral, too, bent his head a little bit and listened, but then had to move on lest the music, like Joshua's horn at Jericho, topple the walls of protection around him, sending them tumbling and shattering to the ground.

E xcept for the colorful window drapery, Meral's Casa Nova room could have been a monk's: a clothes tree, a desk and chair, a single bed without headboard, and a tall stained pinewood wardrobe, on top of it a statue of the young boy Jesus handing a single red rose to his mother. When Meral had first moved into the room, he had requested that the statue be removed. But then a few weeks later he had it brought back. No explanation was given at either time. Meral looked at it now as he sat on the side of his bed, exhausted, then turned his head to stare at the dark bronze crucifix hanging on the wall just above the room's door. Was that the highest aspiration of man? To suffer? Why? To what end? The answer of a priest at his table months before had been a mere two words: "soul formation." It had given Meral light for a time but little warmth. Was there no other way? He looked down at the terra-cotta tiles of the floor and then lifted his stare to the array of framed photos that were propped on a desk set against the wall. His parents. His beloved wife. And then his gaze settled onto the son he had loved with an intensity that surprised him, that at times he had even feared, although never knowing why until that day when the uncaring sky had birthed death and he at last understood that the thing he had feared was the essence of hell: the pain of loss. Standing with his legs wide apart on green grass, dark ringlets of curly hair banding his brow like a Grecian Ephebe of Marathon raised up from the floor of the sea and given breath, Meral's son stared out from the photo with the love of angels shining from his face as he proffered a long-stemmed red rose to the camera.

Meral stared. He would cry now yet he couldn't. The Wall. He saved all his tears for his dreams.

Meral lowered his face into his hands. Why had he come home so early that day? Why not five minutes earlier? Five minutes later? Two? One? The litany of guilt and recrimination had been faithfully repeated every day now for years. Meral looked up and turned his head, staring pensively at something on his bedside table. He reached over and picked it up. It was a book about Einstein, God, and quantum physics. Though never the grail of complete assurance, Meral did find help in such books. But it wasn't this one's content that had his interest. It was something else. He stared at the cover for a moment and then opened the book to the page where on the night before last, before getting into bed, he had placed a narrow Casa Nova paper bookmark—it had a photo of the hostel on one of its sides and a spiritual quotation on the other—into the book to mark his place. When about to fall asleep that night, the policeman had murmured, as he had every night for the last four years, "One more day, son. One day closer." He had tired of asking for signs that never came, although even were the sun to hold still in the sky, days later his doubts would all return. But on this night he had decided to petition his son: "If you live, if you hear me, please come to me. Visit me tonight in my dreams." The son didn't. He never had. But on the following night when Meral had again picked up the book, he found the Casa Nova bookmark no longer there and in its place there was a freshly picked bright yellow sunflower, the favorite of his son. This early morning when Meral asked the gray and green uniformed housekeeper regularly charged with the care of his room if she had made the exchange, she had looked him askance and with a smile of bemusement had told him, "Why would anybody do such a thing?" Afterward, heading to the dining hall for breakfast, Meral had stopped, spying Wilson with his head bent low at the reception counter where he was resting his weight on folded arms, perhaps waiting for the tiny nun in charge to give him instructions. For a moment Meral stared at the cluster of room keys attached to Wilson's belt of tools, and then, on a sudden impulse, walked over to him.

"Oh, Wilson!"

Wilson lifted his head with a look of warm trust and recognition.

"Sergeant Meral!"

"Was it you?" Meral quietly asked him.

Wilson's brow crinkled up with an innocent bewilderment.

"What do you mean, Sergeant Meral?"

Suddenly embarrassed, Meral answered, "Never mind. Have you a monkey wrench I could borrow? A small one, the smallest that you have."

"Oh, well, sure!"

"I haven't seen you here in quite some time."

"Yes, I know."

Wilson was wearing leather workman's gloves, and when he'd slipped one off so that he could grasp the tiny wrench at his belt, Meral noticed there were bandages wrapped around the palm of his hand.

They were red with a seepage of blood.

"Hurt yourself, Wilson?"

Looking down at his belt as he reached for the wrench, the handyman had shrugged and smiled faintly.

"That's the job, sir," he'd said. "Getting hurt."

M eral picked the sunflower out of the book and for moments held it up to his probing stare. He wondered. But could go no further. "One more day," he murmured into his pillow. "One day closer." He wanted time to sweep him up into its arms and then to carry him, to race with him, at blinding speed to a place where he might find something other than this sadness that clung to him on and on without end.

He slept. And did not dream.

The next morning after Meral had awakened he picked up a message slip from under his door. Moses Mayo had called him just before midnight. After Patience had explained to Mayo that in addition to the hostel's 11 P.M. curfew, he had orders from Meral never to knock on his door after ten, and then referenced "the raveled sleeve of care," the besieged Abyssinian finally buckled under Mayo's irritated shouting and agreed to slip a message under his door—"very quick, right now," he told Mayo—but then deflected a request to "gently rap on the door" as well.

Patience told him he would cough. "That is all I can do."

Meral unfolded the message slip. Laboriously inscribed by Patience in pencil and in thick block letters tilting this way and that were the words:

COME SEE ME! IMPORTANT!

And below that:

. . . SHAWR . . . INAXPLIKABLE . . . DEAD.

CHAPTER 6

I'd followed you at a distance. Then I stopped and just watched when you pulled into that little Paz gasoline station, and then when I saw you getting out of your car, why then my blood began to sing in excitement! Not a passion for your death, understand: just the thrill of completing one's duty to perfection. Then this bird with an owl chasing after it flew into the cab of my car. A mad flurry of wings and chasing and squawking. I didn't care, though: I just had to embrace the moment's chance and I accelerated forward and was heading right at you when the tip of a bird's wing hit my eye and I missed you and I crashed and burned. Thank God!"

"Let me help you move a bit forward. I want to put these pillows behind you."

"Oh, thank you."

"And the pain? More morphine?"

"No. No, I'm alright for now."

"That's good."

"Who are you?"

"What?"

"Who are you?"

"Haven't we been through this all once before?"

CHAPTER 7

Dearest Jean,
So many things. A sort of Cyrano's Last Gazette.

First, Moses Mayo. You remember? The funny doctor at Hadassah Hospital that I went to for a checkup the first month I was here? I've had drinks with him a few times and he's finally opened up to me and now I know his whole story, the reason he gave up the job of chief physician and then suddenly started to lose so much weight. After coming to the

States on a cultural grant and doing his internship at UCLA, he went back to Israel where he worked on staff at Hadassah in general medicine and neurology and found himself in a position to play the male lead in the second most touching and transcendent love story that I honestly believe I've ever heard. An American film crew came into town to shoot a major motion picture, a spy thriller starring the young and very lovely Jane Ayres. She met Mayo at a cocktail party and reception at the home of the Minister of Culture. They sat in a corner and talked, I'm told, and were instantly attracted to one another despite the wide chasm between their ages. There was lots of laughter between them. Then at some point the starlet asked Mayo if Israeli medicine had made any new discoveries concerning infertility. Married and barren, unable to conceive, she told Mayo how she desperately wanted a child without which, she was certain, her marriage was destined to collapse. "You're sure it's you and not your husband?" Mayo had asked her. "No, they've ruled him out. It's me." Mayo called her in for a complete examination and a series of tests, and then, somehow, improbably, while the motion picture filming was proceeding, the two became romantically entwined.

"What could you possibly see in me?" Mayo once asked her at a time when it seemed to him abundantly clear that if her marriage fell apart it was likely she would instantly settle at his side. "I'm so much older and not anywhere near good-looking." She took his arm in hers and looked into his eyes. "Funny is forever," she told him. But then, as the filming was

nearing completion and after many weeks of tireless study and late-night hours spent in intense and unbounded thought, Moses Mayo awakened one April morning with his eyes wide and staring at the ceiling of his room and the strangeness and unpredictability of life, got out of bed, went immediately to his desk and started feverishly writing on a large yellow notepad. Many nights of pacing in his quarters followed as he struggled with an incredibly difficult decision. And then suddenly, the filming completed, there they were at Lod Airport saying good-bye: the star-crossed Mayo and the love of his life who was just about to board her flight home to the States. As they stood looking into each other's eyes, Mayo asked, "Are you still desperate to have a child?" And when she lowered her head and said, "Yes. Yes, that would have been best," Mayo reached into a pocket and handed her an enve lope. "Don't lose this," he cautioned her gravely. "Give it to your doctor." "What is it?" "Never mind," he replied. "Just don't lose it."

It was a recipe for curing her infertility.

Later she conceived and gave birth to a boy.

Mayo never saw her again. Except in movies.

Mayo, Meral, and me. We have all lost the loves of our lives. Mayo tries to recapture his in healing, Meral in keeping others safe. And me? Well, that's not for me to say. Not yet. And so let me turn the page in this final gazette to a topic that I've lately been reading about and that I wish I had known before. It's so strange.

The star Sirius, you see, possesses an invisible companion

that today we call "Sirius B." Unless you view it through a telescope you can't see it. It's totally invisible. No one even suspected that it existed until around the middle of the nineteenth century. But the Dogon tribe of Mali has known of its existence for hundreds of years! They call it "Digitaria." A beautiful name, don't you think? The Dogon have known that its orbit is elliptical, that its orbital period is exactly fifty years, and that it rotates on its axis. They have also believed it is the smallest of all heavenly objects, and yet, paradoxically, also the heaviest. Well, it now turns out that this type of star is in fact the smallest that we know of and is made of a matter that is super dense, one whose kind exists nowhere on the face of the Earth. How could the Dogon have known these things? Sirius B is ten thousand times dimmer than Sirius A, and yet for centuries the Dogon have believed that it's the most important star in the sky, which might explain why they've built their religion on it. Astronomy, cosmology, biochemistry—the Dogon have knowledge of all these things and insist they were taught by alien beings they refer to as "the Nommo" and whom they divide—at least according to an ancient Dogon text—into separate kinds: the Nommo Die, who is God; the Nommo Titanye, who came to the Earth in spaceships and are the Nommo Die's messengers and deputies; and then finally there's someone they call "O Nommo" who's going to be sacrificed for the sake of the purification and reorganization of the universe (This made me think of my "Red Light" dream!) and will enter human form and then descend upon the Earth. And then the even more stunning thing. I'll quote it: "The O Nommo divided his body among men to feed them, and as the universe had drunk of his body, the O Nommo also made men drink, and he gave his life principle to human beings." A little later in the text it says he was "crucified on a kilena tree" and soon afterward rose from the dead.

Had I known of this before it might well have impacted my "special thinking" as well as my hunt for "Target X," which by the way is the most difficult of my career, although I still have no doubt that he is here and that I will find him. Unless he finds me first. Speaking of that, something curious. Though I didn't see the person, I did hear footsteps just a few days ago that I could have sworn were unmistakably Stephen's. It must have been a wish. How often in my dreams have I lived it over, the explosion that took your life and his? At long last are my senses beginning to dull? Perhaps they have altered along with the rest of me. I am changing, Jean. Something is happening to me. I feel myself becoming new. I'm not sure yet what it is, but I've a sense—you could call it a premonition—that I might very soon be joining you in that place where we've been promised "every tear will be wiped away."

Dawn is seeping through the window in front of the little wooden table where I write and my eyes sweep the watching street below. There is still another killer out there somewhere. Please don't worry though, my darling. The worst that can happen is there'll be no more letters.

There'll be you.

N o, I'm not imagining it! These are *facts* I am giving you! *Facts!*"

Mayo paced back and forth behind his desk in agitation while Meral sat patiently listening and doubting. Eddie Shore was found dead of a cardiac arrest very early in the morning on Tuesday, 11 March.

"Myocardial infarction," the autopsy had concluded.

But Mayo was convinced there'd been foul play.

"For what reason?" Meral asked.

He wasn't in uniform. It was Sunday, Meral's day off.

"I don't know," Mayo fretted. "But those two CIA guys at the American Embassy—everybody knows who they are— they came storming into Eddie's room and sealed it off until forensics finally showed. Theirs. Not ours. And now they say they want his body shipped back to Langley for a second autopsy. And so why would that be? Want to tell me? Look, it smells, Meral! Really! It stinks!"

Mayo flopped down into the chair behind his desk.

"Okay, now listen," he said in a voice now calm and low. "Every now and then somebody comes to this hospital with the symptoms of salmonella poisoning. I've looked it all up. It's in the record. They come here and they die. The last one was a year ago. Vladimir Secich. He was a high-level Soviet consul who turned out to be a spymaster. Everyone was saying he was about to defect. And then there was another one here for salmonella, a Bulgarian security official who might have had connections to the Russians. Salmonella doesn't kill people, Meral. It's benign."

"But you said they died of heart attacks."

"You remind me of my mother. No matter what disaster you told her had happened that day, she'd wave it off and say, 'Worse things happen at sea.' Listen, death that looks like a heart attack can be brought on at any time by injecting a person with insulin. Okay? A tiny hypo could be rigged on the bottom of a ring on the killer's finger. He could tap the victim's leg in a consoling way, or just a friendly good-bye kind of thing, and the victim wouldn't feel it. Secich had security twenty-four hours, a guard inside his room and another one outside by the door, but then even the guard inside could be looking right at it and think nothing of it."

"Wouldn't insulin show up in the autopsy?"

"Sure it would, but only if it's done right away: within eighteen hours, maybe less. With Secich the Russians hauled him out of here and then flew the body straight back to Moscow before there was any autopsy. Besides, the murders could be done another way. It takes a little more finesse, some basic knowledge of human physiology, but the advantage is it wouldn't leave a trace of any kind! All you'd need is to inject a little air bubble, Meral. When the bubble hits the heart it's instant death without a trace. Come on, I know all different ways where there'd be no suspicion, where the cause of a death wouldn't show up in tests."

Meral's eyes began to narrow with concern.

"You really think that all three of these deaths were murders?"

"So what else am I to think? That they'd just seen their hospital bill?"

"You seem so emotionally invested in this, Moses."

"Eddie Shore was a wonderful person."

"Then if so, why would anyone want to kill him?"

"I don't know. All I know is those CIA agents came around, and that if you want to have somebody killed, then a hospital's the absolutely perfect place to do it. People die here. They die here all the time." He looked off for a moment, and then back. "And then there's this other thing."

"What?"

"About an hour before he died someone came into Secich's room with the 'lytes, his electrolytic balances. Sometimes we send down to the lab and we order them to see if the patient's maybe losing too many nutrients from vomiting or maybe diarrhea. The 'lytes are tested, then sent up from the lab."

"What are you getting at, Moses? That some doctor killed these people?"

"Now you're talking like you did back in school in Ramallah when you suspected Sister Joseph had stolen your lunch. Doctors *order* the 'lytes, they don't deliver them. They're brought up by one of the attendants. Do we really need an Arabic Inspector Clouseau?"

Meral turned his head and looked out of a window.

"So now help me to figure out *this* one, Meral. Two days after Shore dies, I run into Dave Fuchs, Shore's doctor, and we're talking about how we couldn't guess this was coming. Then Fuchs tells me something very strange: he says one of our volunteer attendants—I think you might know him from the Casa Nova. He works there part time. Name's Wilson?"

Meral turned back to Mayo.

"Oh, yes, Wilson. Yes. Yes, I know him."

"Well, he tells me Wilson came to him the next day and he wanted to know what had happened, and that Fuchs had called down to the lab about an hour before Shore died and ordered his 'lytes and said to send them straight up to Shore's room, and not as usual to the desk, because that's where Fuchs said he was going to be. But when Wilson went up there the room was dark, he said, and there was only a night light on and Shore was sleeping. Fuchs told him that he didn't know what he was talking about, he wasn't even in the hospital that night! It's all crazy, Meral. Weird. It's all wrong."

Meral stayed silent and impassive.

Mayo leaned forward intently, hands flat on the top of his desk.

"I'm not delusional, Meral. Understand? I've got a strong instinct about this thing. You know all about instinct don't you, *boychick*? You invented it. I know there's something wrong here. I know it in my blood. Why would someone fake the ordering of 'lytes to Shore's room?"

"I think I've read enough Hercule Poirot novels to guess at that one."

"Let's hear it."

"I don't know if I should tell you. It might only feed into your paranoia."

"Meral, where did you learn such big words? Did those mischievous sisters at Ramallah teach you that one and then told you it's a fish with little razor-sharp teeth? Those Catholic nuns will stop at nothing to break a man's mind. Okay, come on now! What's your theory? Or Hercule Poirot's. Or whoever's."

"Well, if Shore was really killed in the way that you imagine, it could be because the killer wants suspicion thrown on Wilson. It would be someone who wants Wilson put away or even dead."

"Throw suspicion on Wilson for a murder?"

"I'm just entering your fantasy, *habibi*."

"It's not a fantasy, *bubbi*."

Meral gave a diffident shrug.

"Why don't you bring this up with Shlomo?"

Mayo leaned back in his chair, aghast.

"Shlomo? Shlomo Uris, my idiotic nephew and totally use-less boy Inspector of Police who went tapping on the walls of the Tomb of Christ once looking for an entrance to a secret passage? Please be serious," Mayo said sharply.

"I've heard he's quite sharp," Meral told him. "The point is Hadassah is Jerusalem Sub-District, Moses. That's his province, not mine. I can't intrude."

"But you did with that crazy Christ killer!"

"That was personal. I did no investigation. And besides, Moses, murders are rare in my province, most especially something as exotic as this. I solve murders in novels. This is life."

"Well, I'm not letting go of this thing. Not by a long shot. I'm going to keep digging."

"Yes, do that. You're good at that, Moses. You should."

"What's the matter with you, Meral?"

"What do you mean?"

"Your face, Meral! Look at your face! I've never seen such unhappiness in all my life." Mayo stood up. "That's the trou-ble with doctors these days," he declared. "You come into the examining room and they're flipping through pages in your file checking blood test results instead looking at the patient's face, which is where the whole story is at times. *Lots* of times. Okay," he said, moving, "come on."

"Come on what?"

"Come on into the examining room. I want to check a few things."

"Afraid I haven't got the time."

"Then make it!"

Twenty minutes later Meral was buttoning up his shirt while Mayo was folding up a blood-pressure sleeve. "Well, you're healthy," Mayo said. "Does that depress you? Look, you've got to start taking medication. I keep telling you to see someone. Do it, Meral. Please! And then this guilt you keep carrying around. You know, they're saying now when somebody's dead a few minutes and we're able to do something right for a change and we bring them back to life, they say they saw this bright light at the end of a tunnel and it helped them review their whole lives, all the things they did wrong. *You* have a life review every ten minutes!"

Back in Mayo's office, Meral plucked his policeman's beret from a wall hook, walked over to the front of Mayo's desk and looked down at his boyhood friend, who was sitting with his elbows propped and the sides of his head lowered into his hands.

"I'm not letting go of this," he vowed. "I am not."

"Take care," the policeman said softly, and then he turned and walked slowly to the open office door where, before stepping out into the bustling hall, he stopped and turned around for a long look back.

CHAPTER 9

W here do you get these things?"

"What things?"

"You know, the morphine. Syringes."

"Does it matter?"

"Then they're stolen, I presume?"

"Are you interrogating me?"

"Ah, you're smiling that archangel's smile!"

"Let's replace these old dressings. Come on now. Sit up."

"You've changed."

"Yes, I know."

"It's much stronger now."

"What?"

"That light. That terrifying inner light of yours. It's stronger and worse, much worse, than before."

"How worse?"

"More painful. It feels like forgiveness."

CHAPTER 10

A nd so Shore comes to Israel, mysteriously dies, and you're telling us he wasn't on a mission? Always traveling, researching, giving speeches: he's your perfect secret errand and delivery boy. Come on, we know that. My question is, what was he delivering *here*?"

They were in the office of Moshe Zui, the forty-three-year-old lawyer-investigator with Shin Bet, the Israeli internal security agency whose fifty-two office complex was blandly hidden behind a single fortified entry door on the second floor of a Tel Aviv building housing fast-food shops and a variety of stores that offered everything from eyeglass repair to women's clothing. A plaque on the agency's door bore the anonymous legend BEST PRODUCTS.

"Come on, come on," Zui prodded. "We know you tore ass to his hospital room. Own up! We're all friends here, not so? What's the problem?"

Zui was speaking to William Sandalls, a high-ranking agent of the CIA with the cover of American embassy "attaché," who now sat in a chair in front of Zui's desk. An ex-Army full colonel with years of duty in Japan, Sandalls was tall and slightly chubby, favored blue-tinted seersucker suits, and had crew-cut blondish hair, a freckled face, and a little snub nose that helped to give him the look of boyish innocence he was constantly trying to project, although the mischievous twinkle in his eyes always fought it. He held his hands out to Zui, palms up.

"Listen, what can I say?"

"Quite a lot. But you won't."

Zui turned his head to meet the gaze of another Shin Bet agent in the room, Lod Evert. He was standing with his back against a wall with folded arms. Zui lifted his eyebrows at him. Evert nodded and Zui turned his attention back to Sandalls. "So okay, we *do* know what he was up to," he admitted. "He was carrying information so explosive you couldn't risk it being intercepted, or maybe being compromised by a mole, and so Shore had to carry it in his head and was supposed to transmit it to your ambassador in person."

"Oh, so you know that. Big surprise."

"We try. Now what was it Shore was going to tell him? Some attack about to come? Some information that could topple the State? Our prime minister, Golda Meir, dyes her hair?"

"Look, whatever it was, no one knew it but Shore. Not even us."

"What *color* she dyes it?"

"Oh, come on!"

Zui turned an expressionless stare to Lod, then looked back at Sandalls, and with his fingertips slowly pushed an open tin of Swiss chocolates toward him. "Here, take three or four of these back to the Embassy with you—even eat them on the way if you like—and then come back here."

Sandalls reached into the box.

"Come back?"

"Yes, right away. We've injected the chocolates with truth serum."

Sandalls drew back his hand.

CHAPTER 11

With most of his Sunday still before him, Meral boarded a noisy old bus to Ramallah where, at a Catholic cemetery far from the tumult of the *suqs*, he placed flowers on the graves of his parents, his wife, and his son. Earlier a drizzle of rain had fallen, further moistening the grass and the tombstones and the air of a place still so damp with the memory of loss that the earth seemed even stiller than the hearts beneath it. *Do they know that I am here now?* Meral wondered. He didn't know. He knew only that he had to come. Afterward he walked to a leprosarium to visit its head, Sister Elena Karina, who once taught him in a Catholic grade school here. They had tea and remembrances. Many silences. And that was alright.

"You've kept the faith, Peter?"

"Yes. What else is there?"

He knew that would please her.

Just before leaving, Meral asked about the leper who'd regained her sight. "Oh, Reema," said the nun with a tilt of her head. There was a touch of sadness in her eyes, as well as something else that Meral couldn't quite place, though he was sure he had seen it before, and quite recently. But he couldn't remember where.

"Why, she died a few days ago, Peter."

"Oh, really? How sad."

"No, it wasn't. She was happy."

Once back in Jerusalem, Meral visited Fuad's, his favorite coffee shop, on Christian Quarter Street, where in mild weather he would sit outside across from the massive and only entry door to the Church of the Holy Sepulcher. A late fourth-century block-stone structure, it was built above the site of the crucifixion and the burial tomb of Christ. Every morning at precisely half past four and again every night at sundown, a ritual unlocking of the door was played out by two members of different Muslim families, the Joudehs and the Nusseibehs. The Joudehs had been appointed by Saladin to be "keepers of the key," and later the Nusseibehs to be their "helpers." At appointed times of morning and night, a Nusseibeh would carry the ten-inch key to a Joudeh, who would then climb a ladder and either unlock or lock the door.

Meral sometimes would be present at the closings, and then often the Nusseibeh or the Joudeh, or both, would come over to his table and join him for a coffee. They basked in his presence. Meral the Good. The Protector. He could not tell them that their visits were an interruption, for he came there not for coffee but to stare at the site of Christ's Tomb while he checked off facts about the resurrection as if conducting the most methodical of police investigations. It didn't matter that the process never turned up fresh insights, never spawned a new theory or unearthed new facts. All he wanted was the comfort of the old ones: the credible restraint of the gospel accounts, so minimally narrated and so utterly lacking in drama and fanfare that they seemed to presume that the facts were not only well known but also believed and not in need of any effort at salesmanship; that the appearances were never at night, but in full daylight; and that the notion of a resurrected Messiah— much less a Messiah who had disastrously failed—was a novelty, if not totally unheard of, in the Jewish traditions of that time. Meral sipped at his coffee and stared at the church, again running through his favorite imagined interrogation: *"Now, Saint Paul, would you tell us again what you said to that crowd that was gathered by the hillside?" "Oh, well, I told them some five hundred people saw the risen Christ all at one time, and that most of those who saw him were still alive." "Were any of the ones who saw him present in the crowd that day while you were preaching?" "I don't know. Maybe so, maybe not. Pretty likely that some were, though. Most believers were teenagers. Avid. They would come. And if not, they'd surely soon enough hear all about it." "You weren't worried that they'd stone you for lying?" "No one did."*

"Your mind is elsewhere, brother Meral."

"Forgive me."

"What you are thinking, does it give you so much pain?"

"No, my brother. What it gives me is comfort and hope."

"God be with you, then. We'll leave you with your thoughts."

Dinner at the hostel that night excelled: veal française with scalloped potatoes and peas. But no priests were at Meral's table and the dining room, barely half full, was much quieter than usual. Later, Meral caught a bus into West Jerusalem where a cinema was playing the American western, *Shane*, with both Hebrew and Arabic subtitles. Meral liked it because of the sacrifice at the end. He thought it somehow spoke to him of transcendence, although in what way he was unable to define. Nor was he certain that such sacrifice occurred in real life: that what looked at first glance to be a reflection of C.S. Lewis's "love that made the worlds" was instead, when one scratched at the surface of things, not so selfless as one had supposed. Perhaps there were such things, but he knew of them in books and in the news and in movies but not in real life. *His* life. All he knew was that the need to encounter such a case was a cold dark fire in his soul that burned without light or heat and yet could no more be extinguished than the lights in the sky that were the stars.

"Shane, come back!"

The cry struck at his heart.

Once back at the hostel, Meral read for relaxation—another Hercule Poirot—and at last bedded down a few minutes after ten. At 11:32, an urgent telephone call came into Reception, someone from the Church of the Holy Sepulcher vehemently demanding to speak to Meral. This time Patience pounded loudly on his door. The dead body of a man in a suit and tie and with a face that was disfigured by the scarring of burns had been found lying peacefully resting on his back atop the burial slab in the Tomb of Christ. No cause of death was immediately apparent and no suicide note had been found, nor any identifying document except for the international driver's license discovered in the dead man's wallet and an empty but postmarked envelope found in a pocket of the dead man's jacket. The name on the letter and the name on the driver's license were the same.

Joseph Temescu.

CHAPTER 12

L ed there by the envelope addressed to Temescu, Sergeant Meral and Corporal Issa Zananiri entered an apartment in Jerusalem Hills that the dead man had rented weeks prior to his death. The apartment was dreary and sparsely furnished and, after walking through it for a quick inspection, the policemen undertook a long and thorough search of every closet, every cabinet and drawer. Many items of great interest were found, a few of less, and all were placed into evidence bags. But instead of bringing clarity and answers, they were destined to confound the normal mind with their strangeness. Among them were an eyeliner pencil, rouge, and a silvery tin of Clown White face paint. There were also three orange-colored vinyl juggling balls.

And a circus clown's frizzy red wig.

CHAPTER 13

INTERVIEW OF SERGEANT MAJOR PETER VINCENT MERAL
21 MARCH, 1974, AT INTELLIGENCE H.Q., TEL AVIV

Present: Charles Bell and William Sandalls, American Embassy;
Moshe Zui, Israeli Intelligence. I.I. stenographer: Deborah Peltz.

ZUI: Good morning, Sergeant Meral. Nice meeting you.
Sorry we're all late. Good, I see you've had some coffee.
MERAL: Yes, a bit.
ZUI: I've heard some wonderful things about you.

MERAL: I'm quite sure they're undeserved.

ZUI: You know Bill Sandalls?

MERAL: I don't think so. You're with whom?

SANDALLS: We're American Embassy attachés.

ZUI: He tells me that, too. It's total bullshit. He's CIA. So's his buddy, over there, Charlie Bell. They think it's funny. Look at them snickering over there like two kids with a closet full of secret decoder rings.

SANDALLS: Nice meeting you, Sergeant.

BELL: Good morning, Sergeant Meral.

MERAL: Yes, good morning to you both.

ZUI: Some more coffee, Sergeant?

MERAL: No thank you.

ZUI: The girl who usually makes it is out sick today.

MERAL: That's a pity.

ZUI: I know what you mean. Now, again, I want to emphasize this isn't a grilling. But our American friends here have asked to hear a number of things from you directly and be able to question you about them. Okay?

MERAL: Yes, gladly. But why?

ZUI: They don't trust us.

SANDALLS: Oh, come on, Zui! We just need to be absolutely sure.

MERAL: About what?

ZUI: Well, your report about the body in the Tomb has raised an issue that you couldn't have been expected to be aware of, so they'd just like you to lay it all out for us again. As you talk, something new might occur to you that you might have overlooked in your report, or that you just didn't think was relevant but which could be explosively so to us. So alright, now, that's clear?

MERAL: Yes, it's clear. But can you tell me what you mean by that last thing you mentioned? You said "explosively relevant."

ZUI: Oh, well, perhaps I've overblown it a bit. So no more coffee, now? You're sure?

MERAL: I'd stake my life on it.

ZUI: Fully understood. So now we've read your report on this Remle Street incident, and we think that was covered rather well. *Very* well. So let's go right to the body in the Tomb that at first was identified as Joseph Temescu.

MERAL: At first?

ZUI: Things change. So you're awakened because of a call from the church that came straight to your hostel, and not to the station or to paramedics. That right?

MERAL: No, they did call the paramedics. They called them next. But, yes, they did call me first. Wajih. Wajih Nusseibeh of the family with the key.

SANDALLS: What key?

MERAL: The key they use to lock and unlock the church.

SANDALLS: He's the one who found the body. Am I right? Wajid?

MERAL: Wajih. No, it was actually one of the Greeks, the Greek Orthodox monks. Beginning at midnight, there are services all through the night until dawn. The Catholics— Franciscans—they start it all off with a Latin Mass. The

Latins, the Armenians, the Copts, the Greek Orthodox: they all share in making sure all the lamps and the candles in the Tomb are lit and that there's no debris. And so it was now the Greeks' turn and this monk went in to check about a quarter to twelve because after the Mass the Franciscans were to make a procession into the Tomb and—

SANDALLS: Awfully tight for that, isn't it? Excuse me. Fits ten, twelve people, maybe? Max?

MERAL: They seem to manage. They enter and exit single file.

ZUI: But are you sure it was the monk and not someone else? I've got your report right here and I seem to recall—Oh, no, sorry. My mistake. It *was* a monk. Anastasios Scorpus. Go ahead, Sergeant. Sorry for the interruption.

MERAL: Quite alright. So now the monk saw the body and he gave a great shout, I was told—he couldn't tell if it was dead, or alive and about to jump up at him like in some horror film—and he ran from the Tomb still shouting and woke up Wajih, and when Wajih came and saw that the man was dead, that's when he called me at the Casa Nova.

ZUI: [Turns to look at the Americans] Yes, they trust you.

SANDALLS: Quit *utzing*.

ZUI: Couldn't help it. Go ahead, Sergeant Meral. He called you, you said. What happened next?

MERAL: Can we go back to something?

ZUI: What?

MERAL: Well, your mention of a change in Temescu's identity. I can't get it out of my mind.

ZUI: I understand, but there's no need for you to know. At least not at this time. Please go on. Wajih called you. And then what?

MERAL: I called the station and requested forensics and then I rushed to the church. It took me only six minutes, it's so close to where I live, the Casa Nova. They were expecting me and had already unlocked the door. Inside there was bedlam. Monks and priests of every sect with their hands in the air, full of questions, full of fright and confusion: Did the body on the slab have some meaning? Should they remove it or continue with their services while leaving the dead man resting on the slab? A Russian Copt had thrown a white sheet over the body while the head Armenian thought that the dead man might be an "incorruptible" and that maybe they could keep him as a permanent exhibit. This last almost started a brawl. And then the Greeks, the Greek Orthodox, they started talking loudly about the possibility that somehow the body was a sign from God that members of the sect about to use and enter the Tomb were intending to commit some abomination. As I said, it was madness. Only the dead man seemed to be calm. In fact I'd say he looked serene. He was all dressed up in a suit and tie with a pink and white flower in his jacket lapel as if laid out for viewing in a mortuary by his family and closest friends. He had his arms folded and crossed on his chest like in some photos that I've seen of dead saints. Do you mind my asking, by the way, what killed him?

ZUI: We haven't quite nailed it, Sergeant. There's a second autopsy underway. The first one found a terminal cancer. The incurable one. Pancreatic.

MERAL: That's what killed him?

ZUI: We're looking at something else.

MERAL: Then he was murdered?

ZUI: Suicide or murder, it could go either way. Let's go on now, Sergeant. Let's pick up. You found something on the body that led you to a furnished apartment that Temescu had rented in Jerusalem Hills for some—what?—some three weeks or so?

MERAL: Thereabouts.

SANDALLS: You went in there alone, Sergeant?

MERAL: No. I had Corporal Zananiri with me.

SANDALLS: So there's a witness.

MERAL: A witness? A witness to what?

ZUI: To the fact that you found what you *say* you found there. Sandalls thinks we sit around here all day munching matzohs and dreaming up schemes to salt evidence just to make him and Bell even crazier than they already are.

SANDALLS: Moshe, I wouldn't put it past you.

ZUI: Sergeant Meral? You'll continue with your *witnessed* story?

MERAL: The concierge let us into the apartment. It was small: two rooms, a kitchenette, and a bathroom. Very dreary. It had some old rental furniture in it. Anyway, we made a thorough search. There was hardly any clothing, just a jacket, a shirt, and a pair of trousers hanging in a closet.

No labels. They'd all been cut. Things were covered with dust. But as you know we did find a few items of interest. The passports and the I.D. card, mainly.

ZUI: And the juggling balls and circus clown items.

MERAL: They're of interest?

BELL: [To Sandalls] That's our boy, alright!

MERAL: I feel that I'm missing something.

ZUI: No. Let's move on.

MERAL: Yes, of course. So we went about knocking on doors and asking questions about him. About Temescu. There were just a few apartments. It's a four-story building. Some of the occupants weren't at home and those who were could tell me little, almost nothing in fact. They all said that except for one time when he first moved in they never saw him; never heard him, in fact: No sound of water running ever. No radio. No footsteps. Nothing. But then a woman on the second floor in the apartment across the hall from Temescu's, a pretty young housewife, she came home as we were just about to leave and she told us that she'd heard someone going into Temescu's apartment on the morning of the day Temescu's body was found in the church. He stayed only a few minutes, she said, during which she thought she heard a closet door being opened and then afterward a drawer sliding open. And then a few seconds later she heard it being pushed shut. Then she heard him leaving.

SANDALLS: She never saw him though?

MERAL: No. No, she didn't. But the odd thing . . .

ZUI: Yes?

MERAL: Well, it seems there was a repetition very late that night: someone entering the apartment for a very brief time and the sound of a drawer sliding open and shut and then the footsteps of the person leaving.

ZUI: One drawer only?

MERAL: Just one. But Temescu was dead by that time. So who was it?

SANDALLS: So once again she doesn't see the person? Right?

MERAL: She's in bed. And she also couldn't swear it was a man.

ZUI: Is her bedroom so situated she could really tell for sure that the sounds were from Temescu's apartment?

MERAL: No, her bedroom was a bit down the hall from there. She herself wasn't positive, she said.

ZUI: Let's go on. Now you made a passing reference [consults notes] to a woman, to a nurse who also lives in the neighborhood. A nurse named Samia. . . .

MERAL: Yes, Samia Maroon. We're acquainted: friends of a friend sort of thing. She was walking up the street when she saw us going into the building, and when we came down from the apartment she was standing beside the patrol car. She gave us a "Hello," and then asked what was going on. She's a naturally inquisitive sort of person.

BELL: You mean a busybody, Sergeant?

MERAL: Oh, no! Not at all! She's quite nice, in fact. I showed her the driver's license with the photo of Temescu on it and I asked if she had seen him around. Well, she squinted at first, as if she couldn't make it out. It's in very soft focus and blurred. She kept staring and staring and she began to look troubled. She looked up at me, then, and had opened her mouth to give an answer, but she never got it out. She just stopped and very quickly closed her mouth. There was that worried look still on her face and her eyes seemed to study me, flicking back and forth and scanning mine. And then she asked me a question. She—

SANDALLS: Hold it, please. Sorry. This is one of the things that we want to be absolutely sure of. Okay? Please repeat word for word what she said, would you, Sergeant? At least as you *now* recall it.

MERAL: What she said was, "Does this have anything to do with a murder or something? Some really really serious crime?"

ZUI: And that's precisely what's in your report. Please go on.

MERAL: I told her yes, and that a serious crime was a possibility, and then right away she gave me an answer. No, she told me, she'd never seen him. And then something about wanting to meet for a drink or a coffee that night. That's not in my report.

ZUI: No it isn't. Do you socialize with her?

MERAL: No. I never have. Though she sometimes asks me to meet in that way on some pretext or other.

ZUI: Did you do so that night?

MERAL: No, I didn't. I gave her request no significance.

ZUI: And so what do you think was going on with her, Sergeant?

MERAL: I'm not sure. But I suspect that she actually *had* seen Temescu.

ZUI: Any reason she would lie about that?

MERAL: Oh, well, she could be one of those people who just doesn't ever want to be involved.

ZUI: You think that's it, then?

MERAL: Actually, I don't. Assessing her manner, her behavior—as I said, I do know her a little—my instinct says she might be protecting someone.

ZUI: Right. Now it's been mentioned to us that there's a bit of a lapse in your written report.

MERAL: Is that so?

SANDALLS: Wouldn't someone at the church remember seeing the dead man going into the Tomb? I mean, although it's not entirely out of the question, it seems whacko to imagine someone carried in a corpse. There must be someone from the church who's always posted by the entrance to the Tomb. Not so? Someone checking for crazies with a bomb or something and making sure not too many are going in there at once?

MERAL: Yes, there is such a person. There are three, in fact, working in eight-hour shifts.

SANDALLS: Don't they need to be questioned? They can confirm that our man wasn't carried in there, and they can tell us if he came into the church all alone or with someone else.

MERAL: You're entirely correct. But as it happens I've already questioned two of them and neither one has any memory of Temescu entering the Tomb. Before drawing a conclusion, I was waiting to interrogate the third one, Tariq Maloof, but he was visiting family in Amman. He's coming back today and he'll be on duty tonight, which is when I'm going to question him, and if he saw something meaningful, why, certainly, I'll give you an immediate further report.

ZUI: Yes, we'll want you to refresh us from time to time anyway.

MERAL: Gladly.

ZUI: Bill? Charlie? Anything more? Alright, Deborah, that's it. You can go. And you, too, Sergeant Meral. Thanks so much for your help. And your patience. We'll be in touch.

MERAL: One more question, please. May I?

ZUI: Go ahead.

MERAL: You said you were looking at "something else" as the cause of Temescu's death. Something other than the cancer. Can you tell me what that is?

ZUI: No, not at this time.

MERAL: You don't know yet?

ZUI: We know but we can't quite believe it.

[INTERVIEW ENDS 1106]

CHAPTER 14

Outside the inner chamber of the Tomb of Christ, quiet voices could be heard from within by the two policemen slowly pacing back and forth in front of it with heads bent low and hands clasped behind their backs, their measured footsteps reverberating softly on the diamond-shaped rose and black marble tiles that shimmered with the light from giant candles amid the thick sweet smell of hot wax and incense and the lingering whispers of a million warm prayers. Leaving his hostel at ten-fifteen so that he wouldn't interfere with the start of night services, Meral had walked quickly up a narrow street that once had shuddered with the clang of Roman armor and the terrifying stamp of marching feet. Only the quietest of sounds were to be heard now: the whirring of a turning TV antenna, the quiet rapping of knuckles on corrugated steel as municipal guards checked the shutters of shops, and, as Meral neared the church, the lilting, satisfied atonal singing of a baker who just before dinnertime had given to the poor, as he did each night, by baking their unbaked bread without charge.

"Was he here? Did he come into the Tomb?"

Meral was questioning Tariq, the third and previously unavailable checker of those who would enter the space where they were standing: a quadrangular chamber hewn out of rock and plated in marble. Six feet wide, seven long, and seven high, it was the burial chamber of Christ. The light of candles and forty-three lamps made of gold and silver danced faintly in Tariq's dark eyes as his fingers cupped his stubbled chin and he studied Temescu's driver's license.

He handed it back to Meral.

"Yes, I think he was here. I think I saw him."

"Was there anyone with him?"

"Yes, I think so. Absolutely. Maybe."

"Which is it, Tariq?"

"Yes."

"Yes, what?"

"There was somebody with him."

"A man or a woman?"

"A man."

"And they were together, you say?"

"Yes, together. I had seen them come in and they were talking. Maybe arguing."

"Arguing?"

"I think so. Maybe. I'm not sure. There were gestures, the one who was with him always leaning in close to him. Whispering. Excited."

"And the dead man? The man in the photo?"

"He was calm."

"Can you describe the other person?"

"Yes. He had a beard."

"Tariq, look at me. Look me in the eye. How helpful a description is that in Jerusalem?"

"I don't know what you want me to say."

"I would like a full description."

"I cannot remember."

"You wouldn't know him if you saw him again?"

"Maybe yes, maybe no. Very possibly."

"Was there anything distinctive about him?"

"I don't know."

"Tariq, try."

"Alright, one thing perhaps. He looked sad. I saw him crying."

"Crying?"

"Yes, a little."

"And what time was this, Tariq?"

"I don't know that exactly. But the end of the day. The last people were entering the Tomb."

"Did they enter together?"

"It could be."

"It could be?"

"I think maybe."

"And the man with the beard. Did you see him coming out?"

"I don't know. Someone called me to the entry door."

"Who?"

"Someone selling falafel."

Meral watched Tariq leave, and then crouching down to fit through the low arched access to the Tomb, he entered the chamber and then pensively looked down at the burial couch. Roughly two feet high from the floor, its primitive rock had been long ago covered by a mottled pink and ivory marble slab that was silken and slightly warm to the touch from the crowded profusion of candles and lamps, softly flickering sentinels, overlooking the burial couch. Meral reimagined Temescu lying there, as he pondered the puzzling documents he had found in the dead man's apartment. Among them was another postmarked envelope addressed to Temescu in an unknown hand, this one containing a letter that, in spite of the name on the envelope, was written to someone other than Temescu, or so its salutation seemed to indicate. And there were six other puzzling items. Five of them were passports: one Italian, one British, one Swedish, one Cambodian, and one American, all issued in different names, although none in the name of Temescu; and all bore the photo of a man who, while generally resembling Temescu, also differed from the photo on his driver's license, just as each differed one from the other: length, style, and color of hair, as well as skin and eye color, in particular in the Cambodian passport photo. Even eyebrow thickness and the prominence of cheekbones differed. Beyond that the expression staring out from the photos was so different in each of them that they were able, at least for some moments, to create the impression of a totally separate and distinct personality. Meral found this especially true of the somehow affecting photo on yet a sixth document. It was a faded Albanian identity card of someone named Selca Decani.

CHAPTER 15

Zui lifted a dismal glance to Sandalls, who was sitting next to Bell on the camel leather sofa directly across from Zui's desk.

"And so what was he doing here?" Zui demanded.

Sandalls threw up his hands and shook his head.

"We don't know."

"You don't know? The deadliest assassin in your agency's history and you're telling me you haven't got a clue why he was here?"

"Look, we haven't been in touch with the guy for years."

"Oh, please!"

"No, Moshe, really! He dropped out! He disappeared!"

"Come on, spooks don't retire. They just go from cover to cover. He came into the country on a phony passport. And the cowcatcher, Bill? What was *that*? He was planning to go work on a kibbutz? Quit the bullshit. He was here on a mission. Now what was it?"

"Moshe, I swear to you, we didn't even know he was here!"

"Should I bring out the truth serum candies again? Better watch it. They could ruin your careers. They're addictive."

"Thanks for the coffee."

That night, Zui went home to the small apartment, close to the shore in Tel Aviv, where he lived with two young children and a wife with some renown in the city for having cheated death at Auschwitz when the guard in charge of admitting a line of doomed prisoners into a gas chamber studied her face and then said to the guards who had brought her, "No, no, take her away from here! Take her! She looks just like my daughter!"

"Have an interesting day?" she asked Zui as he came into the kitchen. Zui shrugged and shook his head. He took off his jacket and loosely draped it over a breakfast table chair.

"Just the usual routine."

"Same here. God, we need some excitement in our lives."

Zui turned and appraised her ironic smile.

And then he went to her and hugged her soul.

"*You* are the excitement in my life," he said to her.

Life was the excitement in hers.

There would soon be enough to go around.

CHAPTER 16

Mayo stood behind his desk with a phone at his ear.

He checked his watch. He was late for an appointment.

"Your housekeeper?" he repeated.

"Yes."

"What's her age?"

"Does that matter?"

"Yes, it matters."

"Early forties."

"Any swelling of the legs and ankles? Nasal stuffiness?"

"Yes. I've noticed both. And there are these tiny pale spots on her face: does that sound like it, Mayo?"

"Any numbness? Loss of feeling in her fingers or toes?"

"I don't know. I'd have to ask her. I'm here on the pay phone at the post office. I'm so worried, Mayo. The woman's so miserable. She's sick as a dog."

"There's no one local who could deal with this?"

"No. Not like you. I don't trust them."

"Can't you bring her in here? We'd be able to run tests."

"Oh, I would but she's feeling so out of it, Mayo. She's got it coming out of both ends. It would be such a mercy if you'd come. Will you come? Incidentally, if you do, you can't say anything about this to anyone. I've heard it's highly curable now and that's fine, but then someone hears leprosy, even today, and you know what would happen to us here. Can you come right away? It won't take that much time. You could take her blood or whatever you need and then run your tests back there. Isn't that right?"

"Yes, I suppose."

"So you're coming?"

"Oh, well, alright, then; I'm coming. Not today, though. Too late. Tomorrow morning."

"Bless your heart. And by the way, I'll have a treat for you to take back home. The trees in our yard are in fruit and I swear they're the best I've ever eaten."

"The best what?"
"Never mind. It's a surprise."
"How nice."
"It's the least that I can do for you."
The *very* least.

CHAPTER 17

William Sandalls ushered Zui into a room on the second floor of the American Embassy in Tel Aviv and then led him to a chair at the end of a highly polished dark pine conference table where he placed an untitled file folder in front of him stamped TOP SECRET.

"Of course we had to redact some," said Sandalls. "Oh, well, a lot. But there it is. When you're all done reading it, you'll finally understand that we know nothing about any mission for him here, or for that matter, anyplace else, for at least the last three years. But no notes, Moshe. Okay? You won't need them. Let me know when you're done and we'll talk."

He pointed to a button on the side of the table. "Here's the buzzer."

"Where's Bell?"

"Busy-busy. Might pop in on us later. By the way, we want the body flown back to D.C. We'd like to run another autopsy."

"Fine. Yes, alright. Of course."

Zui watched as Sandalls trod noiselessly on thickly piled brown wool carpeting, opened a door and then quietly closed it behind him. It had been four days since the autopsy's final conclusion that the name on death's calling card for the man found dead in Christ's Tomb was undoubtedly "pulmonary edema," the result of the venom of an Omdurman scorpion, abundantly found in the Israeli desert and known by the alternate name "The Deathstalker." Also discovered by the drug screen were massive amounts of chloral hydrate, the so-called Mickey Finn, which together with the venom would kill within less than ninety minutes. There were also residual traces of morphine tied to the multiple scars of injection sites on the dead man's arms and legs that were likely related to his trauma from the burns, or the cancer, or both. Was it murder or suicide? No one could be absolutely certain.

What was clear was that the dead man's name was not Joseph Temescu. The damage to his face from third-degree burns rendered photo comparisons of less than perfect use, and while due to the burning of his hand a complete set of fingerprints could not be had, this was actually irrelevant inasmuch as the agency the dead man had worked for didn't have them on file, nor were any photos of him extant, this against the chance that a mole might one day copy them and compromise the life of their most valuable asset. But there were other things helping to establish his identity, beginning with a tracheotomy scar, and the multiple passports in his possession, as well as the Iron Curtain dentistry and the letter with its brief and innocuous content, discovered in the inside pocket of his jacket, that began with the words "Dear Paul." But the proof that some would deem to be finally dispositive was the worn and faded identity card of a country where the dead man had performed two missions.

There was also something else to be added to the proof that, because of the burns on the dead man's face, was not totally dispositive, but when taken together with all the other evidence seemed to be the turn of the screw on all doubt. To the morgue where the body was kept, Shin Bet agent Hyam Dov brought a one-time British Special Intelligence agent, who among his frequent alcoholic blathers had been heard to drop the name of the mysterious dead man, indiscreetly asserting he had worked with him once on "a frightfully dangerous mission, you see" in Nazi-occupied Poland.

"Is this anyone you recognize?" Dov asked.

"I can't say," Scobie answered. "I think no. No, probably not."

"What about these passport photos? Even seen this person?"

"These persons, you mean."

"No, they're all the same person."

"Oh, yes. Yes, I see that now. Really. Quite. Alright, let me look."

Scobie sifted through the photos.

"No. No. No, none of these photos ring a bell. I'm so sorry."

"Take a look at the body again."

"All those burn marks don't help. And would you look at those hands! Good God! Was it the fire burned his fingernails off?"

"Look more closely at his face, please."

"Yes, yes, I'm looking."

"Do you recognize him?"

"Vaguely. Yes, a little bit, now you that you mention it."

Dov gave him a name.

"No, I've never known any such person."

Dov gave him a second name.

"No."

And then another.

"What's that you say? What? Oh, my God! Oh, why, *yes*! Yes, of *course* it is! It's *him*! It's most *definitely* him! My God, what's happened to my brain? Too many bloody Pimm's Cups, I'm afraid. Oh, well they finally got him, did they? Too bad. Brave bugger."

What Scobie had just confirmed was that the dead man thought at first to be Joseph Temescu was in fact an American clandestine agent referred to in some quarters of the world as "legendary," while in others as "the agent from hell."

Paul Dimiter.

Zui looked down at the folder. He was still skeptical. Dimiter had entered the country surreptitiously. And so how could his intent have been innocent? Especially an agent so notorious, so invincibly lethal that there lingered among the world's intelligence community the persistent rumor and belief that the charismatic Viet Cong leader, Ho Chi Minh, didn't die a normal death in his bed from heart failure as had been put out by the North Vietnamese, but in fact had been the victim of a hit by Dimiter while attending a banquet in Albania where Ho was in meetings with the Albanian leadership and Soviet military officials. Having been in deep cover, ran the rumor, the agent had infiltrated the kitchen and dining room staff of the Hotel Dajti in Tirana and on the night of the banquet rubbed a deadly and slow-acting poison on the inside surface of a wooden salad bowl, which he then set down in front of Ho. Albanian security men hovered at the scene both in the kitchen and the banquet hall all through the dinner. Although not to any noticeable avail. On the plane flying back to Hanoi, Ho experienced a minor stomach disorder and then six days later was dead, an event for which the North Vietnamese blamed the Russians. Zui wondered if some reference to the exploit, however oblique, would be found in the pages now before him, although he expected it would not.

Nor was it. Nor, to Zui's frustration, was there anything else in the folder's contents that did not go directly to making the case that the CIA had nothing to do with, nor even any knowledge of, Dimiter's presence in Israel. Almost everything else was either missing or redacted. Even Dimiter's age was not noted.

Shaking his head, Zui combed the pages for whatever there was: World War II O.S.S. combat officer 1941 to 1945, and then immediately recruited by the CIA and assigned to Clandestine Services; Special Training (unspecified) in 1946; various missions; unspecified service in Vietnam in the sixties at which time, during the earliest days of the war, he received paramedical training while aboard a Swedish prisoner exchange ship; secret (and against regulations) marriage to another agent, who later, along with an agent whom Dimiter had trained, met her death while on a covert mission led by her husband in 1972. A deep depression followed. And then in 1973 he completed a second and highly unusual mission in Albania. Zui frowned. The next two pages were completely redacted and the body of the main report at an end. An appendix was attached. It was Dimiter's final report on the mission that had ended in the death of his wife and agent Stephen Riley, a biochemist, trained killer, and explosives expert.

Dimiter's wife, an experienced pilot, had flown the trio to a narrow and well hidden dale on the outskirts of Dolacio, a small city in the Los Lagos district of Chile that had always attracted strong German immigration. The target of the hunt was Erik Klar, a German scientist who had invented and sold to the United States government the working plans for a new technology giving military aircraft the ability to completely escape radar detection. But then a fully confirmed report came through that Klar had just duplicitously offered the Soviets a countertechnology that nullified the radar defeater. Finding Klar in a house very close to a number of low-rise apartment buildings, the agents, after killing both of Klar's bodyguards, forced him to give up the location and combination of a safe in a nearby building that Klar said contained all the plans and schematics for the counterdevice. While his wife went with Riley with instructions to retrieve them and place them in one or, if necessary, both of the two black valises that Riley all along had been in charge of, and then to go directly back to the plane, Dimiter stayed behind to kill Klar, for the plans for his device were still in a head where there also resided a treacherous intent. Dimiter broke his neck. Next, he made a thorough search of the house in case Klar had been lying and the plans were really here, or perhaps a second set of them made as a protection against loss of the first. Finding nothing, Dimiter set about obtaining the proof that the man he had killed was indeed Erik Klar. First he wrapped adhesive tape around his own forefinger. Next, he wrapped a second piece of tape around Klar's, then pressed firmly, removed it, and then carefully wrapped it around and on top of the tape on his own forefinger, thus concealing and protecting Klar's fingerprint. Just as Dimiter had finished this procedure, the blast of a tremendous explosion shook the house. Dimiter raced out into the street, or so read his report, to see a nearby apartment building crumbling to the ground in a titanic shroud of soaring flame. It was the building in which Klar had said the plans were stored.

There were shouts and screams, although not from the building. It was impossible for anyone to have survived. But Dimiter waited. Agonized. Watching. And passionately hoping that he was mistaken, that this wasn't the building that Riley and his wife had been told contained the plans, or that they'd retrieved them so very quickly they were out of the building before the explosion and were patiently waiting for him back at the plane.

They were not.

Two photos were attached to the file, each with a name imprinted at the bottom. One photo was of Riley, a tall and handsome redheaded man, while the other was of Dimiter's wife, a pretty blonde with a look of innocence and a winsome schoolgirl smile.

There was no photo of Dimiter.

The name of his wife was Jean.

Zui turned back a few pages, scowled, and then closing the folder he slapped it down on the table and buzzed for Sandalls, who a few moments later hurried into the room with a document folder in hand and sat down across from Zui with a satisfied grin.

"And so what was this mission in Albania?" Zui asked. "It's redacted."

"Yeah, it's sensitive."

Sandalls held up the folder he'd come into the room with and handed it to Zui. "Here it is! The whole story! I'd hoped we'd have the clearance last night but it just came in. Read away. I think it's going to ease your concerns."

"What clearance?" Zui asked. "From who?"

"From the Vatican."

"From the *what*?"

Sandalls shifted a gumdrop to the side of his mouth.

"It's all there," he said, indicating the folder while his other hand crushed up the gumdrop wrapper. He stood up and said, "Buzz me when you're done."

"I will."

Zui waited until Sandalls had closed the door quietly behind him, and then he opened the folder and began to read with fascination the riveting report that it contained. In 1973, it was stated, the Agency was secretly petitioned by the Vatican for help with a dire situation in Albania. As had happened in Mexico in the early part of the century, Catholic priests there had been killed, imprisoned, or deported and whenever the Vatican tried infiltrating a bishop with the power to ordain new priests, they were almost immediately caught. And killed. So now the Vatican asked the CIA for the services of one of their agents, one with the ability to evade capture and then to carry out the mission. If either born or baptized Catholic, he would be ordained — temporarily — a bishop.

Remarkably, the CIA granted their request, and based on his Albanian expertise, they gave the Vatican Dimiter, who then carried out the mission. But on returning to Rome to have his faculties revoked, he unexpectedly — and shockingly, according to some — retired from the Central Intelligence Agency and vanished from the face of the earth. Answers had been sought, though never received, from a Cardinal Vittorio Ricci, Dimiter's Vatican mentor and ordainer, who said he had no notion of Dimiter's plans or of where he might be. The only light that he could shed on the agent's state of mind was something Dimiter had told him on returning from Albania about a "mystical experience" that had occurred near the end of his Albanian mission, something that had shaken him profoundly but that either he would not, or could not, describe that now made it impossible for him to kill, an impulse, he told Ricci, that he had already felt coming on long before.

"It was after we had baptized and ordained him," Ricci related. "I think somewhere near the start of mission. At least that's what he told me. And then there'd been the death of his wife. Sometimes suffering turns out to be the dirty window that at last allows grace to enter the heart. Oh, and yes! Yes, something else I recall now, now that I think of it: his remarking there was something that he needed to find out. A sort of mission, if you like. Not one of yours, though. No. Not one of those. Something else."

Zui closed the folder, set it down and buzzed for Sandalls.

"Satisfied, Moshe?"

"Yes and no. It's still a mystery, is it not? Why he was here?"

"I'll grant you that. Yes, it is."

Zui tilted up the folder to his gaze.

"So the guy was a freak," he said.

"How?"

"Inability to feel pain, for one."

"Lucky boy."

"Maybe not," Zui remarked. "Bell coming?"

"I don't think so."

"One on one, then, let me ask you something, Bill."

"Go ahead."

"You know this rumor about Dimiter killing Ho Chi Minh?"

"Yeah, it's out there."

"Did he really?"

"I couldn't say."

"You just did. You're smiling."

"I was looking at your tie."

"Well, while you're at it look at this."

Zui had lifted out a page from the heavily redacted CIA folder.

"All these different kinds of looks in the passport photos. And yet no sign of plastic surgery scars. That's what the Arabs call a *ghaimetsayfiyyeh*, 'a tiny cloud of summer.' "

"I like the season, at least."

"It's still a cloud. How do we explain it? Maybe inserts, bits of sponge in the cheeks? Subcutaneous injections to darken his skin?"

"Could be that. Or maybe it was just something inside him made the difference. He was special. Very special. An extraordinary person."

"Then you've met him?"

"No, I haven't. Or maybe the correct thing to say is, 'Who knows?' "

Zui let the slightest of smiles curve his lips. "Yes, and speaking of things not known . . ." He picked up the folder and held up its cover to Sandalls. "Here we're given tons of tiny and irrelevant details, like his marksmanship scores, his love of classical music, and so on, or how a Cambodian former circus clown on some cockamamie prisoner exchange ship taught him how to juggle and put clown makeup on to keep the mice in the hold from being bored. And yet we're not to be privileged to know his age? Place of birth?"

"We don't know."

"You don't *know*?"

"No, it isn't in the file. *Any* file."

"Bill, this is farce. I mean, really. Am I to assume the man *landed* here on the planet?"

"I am telling you the truth."

"Do I get points for not quoting Pontius Pilate?" Zui opened the folder and started turning pages. "Oh, no, sorry. What he said isn't here in the file." He dropped the folder to the table with a splat.

"All this venom over a tie?"

Zui leaned back in his chair and smiled slightly.

"Oh, you're good. And incidentally, you just said the secret word."

"You mean tie?"

"No, venom. Who on earth would choose to die by the venom of a Deathstalker scorpion, Bill? They say the pain is horrific."

Sandalls shrugged.

"Oh, well, who the hell knows. I've heard he was carrying a ton of guilt about his wife."

"About his wife?"

"That's what they say. Or rather 'he.' Our man at the Vatican. If Dimiter hadn't broken the rules about marrieds not teaming together, she wouldn't have died. *Capiche?* She wouldn't have been on that mission."

"And so?"

"And so maybe he just wanted to suffer."

"Oh, so now we're psychiatrists, Sandalls?"

"Come on, Moshe. It's *got* to be suicide. The guy was dying. Why try to kill him? Why take the chance?"

"All good questions. Still, I'm asking the National Police to have Kishla keep that Meral fellow on it for a while. I like him. I like the way he thinks. Could be Dimiter was killed. If he was and we find out who did it, that could lead us to what Dimiter's mission was here. Where he goes, death follows. But whose?"

Sandalls looked away and shook his head.

"You just won't get off that," he muttered.

"No."

Zui picked up a newspaper from his desk. "I guess you've seen the bloody headline in the bloody *Jerusalem Post* today: 'Man found dead in Christ's Tomb was top killer for CIA'?"

Zui tossed the paper back onto the desk.

"Any notion who leaked this, Billy-Willy? I swear I'm going to find out and have him fed to giant ants."

"The guy's dead, Moshe. Come on."

"Come on what?"

"The only cover you can blow now is the lid on his coffin."

Which, in its way, would later prove to be prophetic.

CHAPTER 18

Mayo stared at the priest with incredulity.

"You're not serious! I drive all this way and she isn't here?"

"I'm so sorry, Mayo. Really. I woke up and she was gone. Scared of doctors, maybe. Young Palestinian woman. Scared of anyone with knives. Come on, sit down. She might be back here any minute. Who knows? Come on, I'll make us some tea."

"How could she do that and be all that sick?"

"Oh, who knows?"

"You couldn't call me?"

"There's no phone here. We have to make our calls from the local post office, and the lines have been down all day. Sorry, Mayo. Really. And would you please have a seat, for heaven's sakes?"

Mayo sighed and then nodded. "Okay."

He sat down at a small round wooden table.

"How can you not have a phone?" he asked Mooney morosely.

"They never laid in the lines. We'd have to pay for it ourselves and we can't afford it. It would cost us a fortune. Much better to use it for the poor."

For the poor? wondered Mayo.

He'd remembered the priest's chunky gold Rolex wristwatch.

"Okay, I'll brew up the tea and then bring out the surprise."

"Surprise?"

"The one I promised you. We grow them out back."

"Grow what?" Mayo asked.

"Some lovely figs."

CHAPTER 19

The young Syrian soldier who had killed the rival Christ at Hadassah Hospital tightly gripped the bars of an observation window in the door of a padded cell, his dark eyes pooling with a plea for understanding and with gratitude for Meral's presence. After getting into bed that night, the policeman had grown restless and unable to sleep, his mind awhirl with the mystery of Dimiter's mission, until at last he got up out of bed, dressed in uniform, called for a taxi, and went to Kfar Shaul to see the young soldier who had killed the rival Christ.

"I am here with you, son. I am here. Are they treating you well?"

No answer. The soldier kept staring into Meral's eyes.

"Are they giving you books? Things to read?"

In the standoff in the Psychiatric Ward, the ravings of the lunatic killer had displayed a keen intelligence and knowledge of theology far beyond his years and education. Certain states of brain disorder, according to the Kfar Shaul psychiatrists, at times created heightened intelligence, and as for the soldier's knowledge of theology, it was presumed to have come from the books he was always seen reading in the Hadassah Psychiatric Ward.

"Are they?" Meral repeated.

The Syrian soldier's wounded gaze never wavered.

But again he stayed silent.

"I have a question," Meral at last said quietly. "And the answer is very important to me. You would be gifting me greatly with it. Very much. That time when I told you that now you were the only Christ in the city: You remember? It was on the way here. And you said to me, 'No. There is another.' Tell me, what did you mean? Who is the other?"

More silence. The mad soldier's stare was unblinking.

"Tell me *some*thing. Tell me *any*thing," Meral asked urgently.

Unexpectedly the soldier spoke, saying cryptically, "They wanted to kill him but He passed through them."

And with this, he turned slowly away and lay down on a mattress on the floor against a wall, with his face turned away.

Meral stared at his back. "Who is he?" he asked.

He waited, then at last said quietly, "God be with you."

He turned away and left, convinced that he was never going to get an answer. And he wouldn't.

At least not from the soldier.

The nurse at the reception desk watched with folded arms as Meral carefully signed out in a ledger. "I can't help feeling sorry for him," she said. "He's so young. And he seems so wounded."

She picked up the ledger to put it away.

"I'm really glad that he's got another visitor."

About to turn away, Meral stared.

"Someone else visits him?"

"Oh, yes. Fairly often."

"Who?"

"Forgot his name. Do you want me to look it up for you?"

"Oh, would you? Yes, thank you. Thank you very much."

The nurse retrieved the ledger, opened it, flipped through its pages to a recent date, and then stopped and ran her finger down the page.

"Oh, yes, here. Here, I've got it. Last name's Wilson."

His thoughts a sudden whirlpool of conjecture, Meral returned to the Casa Nova where Samia the nurse was waiting for him. She was sitting in the entry lobby. When Meral walked in, she stood up and waited for him to approach her.

"Why, Samia! What is it? Something's wrong?"

"No, I just need to tell you something very important."

"What is it?"

"Not in here," she said, lowering her voice. "Outside."

Meral turned to see Patience watching them intently from behind the reception counter. Leaned over, he was resting his weight on folded arms.

"Yes, come on. We'll take a walk."

Once down the few steps to the Casa Nova Road, they stopped.

"Yes, now tell me, Samia. What is it?"

"Well, you remember that day that you were working on a case in my neighborhood and you showed me a picture of someone and you asked me if I'd seen him before?"

"I remember."

"Well, I lied."

"I remember that, too."

"You knew I lied? I guess I'm not a good liar!"

"And that's good. And now you've come to tell the truth?"

"Look, I just didn't want him to get into any trouble."

"Who?"

"Wilson. I think I've seen him with the man in that picture you showed me."

Meral looked incredulous.

"Wilson?"

"Yeah, Wilson. I mean, he wasn't just *with* this guy. I think the guy *lived* with him for a while. I'd see him staring out the window now and then."

"Samia, the photo I showed you is blurry. Are you positive?"

"Positive? No. But I think so. Oh, well, now I'm not sure."

Meral slipped a notepad and pencil from a pocket of his shirt.

"Let's assume that you are."

"Yeah, okay."

"For how long?"

"How long what?"

"How long might the two of them been living together?"

"Couple of months. Started January."

"Date?"

"Around the middle of the month."

"The fourteenth, by any chance?"

This was the date of the Remle Street incident.

She shrugged. "I don't know."

Someone opened the hostel front door and was coming down the steps to the street. Meral put a hand on the nurse's shoulder, turning her to walk with him a little, and then stopped. "Yes, go on," Meral urged her.

"Well, when I'd see him at the market he'd be buying almost twice as many groceries as usual. You know? Like for two. Those creepy people at the market, by the way. They're really snots. A bunch of racists. Oh, well, forget it. You want to know where you can find him? Find Wilson?"

"Oh, I know," Meral told her. "He does handyman work here at the Casa." He lifted an arm and glanced at his watch.

"But not this late," he said. "Too late."

"I can tell you where he likes to hang out."

CHAPTER 20

Meral walked through the quiet dark streets to the flashing colored lights of the Club 2000, a disreputable coffee parlor with video and pinball machines, which at night was filled with boisterous and largely unemployed young men, as well as others with nefarious pursuits. Wilson was sitting with a group of them, laughing and talking and in very high spirits, but seeing Meral approaching in uniform, the group's lively conversation fell away to silence. "It's alright," Meral told them, "I have come to have a coffee, nothing more." The group's chatter resumed, although at a level that was just above an undertone. When Meral saw Wilson looking up at him, smiling, he lifted his eyebrows and gestured toward the tables and chairs outside the club. Wilson nodded, then stood up and followed Meral outside. There was no one else there. Meral pointed to a table that was farthest from the door.

"Over here?"

"Yes, that's fine."

They sat down.

"Nice seeing you, Wilson."

"You, too. So what's up?"

"Oh, well, we just need to talk a little bit."

"Oh, well, sure."

"Incidentally, you're a relative newcomer here. You should know that this club is a hangout for criminals. Some of the men you were sitting with, in fact. So be careful."

"Oh, I know about that."

"You know?"

"Healthy people aren't the ones who need a doctor."

Meral stared for a moment.

"I'm afraid I'm having trouble understanding your meaning."

Wilson smiled and looked off to the side.

"That's just me," he said amiably. "Can't have people understanding me until they're really ready."

Before the baffled policeman could speak or react, a slender waiter named Yunis had come out of the club and now hovered. Two coffees were ordered.

"*Sichar wasat*," Wilson specified: medium sugar.

Then he turned back to Meral with an archangel's smile.

"I'm really so glad to be with you like this," he said effusively, a seeming honest gladness glowing in his face. "You have some questions, Sergeant Meral? Sure, what are they? Go ahead. Is this police work or something about the Casa Nova again?"

"Oh, well, police work. A case I've been on. Someone told me that you might be somewhat helpful."

"Oh, really? Who was that?" Wilson asked.

"It's not important," Meral answered.

He had slipped out a photo from an inside jacket pocket. He held it out to Wilson's view. It was a blowup of the soft-focused photo on Joseph Temescu's driver's license.

"Have you seen this man before? I think you have."

Wilson took the photo and studied it gravely, his smile now faded away. "It's rather hard to make out."

"Although not to the eye of truth. His name is Joseph Temescu. It's been reported that he lived in your apartment for a time."

Wilson looked up and met a steady, strong gaze.

"Alright," he said. "I did take a few things from Hadassah. Is that it? Is that what this is about?"

Meral's brow furrowed in puzzlement.

"What are you talking about, Wilson? What things?"

"Oh, come on now. The bandages. The morphine. Dressings. Syringes. Antibiotics."

"These are things you say you pilfered from the hospital?"

"You knew that."

"No, I didn't. Was the pilferage on January fourteenth?"

"Why then?"

"Please just answer, Wilson. Was it?"

"No. No, I don't think so. It was later. Maybe two or three days. I didn't have the money to buy them and I really had to have them. I *had* to!"

"Why? Do you sell them?"

Wilson stared at Meral worriedly.

"Am I going to be in trouble? In a way I think I've paid for those things. I mean, really. All the hours that I donate over there. Over there at Hadassah. Are you going to charge me with something?"

Meral stared with a distant bemusement in his eyes. Despite his strong rugged features and an almost imposing physical presence, Wilson seemed a little boy caught stealing pencils and erasers from a schoolbag.

"Hadassah is not my jurisdiction," Meral told him, "and the supplies are of no interest to me. The thing I am interested in is Temescu. I want to hear everything you know about the man. Everything. Your impressions. His habits. Whatever he divulged to you about himself."

Meral slipped the photo out of Wilson's hand.

"Will you cooperate?"

"There won't be any trouble about the hospital supplies?"

"There will not."

"Well, okay, then. I'll tell you. I will. But not now. I'm with these guys." Wilson lifted his thumb back toward the club's interior. "Can we do this tomorrow, Sergeant Meral?"

"Yes, we can. And we will talk in great depth. You have quite a lot to tell me, I think."

"Yes, I do. You need to hear it."

For a moment Meral measured him in silence. Wilson had a way of making the most ordinary statements sound cryptic, as if they had a hidden and deeper meaning. Or was he just imagining this?

He stood up and Wilson followed.

"Tomorrow morning," Meral said. "Nine o'clock?"

"Yes, that's fine. At your office?"

"No, why not Fuad's for a coffee? It's close to the Station and right across the street from the Church of the Holy Sepulcher."

Wilson flashed a brilliant smile

"Oh, that's a *fine* place to meet!"

Meral nodded. "Yes, that would be best."

Meral watched as Wilson hurried back into the club. *Morphine. Bandages. Antibiotics.* Was it possible that Wilson was Temescu's rescuer from the burning Land Rover that night? And if so, might there not also be at least some degree of probability that he'd been with him when he died in the Tomb of Christ?

And done what? wondered Meral.

A chilling possibility entered his mind.

Nothing was out of the question.

Not in this world.

He started walking toward the Church of the Holy Sepulcher. He had to speak to Tariq.

Now!

CHAPTER 21

Seated at his desk with a hand against his stomach, Mayo grimaced as if he had tasted sour wine. "I don't know what it could be," he groaned softly, "but I'm suddenly feeling so punky."

"And so what did you eat today that was different?"

Samia was seated in her favorite low position on the faded green Naugahyde chair. "This is funny," she added. "I mean, *I'm* asking *you*."

"I ate latkes with sour cream and apple sauce, Doctor, and it's never affected me like this my whole life."

"And so what have you got, Moses? What do you think it could be?"

"Must you stare without blinking from that low-down position? You look like a white anaconda with feet."

"Don't change the subject. What is it?"

"I have no idea."

"Well, if *you* don't, who would?"

"Very true."

"Want to hear my opinion?"

"No."

"Well, you're getting it. You're lonely and depressed and that's how that stuff shows."

"I've been lonely and depressed all my life."

"That's not what *I* heard."

"I don't care what you heard."

Mayo turned to stare pensively out through the window.

"Samia, why would a priest have a radical face-lift?"

"Is this a joke? Does it have a joke answer?"

"I hope so," Mayo murmured broodingly.

"What do you mean?" Samia pressed him.

"Nothing."

Mayo turned back to her.

"Would you take a little blood and run it down to the lab for me, darling?" he said weakly. "I'm feeling really, really rotten."

Samia struggled to her feet.

"Poor guy. Yes, of course."

"This is really just the worst," Mayo said.

He was wrong.

CHAPTER 22

"You shaved off your beard, Wilson. Why?"

"Oh, I don't know, Sergeant. Spring cleaning, I guess."

They were sitting having coffee in front of Fuad's. The massive door to the Church of the Holy Sepulcher across the way had been pushed wide open and tourists and pilgrims were already walking in.

"How old are you, Wilson? You look so very young."

"I'm fifty-two."

"Fifty-two? I can't believe it!"

Wilson grinned.

"You know, in bright sunlight and without that beard . . . ," began Meral.

"Without the beard, what?"

"Well, your eyes. They're blue. I always thought they were dark. Almost black. Wilson, where do you come from?"

"California. Didn't you know that?"

Meral's demitasse coffee cup was halfway to his lips when he stopped to study Wilson's face. He was simple, he decided. But hardly dull-witted.

Meral sipped and then set down his cup.

"Yes, I did. I did know that. Of course. And you've been here six months. A little more. So what brought you here, Wilson?"

"Guess I'm searching."

"For what?"

"For the meaning of my life, I suppose."

Meral quickly turned away, his look of tolerance putting up a brave but futile fight against a spasm of impatience. "Yes, one can have romantic illusions about this place, but the reality is envy and noise and hostility and squabbling over coins and cold hardness of heart. Just the same as it's always been." He turned back to look at Wilson. "You haven't learned that yet?"

"No."

"Good for you. Or too bad. How do you live, by the way? You do volunteer work."

Wilson shrugged.

"I've got a little bit of money saved up. Just enough. I guess I'm lucky."

"Lucky how?"

"Money keeps you from seeing."

"Seeing what?"

"What's really there." Wilson picked up his coffee cup, took a sip and then put it down. "Are we going to talk about the hospital supplies?"

"As I told you, they aren't a concern of mine, Wilson. Although at some point I'll certainly want to know why you took them."

"*Ahlan!* May I sit?"

It was Tariq. He was standing by their table.

"Yes, of course, my friend, sit," Meral told him. "Have a coffee."

"You don't mind?" he asked Wilson.

"Why would I?"

Wilson gestured at an empty chair.

"Come on, join us."

Tariq sat and immediately started staring at Wilson intently. Wilson smiled and said, "It's Tariq. Isn't that right?"

Meral stared without expression, trying not to give away his surprise. His mousetrap hadn't failed; it was unnecessary.

"You know Tariq, Wilson?"

"Yes. Yes, we met the other day when I was visiting the church. We had a chat about falafel."

Befuddled, Tariq's eyes were now open wide as they shifted back and forth between Meral and Wilson. "I had a beard then," Wilson told him. "A big bushy red beard. You remember?"

Meral looked toward the church.

"Tariq, I think someone's waving for you to come back."

Without a word Tariq bolted from his chair and began to walk swiftly across the street toward the church, his arms swinging and his heart filled with gladness and relief to get away from it. Whatever it was.

Wilson watched him.

"He didn't get to have his coffee."

"He won't mind."

Wilson turned back to Meral. The policeman was studying him appraisingly, his head tilted slightly to the side as he measured Wilson's questioning look of innocence and utter lack of guile.

"You were in the Church of the Holy Sepulcher on the seventh of March?"

"Oh, what day of the week was that?"

"A Tuesday."

"Oh, I was, then. Yes. I was there when they were closing."

"You were alone?"

"Why are you asking me this?"

"You want to help me, don't you, Wilson?"

"Oh, so much, Sergeant Meral! So very much!"

Meral paused for a moment, surprised by the fervor in Wilson's voice.

"Well, then tell me: Were you with someone?"

"Yes."

"Was it the man who once lived with you? Joseph Temescu?"

"Yes."

"And did you enter the Tomb of Christ with him?"

"Yes."

"What were you doing with him there?"

"He wanted me to help him die."

"What was that?"

"He wanted me to help him die. He asked me to inject him with chloral hydrate to help knock him out and make the end come quicker. He'd brought it all along himself: the syringe, the chloral, morphine."

Taken aback, Meral didn't know what to say next.

And then his stare began to narrow.

"He could have injected himself though, could he not?"

"Sure, he could have."

"Then what need was there for you to be present?"

"Listen, Sergeant, I'd have to explain things for an hour before I could tell you and know you'd believe me. It's just too complicated. Too weird."

"Is that so? Very well. We'll put that off to another time. Meantime, why did he want to die in Christ's Tomb? Or is that too complicated as well?"

"He said he wanted his death to be all over the news."

"Are you serious?"

"That's what he told me."

"Was he mentally unbalanced?"

"Not at all."

"Well, I must say, he certainly got his wish."

"What do you mean?"

"You didn't read the morning paper?"

"No."

"The man posing as Joseph Temescu was in fact an American government assassin."

"He was *what*?"

"Yes, it's true."

"I don't believe it."

"He didn't tell you that?"

"No! An assassin? Are you sure?"

"Yes. It's on the front page of *The Jerusalem Post*. His name was Paul Dimiter. Quite famous in his circles. You can count yourself lucky."

"Lucky? Why lucky? He— Oh. Oh, I see. Yes, a killer. A killer in my apartment. Though I still can't believe it. I mean, the man seemed so kind."

"Yes, as killers often do. And so honest."

Wilson's head tilted to the side.

"What do you mean by that?"

"Nothing. Less than nothing. So let's try now to focus on what this Dimiter was doing in Jerusalem. No. No, let's back up a bit. Tell me how you met him."

"And you're sure there won't be trouble about the hospital supplies?"

That child's look of worry had returned to Wilson's face, and once again it disarmed Meral's latent suspicions.

"There's a connection?" he asked.

"Yes, there is. And I'll tell you. But no trouble? That's a promise?"

"That's a promise. Now then, how did you meet him?"

"He had a terrible accident late one at night at the Paz gasoline station just below the Jaffa Gate."

Meral's eyes widened.

"You're the second man!"

"What do you mean?"

"Never mind now. No, really. Go on, now. Go on. Tell me everything."

"Well, the engine of my car was overheating and I needed some water for the radiator. So I stopped there. Late at night they put water cans out at this station. Tins of gasoline, too. Then you pay the next day."

"Where were you coming from?"

"Ramallah. I was on my way home. So as I said, I made a stop and then all of a sudden I hear this car speeding toward me, and then it veers and it crashes into the gas pump and there's an explosion. It was awful. I ran over and I'm hauling him out of the car and—"

"Hauling who?"

"Oh, well, the driver. The man you call Dimiter. Whoever. He was all banged up. Badly burned. Unconscious. The car was on fire. I got to him as quickly as I could but he was already pretty badly burned. His face and hands it seemed, mostly. So I took him to the Arab Government Hospital. The one for the poor. It was the closest. But Hadassah's much better equipped for burns, and so in a couple of days, when they'd done all the emergency stuff and he seemed to be pretty well stabilized, that was the place where I wanted to take him.

But he didn't want to go. He was adamant. Something about him not wanting to go into the system. About being identified. At Government they're loose about that."

"Yes, they are. But they try. They're good people."

"I could see that. Well, so after two days I checked him out of the hospital and took him to my apartment and looked after him."

"And so here we have the explanation for the pilfered supplies," said Meral. "The return of the 'Good Samaritan.' "

"It tore me up to see someone in that kind of shape. All the burns. All the cuts on his face. And then that god-awful cancer."

"Oh, he told you about that?"

Wilson lifted his head.

"Oh, he told me all kinds of things. He knew he was dying and so he completely opened up to me. A lot. Lots of things about his life. But all lies, though, I guess. Isn't that right?"

"I hope not. We'll be going into all of that, Wilson. It's the main thing that I'm after. But for now, though, just give me the basic narrative right up until the last time you saw him."

"Oh, well, that's pretty much it. What I told you. I took care of him until he was able to walk. Short walks down the street. Just for air. And then one day he wanted me to take him to a church."

"Why was that?"

"Well, I asked him but he just shook his head and wouldn't say. But he seemed so awfully anxious we should go there."

"And you took him?"

"No, not right away. It was raining very heavily that morning. The streets were all flooded. He kept pacing back and forth, back and forth. Very agitated. Tense. He seemed filled with some urgency I couldn't understand. Then by late afternoon the skies cleared and I took him to the church beside the Garden of Gethsemane."

Meral nodded. "The Church of the Agony."

"Yes."

"And so who chose the church, you or he?"

"Oh, it was he."

Here Meral leaned in with sharp interest.

"And once inside the church, what did he do? Did he meet someone?"

"Well . . ." Wilson paused and looked away. "You could say that."

"Meaning what? Who did he meet?"

Wilson turned a soft look back to Meral.

"When we entered the church it was empty, there was no one else there, and at first he just stood in the back for a time, very quiet, very still, and at first looking scared, in a way, and wary, somehow squeezed and pulled tighter protectively into himself, smaller, diminished, as he stared straight ahead through those giant stone pillars at the Rock of Agony in front of the altar. It's the bedrock where they say Christ prayed on the night before the crucifixion."

"Yes, I know that. I've been to that church."

"Oh, good! Well, I followed his stare and then I heard a soft choking sound, a smothered sob, and I turned and saw his face was contorted with grief. And then he lurched a step forward and began to move unsteadily and slowly toward the altar with his arms outstretched, and with those white, charred hands palms up, and when he'd arrived at the metal Gate of Thorns around the Rock, he fell across it and then to his knees in a convulsion of sobs that wracked his body, his head bowed down and with those hands still clutching the top of the gate. It was then I moved forward until I was standing directly over him, and I could hear him still quietly sobbing and repeating, 'I'm so sorry for all that I've done! I'm so sorry!' again and again."

Here Wilson fell quiet.

"And then?"

"And then nothing. I waited for whatever it was to pass, and then I helped him to his feet and took him home. The next day he took his own life. He took the venom."

"You're sure of that, are you?"

"Of course. I just told you I helped him to do it."

"Yes. But there are times when one can help overmuch."

"What do you mean?"

"I meant nothing."

"Oh, no, wait a minute! Hold it! You suspect I might have killed him?"

"I repeat: I meant nothing."

"Some nothing!"

"Alright, *practically* nothing. I'll be honest. Why would he kill himself, Wilson? If he did, he must surely have told you the reason. Why did he do it? To stop the lingering pain of the cancer?"

Wilson looked over at the church, where two parents were dealing with the sobbing and hysterical cries of their very young pigtailed daughter who was terrified of entering the dimly lit interior. She'd been told it was the place where Jesus had been killed and buried. Wilson stared at her.

"Yes," he answered quietly. "To stop all the pain."

The little girl stopped crying and her father had her hand. As they entered the church, she looked over her shoulder at Wilson.

Meral took a last sip of coffee, placed the cup upside down on its saucer, and then started to turn it around. The faint porcelain squeaks drew Wilson's gaze back to Meral.

"Yes," Meral mused, "they say that ever since the death of his wife he was depressed and tormented by guilt."

"He lost his wife?"

"These things happen. And sometimes the pain is so great one cannot breathe." Meral stopped turning the cup. His faraway stare and his fingertips continued to hold it in silence. Feeling Wilson's stare, he looked up to see him studying his face. What was that in his eyes, Meral wondered? Fondness? Compassion? Or was it something that had no earthly name?

Wilson folded his arms across his chest and looked down. "I still can't believe it," he said. "I mean, the man that I saved that night . . . Well, you're mistaken. He just couldn't have been your Dimiter. He couldn't."

"You must face it that he was."

Wilson looked up.

"Are you sure about his wife being dead? I mean, he talked

to me about her as if she were alive. He showed me pictures of her."

"Really."

"Oh, yes!"

"Well, then delirium, perhaps. The morphine."

Meral's walkie-talkie radio crackled. He unhooked it from his belt and pushed TALK. "Meral," he said crisply. And then pushed another button to receive.

"Kfar Shaul needs to talk to you," came a voice. It was the Kishla Station commandant, Zev.

"I need to go there?"

"No, call them. But do it this morning. Talk to Doctor Waleed."

"Acknowledged."

Both sides signed off. Meral glanced at his watch.

"I must be leaving now," he said. "I have a very sick friend plus some difficult Albanians to deal with, as well as a lunatic asylum and the world. Look, don't worry about those things from the hospital. There won't be any trouble. However, you and I have many miles yet to go. *Many* miles. I've been charged with finding out what your patient was doing here. Think about it, please. Make notes. Incidentally, I'm intrigued by your suggestion that he seemed to have a spiritual side." The cowcatcher leaped to Meral's mind. "Although I doubt it very strongly," he amended. "No, I suspect that something darker was afoot with the man. But then who knows? Did he speak of such things at any time? I mean beyond the Rock of Agony incident. I'm just curious."

"Oh, he did. And a lot about life after death."

Meral had raised his hands to clap twice for the waiter, but now he lowered them again to his lap. "Is that so?" he said. "Really?"

"Is there going to be a burial service for him? I'd like to come."

"No, they're sending him home."

Wilson turned his head and mutely stared at the entrance to the church for a moment. Then he softly said, "He's already there."

Something stirred in Meral's eyes.

"We need to set a schedule for when we can continue," he said. "We've just barely begun. Only barely. You don't mind? You'll cooperate?"

Wilson's brows furrowed up. He looked troubled.

"Does it have to be at Kishla Station?"

"Not at all. But not here. You have someplace in mind?"

"My apartment, maybe?"

"Possibly so. Though, are you working at the hostel this evening?"

"Yes, I am."

"Then why not come to my room when you've finished with your work? Any time after seven. Can you come?"

Wilson's smile was pleased.

"That should work out just perfectly."

Meral met his gaze.

That ambivalence again. What does he mean?

Meral clapped for the waiter and the bill.

As they waited the policeman picked up his coffee cup and held it out to Wilson. "Look at what the sludge has done when I turned the cup upside down and around. Some tell fortunes this way. They see pictures that the coffee dregs make inside the cup. Here, take it. Take a look and then tell me what you see."

As Wilson took the cup and bent his head to look closely at its inner white sides, suddenly Meral lost his grip on both himself and on the edges of time so that Wilson seemed frozen in motion like a single frame of a silent film with all the sounds of the world blotted out as a pulsing unearthliness seemed to seep out of him, washing over Meral in undulating waves that at first felt icy and draining, but then left him feeling warm and refreshed. Even new.

"What do you see?" he asked Wilson at last, recovered.

Wilson looked up at him and smiled. "Good news."

T he ever-cheerful and rotund Father Mancini was at Meral's table for lunch that day and was peeling an orange when Meral, who had been pensively quiet through the meal, looked up across the table and asked, "Could this possibly be a line in the scriptures, Father?"

"What?"

" 'They wanted to kill him but he passed through them'?"

Meral had learned to trust the cleric's opinion ever since he had given him an answer to what then was a troubling question of faith:

"You believe that Christ died for our sins?"

"What kind of a question is that? Of course I do."

"And yet Christ said the Father wants mercy, not sacrifice."

"I see where you're going. An old problem of the Father as some kind of implacable Aztec god demanding suffering and blood to propitiate his delicately tuned sense of justice. Is that it?"

"Yes, that's it, Father. How can you believe that?"

"I don't. At least not in the way that many people understand it. Christ died for our sins. Yes, I believe that. I do. But now I'll ask you a question. If Christ had died of cancer or a nasty flu in his eighties and then risen from the dead, do you think there's any chance that we'd have heard about it? No. His death had to be dramatic and public and that's why I think he had to die on the cross: it was so we would know about the resurrection without which our faith would be nothing but incense and smoke."

"Yes, it's Luke," Mancini answered right away. "When Christ preached in Nazareth, the crowd got so angry over something that he said that they dragged him to a cliff intending to throw him down to his death, but he somehow 'passed through them,' Luke says."

Mancini bit into another slice of the orange.

Squirts of juice spattered onto his pudgy fingers.

"What did he say that so offended them, Father?"

"He said that at a time when there were so many lepers in the land the only person that Elisha chose to cure was not a Jew. It was Naaman."

"Who?"

"Naaman. Naaman the Syrian."

Meral stared without expression as a sense of unreality

enfolded him for the second time that day, the world suddenly seeming vague and ghostly, an artificial construct in which anything could happen and nature and its laws were as stable as a whim.

"You look so odd," the priest said to him. "Something wrong?"

After meeting with Wilson that morning, Meral had called Kfar Shaul and spoken with Doctor Waleed.

"*That Syrian soldier who murdered that other crazy Christ at Hadassah? I know it isn't your case but I've heard you've got an interest in the guy, so I thought you'd like to hear the good news.*"

"*Good news?*"

"*Well, good and bad. The bad is someone's going to have to put him on trial. The good is that he's totally sane. He doesn't think he's Christ anymore.*"

The report had stunned Meral. There was no question at Hadassah that the soldier, when admitted, was incurably mad, an opinion confirmed by the staff at Kfar Shaul. But then something had radically changed. What was new? wondered Meral.

He knew of only one possible answer:

Wilson. Wilson and his visits.

Meral took a last sip of coffee, turned the cup upside down and then placed it on its saucer with a tiny click. It made a thin porcelain sound as he gently started twisting it around. "No, no, nothing," he answered the priest. His eyes were on the cup. "Just thinking."

"About a case that you're on?"

"I was just pondering a very strange coincidence."

Mancini bent his head and bit squishily into another plump slice of orange. "There is no such thing," he murmured.

"Sergeant Meral!"

The policeman looked up at Patience.

"Telephone, Sergeant! Very urgent!"

Meral hastily stood up and hurried off, in the process jarring the table so that the demitasse coffee cup fell over on its side.

Nothing good was to be seen in its dregs.

CHAPTER 23

His wide brow furrowed with worry, Meral briskly walked into Mayo's office and went straight to the sofa where the sleeping neurologist lay on his back beneath a red-and-white checked cotton comforter, his arms resting loosely above it. The policeman stared down at an ashen, gaunt face and could hear Mayo's breathing, irregular and shallow.

A whisper from behind him.

"Meral!"

Meral turned to see Samia. She was sitting in the chair

behind Mayo's desk. She stood up and put a finger to her lips to signal silence and then pointed to the hall where, moments later, she and Meral stood in hushed conversation.

"So what's wrong?" Meral asked her. "What has he got?"

"No one knows. Sure, his blood count's not so great, but there's no other indication of anything big. Still, he's so tired all the time and he says feels weaker and weaker every day. And he's been sleeping so much. God, I swear, it's like he's dying of a broken heart. Should I wake him? Meral, someone needs to tell him he should be in a bed in one of those great big rooms in Neuro. I keep telling him myself, but does he listen? No. He's so stubborn. But maybe you he'll listen to, I'm thinking. You're coming back here tonight?"

"No, not tonight. I have a meeting."

"Then tomorrow?"

"Yes, tomorrow. I'll just have to make the time. See you then."

Meral took a step away, but then stopped and turned back.

"By the way, I'd like to thank you very much."

"For what?"

"For letting me know about Wilson and that person."

"Huh? What person?" Samia looked blank, and then, "Oh!" she said. "Oh, yeah. Yeah, that guy he was living with. Right. Oh, well, don't be thanking *me*, though."

"No?"

"No, it wasn't my idea. It was Wilson's."

That night after dinner Wilson came to Meral's room.

"You told Samia to come to me, Wilson?"

"Yes."

"Why would you do that?"

"I wanted to help you."

"Then why didn't you just come to me yourself?"

"That isn't how it works. It's you who has to come to me."

Meral's brow furrowed. "I'm lost," he said.

"Not yet."

Meral met Wilson's cool blue gaze and immediately felt a faintly throbbing panic flowing through him as he sensed that he had entered a maze of thought with twists and turns that he neither could follow nor even guess where they might lead. He dropped the line of questioning immediately and turned to his main concern. "Never mind that now," he said brusquely. "Please focus your thoughts on anything the man now identified as Dimiter might have said or confided to you in the weeks before his death, in particular concerning the reason for his presence in Jerusalem." This shift brought results, with Wilson's answers proving far from enigmatic. He seemed eager to tell Meral every word, every action of the man whose life he had saved, so that these after-dinner meetings would go on for eleven more nights with Meral's eyes growing wider with every session. At the end, when he was making his written report, he had no doubt that it might daze as many minds as it enlightened.

Some things he thought best to hold back.

Meral's Sundays during that time were taken up with day-long visits with Mayo, who now had a bed in the Neurology Ward in the grasp of an illness that had no name, or at least not a name that it wished to give. He grew feebler and more listless with each passing day. Samia tried to spend as much time with him as she could, and on her free time practically never left him, sometimes even sleeping on the chair in his room with Mayo's red-and-white comforter over her. She began to notice a strangeness in Meral's demeanor, for as day by day the neurologist deteriorated, the more alive and refreshed Meral seemed. Would the process now stop? she tearfully wondered early on the morning of May seventeenth? For it was on that day that everyone realized there would be no more Sunday visitations.

N o, this cannot be true," said Meral numbly.
His blue winter uniform had just given way to summery "silvertans" that looked somehow grotesquely out of place as he pulled back the sheet and looked down at the body of his boyhood friend. Samia had called him at the Station to tell him that Mayo was dying, and he'd sped to Mayo's bedside too late for much of anything but grief.

Meral turned to Samia. She was standing beside him with a tear-sodden handkerchief clutched in her hand and held close against her chin. "What happened?" he asked her.

"No one knows. He just died."

"Just like that?"

"He stopped breathing. That's all. Yeah, just like that."

Meral looked sadly down at Mayo again.

"My last good friend," he huskily murmured.

"No. Not your last."

Meral turned and met Samia's brimming stare.

"Thank you," he told her. "Thank you."

Then he pulled a chair over to the bedside where he sat for a time in grieving silence until at last racing thoughts of insidious intent began infiltrating his brain: *I know all different ways where there'd be no suspicion; where it wouldn't show up in tests . . . show up in tests . . . show up in—*

Meral looked up at Samia.

"Do you know what he was doing just before he got sick?"

"Just the usual."

"Nothing out of the ordinary?"

"No. No, not really. Oh, well, one thing, maybe."

"What?"

"He said he wanted me to look up some spy stuff for him."

"*Spy* stuff?"

"Yeah, spy stuff. Lifting fingerprints with tape."

"Whatever for?"

"I don't know."

"Did he ever say anything about what might be wrong with him?"

"No. Not to me. He didn't know."

"Was he asleep when he died?"

"Sort of dozing. And then I saw his eyelids starting to flutter, and I heard him say 'Samia' in this really weak voice. I could barely hear it. I said, 'Yes, I'm here, Moses. I'm here.'

257

And I leaned—" There was a catch in her throat, and for a moment she stopped. Then she went on. "And I leaned over with my ear down close to his mouth and he said something, just a few words. And then he died."

"Could you make out what he said?"

Samia nodded. Her eyes were welling up.

" 'So I'll eat the soup and leave the noodles.' "

"Excuse me?"

"It's that saying on the wall. Over there."

Meral followed her pointed finger to the plaque on the wall with the Kishon quotation on it. "And then—and then," the nurse tremulously began, but a choking sob broke it off and she bolted from the room and then away down the hospital's antiseptic halls. Meral listened to the patter of her quick cushioned steps until they'd faded away into that silence where all of Mayo's heartbeats now were stored. For a moment he lowered his head, and then he walked to the door where he turned for one last long look good-bye, less astonished by the puzzle of inexplicable death than he was by the fact that he was capable of tears.

Something had been chipping at "The Wall."

Samia's return almost startled him.

"Meral!"

The policeman turned around.

"Yeah, he said something else," Samia told him. "At the end."

"And what was that?" Meral asked.

"He said, 'The priest.' "

CHAPTER 24

INTERVIEW WITH SERGEANT MAJOR PETER V. MERAL
17 MAY, 1974, HEADQUARTERS, ISRAELI INTELLIGENCE

Interviewer: Moshe Zui.

Q. So okay, it's just us this time, Sergeant. The Americans
seem to have lost interest.
A. So I see.
Q. Something wrong?
A. What do you mean?

Q. You seem preoccupied, Meral. Thinking hard about something.

A. Yes, I'm sorry.

Q. Moses Mayo?

A. Yes, Mayo.

Q. What's happening there? You've had suspicions, I hear.

A. An intuition. It's in the works.

Q. Want to wait a bit?

A. No. Let's begin.

Q. Well, okay. And so we got your last interim report. Fascinating. Remle Street. The crash. All of that. This fellow Wilson looking after Temescu—that is, Dimiter—and then helping with his suicide. Are you going to press a charge here, by the way?

A. I don't believe so. Wilson is a naïf. Not stupid, mind you. Very far from that. *Very* far. He's just simple. But simple in a good way, not a bad one.

Q. Let me look at this. [Consults file] Been in Israel seven months?

A. Wilson?

Q. Yes.

A. No, now eight.

Q. Okay, eight. So now Temescu was in fact Paul Dimiter. Fine. But the question still is, what was he doing here? It had to be a mission and the fact that the Americans are lying through their teeth means it must have been bloody important. And so Wilson is the key. He took care of him, lived with him for weeks. He must know something, no?

You've had— What? Maybe ten or so sessions with Wilson?

A. More or less.

Q. So I'm guessing they were fruitful, these meetings? He was really that helpful? I mean about finding out Dimiter's mission.

A. Yes, he was.

Q. He was? Oh, well, that's great, Meral! Tell me!

A. Well, it's complicated.

Q. Complicated how?

A. Well, no really hard facts that might bear on that question came up. Very few on any other topic either. And then some of the so-called facts turned out to be not factual at all. I'm talking about Dimiter's statements to Wilson. I think some were either lies or a result of all the morphine in his system. I tend to think it was the latter. He was dying. What advantage could there be for him in lies? Quite the opposite, I would think.

Q. You want to give me an example of what you're talking about?

A. Well, alright. When Wilson asked Dimiter his age he said he really wasn't sure; that he started out life as an aborted fetus that a hospital nurse found in medical trash. A tracheotomy was done and he was put in an incubator from which he was snatched and then smuggled away to her home by the nurse. She was unmarried and of Albanian descent, he said, and so she gave him her name and then raised him until she died.

Q. Why do you think that isn't true?

A. Oh, well, "Snatched"? "Smuggled"? Sounds like fantasy to me.

Q. Except there is that tracheotomy scar.

A. One can build a house of cards on a base that is real.

Q. You're a hard man, Meral.

A. I try not to be.

Q. True. Yes, you do. Any other examples of the lies?

A. Telling Wilson that his wife was alive.

Q. Yes, we talked about that. The wife who died. His wife Jean.

A. That isn't the name he gave Wilson.

Q. Really? Oh, well, maybe you're right, then. The morphine, perhaps.

A. Yes, perhaps.

Q. Well, then Dimiter's mission here. You were saying?

A. Yes. As no reliable facts are in evidence, I thought it might be best to pursue a much more general path toward uncovering what that mission might have been.

Q. What kind of path?

A. Well, religion, if you can believe it. Or rather Dimiter's deep interest in religion. Wilson said he was obsessed with it. Why are we here? Where are we going?

Q. Yes, precisely my question at this point. Where are we going?

A. Well, in a way, to Dimiter's mission. What a man believes colors his purposes.

Q. But aren't we just spinning our wheels here, Sergeant? The world's deadliest government assassin finds God?

A. There is some precedent.

Q. Fine. But is it reasonable, I'm asking.

A. Not at all. But truth and reason are two different things. Something happened to this man that changed him.

Q. Ah, the mystical experience!

A. Exactly. Should I go on?

Q. Perhaps you'd like to take a break first.

A. A break?

Q. You've got that Mayo look again. Come on, we'll take a little break.

A. No, never mind. It's much better if I go on. May I go on?

Q. You'll stay with me?

A. Yes, of course.

Q. Please continue.

A. Dimiter was haunted all his life, Wilson told me, by The Problem of Evil. "A heart-stabbing mystery," he called it. But he came to believe there was a mystery much deeper that he spoke of as the "mystery of goodness."

Q. Now you're losing me.

A. I'm leading up to something.

Q. I hope so.

A. Well, he said if we're reducible to senseless matter, then why aren't we constantly rushing about blindly trying to serve our own selfish ends? Yet what we see is people who give up their lives for someone else. We see self-sacrifice in ordinary lives, not just in heroes. Or so he believed.

Q. And that's it? That's what you think might have colored his motives?

A. Only somewhat. And then there was the mystical experience.

Q. He told Wilson about that?

A. To a point. He said it happened near the end of the Albanian mission. The second one. He'd been feeling something coming on even earlier, Wilson told me: a reluctance to kill if he could possibly avoid it. But as soon as he had finished ordaining those young men— You know the incident I'm talking about?

Q. Yes, I do.

A. Well at that moment some "force" filled him up, he said. Something "bigger than the universe but smaller than a pea." His words.

Q. I see you're looking at notes.

A. Yes, I wrote them right after each meeting with Wilson.

Q. Didn't mean to interrupt.

A. Well, then Dimiter talked about a time he was on mission in Somalia. There was famine in the land, people starving and dying by the tens of thousands. Well, one morning he heard singing, many voices, and then he came upon these Sudanese tribes people, scores of them, all in a circle clasping hands and swaying side to side while they sang, their bodies skeletal, emaciated. They were dying. And yet they were smiling, he said. Their singing and their faces were happy. Full of joy. And sweeping through them, and from them and then into him, into Dimiter, was an overwhelming sense of the rightness and the glory of things. And that feeling, he said, was not even one-hundredth of what he'd felt in

Albania right after he'd finished ordaining those priests.

Q. What, he heard the voice of God or something?

A. No. No, he never said anything like that. Wilson said he couldn't explain it or describe it any more. It was ineffable.

Q. I think now I'm getting it. Finally. Your point. Where you've been going. It's that the man was so changed for the better that whatever he was doing here it couldn't have been bad. Is that it?

A. That's it exactly. Yes, that's all I was trying to convey.

Q. Well, who knows. Maybe so. It would make Bell and Sandalls damn happy. But then the morphine and the fantasies. Maybe lies. Which reminds me. Temescu's wife. I mean, Dimiter's. Wilson told you that her name wasn't Jean?

A. Yes, that's right.

Q. And so what did he say that it was?

A. Moricani.

Q. Really? My wife had a friend with that name.

A. Sounds Rumanian. Is it?

Q. Albanian. So you're all through with Wilson?

A. Not yet. He says he knows *precisely* what Dimiter's mission was here and he's promised that he's going to tell me.

Q. Fantastic, Meral! When?

A. When I'm ready, he said.

Q. Meaning what?

A. God knows.

Q. Shouldn't we put some security on him?

A. To protect him, you mean?

Q. Well, sure.

A. I don't think that will be necessary.

Q. Why?

A. Just a feeling.

Q. Well, okay, then. We're done. Good thing. I see that Mayo look again. You're going to have to get some closure on that, Meral.

A. I intend to.

Immediately after leaving Zui, Meral drove his police car up the Sheikh Garrah Quarter's French Hill Road and then steeply downhill a little farther until he was in sight of the six-story beige-colored limestone cube that housed the National Police Headquarters. Once past the electric gate and the guard station, he parked and soon was pushing on a steel revolving door that placed him in a cool and quiet lobby with mirror-shined white marble floors and a reception desk with uniformed men behind it. Just past them was a bomb display and a burglary prevention exhibit.

There is a tribe on Mount Elgon in East Africa who believe that men have two souls and that one of them exists because the other one is dreaming it. In a dream of the night before, Meral thought that he might have encountered his dreamer. Standing in the burial chamber of Christ, Meral's double was staring into his eyes while at the same time pointing at Mayo's nephew Shlomo, who was frowning in concentration as he softly rapped his knuckles on the chamber's stone wall with an ear pressed against it, listening intently, when a perfectly formed blue rose bloomed forth from the spot where he was rapping. Shlomo plucked it from the wall with a triumphant cry of "Aha!" Then a grating, rumbling sound filled the crypt as large sections of the wall slid away and out of sight to reveal a narrow secret room in which Moses Mayo stood staring out at Meral. Wrapped completely in white burial cloths underneath, Mayo wore a slouch hat and a belted trench coat that resembled Humphrey Bogart's in the film *Casablanca*. He softly blew out cigarette smoke and drawled, "I know all different ways where there'd be no suspicion. Now you know why I never make plans that far ahead." Then lifting an arm and pointing at Shlomo, Mayo uttered cryptically, "Follow the gazelle!"

There the dream ended.

"You're here to see who, sir?"

"Inspector Shlomo Uris."

"Six twenty-two. Go on up."

From the chair behind his desk, Mayo's nephew looked up at his visitor. Tieless, his shirt collar open, he wore wide and aggressively red suspenders over a short-sleeved pale blue shirt. As Meral came in he had his feet up on his desk and was tossing balls of crumpled crime report forms at a green metal wastepaper basket set on top of a filing cabinet in a corner.

"Oh, hi, Meral! Three more shots and that's it. Come on, sit down."

Meral took a seat by the desk and looked around. A little of Mayo's blood was showing: one wall of the office was totally covered with posters, most of rock concerts played all around the world, and all built around a super-sized poster in the center of the comic book superhero "Captain Marvel."

"So."

Meral turned his gaze back to Uris. Finished tossing balls of paper, he had now swung his feet to the floor and was intently leaning forward with his hands clasped in front of him on the desk in an effort to look sorrowful and grave. On the wall behind the desk there was a panoramic black-and-white photographic map of the Jerusalem Sub-District.

"My condolences," said Meral.

"My condolences to *you*. You were so close to him. Like brothers."

Meral's gaze came to rest on a symbol on the side of the telephone on Uris's desk. It was a leaping gazelle.

"Yes, like brothers," Meral answered Uris softly.

"And so, what can I do for you today?"

Meral lifted his gaze back to Uris.

"Find the person who murdered your uncle."

CHAPTER 25

A pattering of rain from a moody morning sky fell in dots on the dust of yellowed windowpanes looking out to a street in Brooklyn, New York. A series of trucks rumbled by over manhole covers with loud and clanging thumps that were barely heard by the elderly woman in a pale pink nightgown and brown woolly slippers. She picked up a photo from the little round table in her tiny living room where she was sitting with a friend, a woman slightly younger by perhaps a few years and whose flowered blue dress and cardigan sweater had the scent and worn look of a thrift shop.

"My little boy," the older woman forlornly murmured. The photo was of a tall and brawny young man with blond hair in the garb of a Franciscan priest.

"Okay," said the friend.

She was holding an ink-fed pen above a sheet of cheap stationery.

The older woman put the photo back down.

"Okay, first tell them I did what they said and I still haven't heard a damn word. They're crazy. Don't put that in the letter. Just—"

"Hold it."

The older woman cupped a hand to her ear and said, "What?"

The letter writer raised her voice a notch, repeating, "Hold it!"

"Oh, 'hold it.' Okay."

The scratching of the pen continued. And then stopped.

"Okay, what?"

"What?"

"Yes. What next?"

"Well, just say that it's the third time I've written them about this."

"Maybe I should call them, Mary. You want me to call them?"

"Oh, would you?"

"Oh, well, anything for you. And for Dennis."

At that moment in Jerusalem, a Teletype machine in the Kishla Police Post communications room chattered out a photo line by line as Meral stood waiting for it, bored and impatient, his thoughts adrift, until finally the photo had come through and there was silence.

Meral lifted it out.

And decided he no longer was bored.

CHAPTER 26

Hands in the pockets of his cargo pants, Shlomo Uris paced restlessly about his office as he waited for the return of a telephone call. For a moment he paused at a long narrow side table under the window behind his desk where framed family photos were propped and arrayed. He picked one up. It was of Shlomo as a boy being held in the arms of his uncle Moses. When the telephone rang he put the photo back down, turned around to his desk, and picked up the phone. "Hello, Uris. Yes? Yes, put it through for me, please." As Uris waited, he looked down at a letter on his desktop. Originally addressed to the American Ambassador in Tel Aviv, it had come from a woman in Brooklyn, New York, gone through channels, and eventually landed on his desk. He'd gone back through the record of Mayo's incoming telephone calls beginning three days before the onset of his illness and up to the day he had first voiced complaints about the problem with his stomach. The origin of one of those calls was striking because of a linkage to the letter from New York.

"Hello, yes? Can you hear me clearly? Good. Look, my name is Shlomo Uris. I'm an Inspector of Police in the city of Jerusalem. Jerusalem. Right. Oh, well, greetings to you, too. Look, I'm calling about one of your people over here. It's rather urgent. I need to ask you to wire a photo of him. No, no, no! No, not anyone. A certain one. I believe you've had inquiries about him from his mother. What's that? No, no telephone number was given. The mother is partially deaf and—"

Uris listened for a moment and then nodded his head.

"Yes, that's him," he confirmed. "Dennis Mooney."

CHAPTER 27

S eated at the little round table in her kitchen, Samia made
a careful notation in her diary. She wrote, "What is love
really?" in electric blue ink and in a small but rounded,
graceful script. Tired and glum and still in nurse's uniform
except for the starched white hat, she had Mayo's checked comforter draped around her shoulders. It was evening and chilly
and something had gone wrong with the building's central
heating system. She looked up as she heard a gentle rapping at
her door. The front doorbell wasn't working either.

"Who is it? Who's there?" she called out.

"It's Meral."

Samia's eyes briefly widened, then relaxed.

She stood up, closed the diary, slipped it into a drawer and shut it.

"Okay!" she called out. "Be right there!"

The nurse hastily straightened her living room, then moved quickly to the door where she peered through a spy eye, then slipped back three separate security bolts before finally opening the door to Meral. His face emotionless, he was in uniform and gripped a black leather briefcase at his side.

"Oh, hi, Meral," she said casually.

"Yes, hello, Samia. Sorry to disturb you. Do you mind if I come in for a moment?"

"Are you kidding?" she blurted. Then she caught herself. "I mean, sure, come on in," she said casually. "Why not?"

Meral entered and Samia closed the door, sharply cutting off the sound of two laughing children running and playing in the hallway upstairs, their thumping steps an unpredictable, happy rhythm.

"Come, let's sit in the kitchen," said the nurse as she led Meral there with a loose forward flip of her hand. "It's warmer from the oven and the burners on the stove. I've got them all turned on. The heating's not working. Creepy landlord. It's probably deliberate. Bet it's working for those Jews upstairs. Come on, sit down. Come, take a seat here by the stove."

"Thanks, I will."

As he sat and set the briefcase down beside him on the floor, the policeman was still gazing around the living room. Three of its walls were pink while the fourth was fully covered with painted blue flowers.

"You have a very nice apartment," he said.

"It's a dump, but I try to cheer it up."

"I like the wall with the flowers."

"Yes, my favorite," she said. "Blue iris. I can't believe you've come by. Want some coffee? I can make some really quick."

"Oh, no, please! Please don't trouble yourself, Samia."

"Oh, come on. It's no trouble at all."

Samia stood up and started plucking the makings of coffee from a cupboard. "You like rosewater in it?"

"Yes, I do, please. If it isn't any trouble."

"So what's up? You've got a case in the neighborhood or what? What's going on?"

"What's going on in your window, Samia?"

"What do you mean?"

"Your window," he repeated. "Over there."

He pointed at the back of the life-sized plastic torso seated on the ledge of a living room window: a long-fanged, grinning vampire, a foot-long dagger in its upraised hand.

Samia looked and then turned back to the stove and the coffee.

"Oh, is *that* what you're here about? Someone complained?"

"No. No one complained. But what's it there for?"

"Security. People see it and they figure someone crazy must live in this apartment and they never want to mess with that. Crazy really scares them."

"Scares who?"

"You know, burglars. Everybody. Them. At night I keep a spotlight on it, Meral. Really spooky."

Meral stared at her back without expression as she measured out coffee, finely ground to brown dust, into a very small long-handled, shiny brass pot. "I know this isn't my district, Samia," he offered, "but to the best of my knowledge this area is the safest in all of Jerusalem, with rarely any break-ins or burglaries reported."

"That's the problem. The law of averages says we're overdue."

Meral had no answer.

The nurse set the coffeepot over a burner and sat down at the table across from him. "So more questions about Wilson for me, right?"

"No, that isn't why I came."

"You mean you just stopped by?"

"Yes, you could say that."

"Are you sick or lost? This is Apartment 2B. My name's Samia."

"Come, I've brought you a gift."

"You're kidding."

"No, not kidding."

"What is it?"

"After coffee," Meral told her.

"Oh, surprise, huh? Like a summons?"

"Not a summons."

"Something good or something bad?"

"I wouldn't ever bring you anything bad."

"No, you wouldn't."

She was staring at him gently, her head slightly tilted to the side.

"You seem different somehow, Meral."

"Different? How?"

"I don't know."

"And you seem a little sad," he observed.

"Oh, really?"

"Yes, a bit. Just a bit. Is it Mayo?"

The nurse shrugged and then nodded, lowering her head as she leaned a little forward and rested her weight on her folded arms. "Yes, a little, I guess."

"Me, too."

"I feel so lonely with him gone."

"You have no other close friends?"

"Not like him."

"And your parents? They're still living? Siblings?"

Samia shook her head. "No, none."

She looked up and turned her head to check the coffee.

"Just like you," she finished matter-of-factly.

Meral stared and was silent.

Samia turned back. "Almost ready," she said. "Now come on, Meral! Tell me! What's the gift? What did you bring me? And why? Come on, what's this all about? What's going on?"

"After coffee," he said firmly.

"Oh, you're just a big tease!"

Soon the coffee had been poured, and for a time they idly chatted.

"Aggravating town, this Jerusalem," Samia declared at one point. "You can't find a Mexican restaurant anywhere. These Jews must think Mexicans are actually just Arabs who call arak tequila."

"Now that doesn't make sense, Samia. Really. There are Arabic restaurants all over Jerusalem."

"Oh, well, sure, closing *them* would be way too obvious."

"Really."

"Well, of course. So they stick it to the spics."

The nurse finished her coffee and then set down her cup.

"Okay, Meral, coffee's finished. What did you bring me?"

Meral reached down to the briefcase and removed two items. He placed them on the table and said, "These. I was able to secure them for you. But I wanted something warm inside of you first."

Her eyes full of sadness and fond remembrance, Samia stared down at the travel poster of the Big Sur coast of California that had once been on Mayo's office wall. She picked it up tenderly. "Thanks, Meral. I'll cherish this. Really. So much. It was his dream, you know. Or maybe you don't. He dreamed of going back there to live someday. Someone lived there that he loved."

"In Carmel?"

"Yeah, Carmel. He said he'd even be happy to see her by chance every now and then, if it came to that, like maybe on the street or in a supermarket or something just so he could smile and maybe wave a hello. Maybe meet her son."

"And so who was she? Do you know?"

"No, not her name. Some movie star. He used to talk about

it lots toward the end when he was sick." She put the calendar down beside the other gift, the photo of the boyhood Mayo and Meral. "And this," she said picking it up. "Thanks, Meral. You're a peach. Or a date. Freudian slip."

"What do you mean, 'Freudian slip'?"

Samia set the photo down and said, "Nothing. More coffee?"

"No, no thank you." Meral glanced at his watch and began to get up from the table. "No, I really must go." Then, "Oh, no, wait," he said, settling back down. "There *is* one more thing." He reached a hand down into the briefcase and picked something out of it.

"The plaque about the soup and the noodles?"

"No, Samia, it isn't anything of Mayo's. It's something else. Not so terribly important, as a matter of fact, but as long as I'm here . . ."

Meral placed it on the table. It was a telecopied close-up photograph of a man in military uniform. Mayo held it up to the nurse's scrutiny. "I've just received this today," he said. "It's quite unlikely, but by chance could this possibly be the man who for a time you say was living with our good friend Wilson?"

"Oh, my goodness!"

"It's the man?"

"Yes, I think so."

"Are you sure?"

"Well, pretty sure. Let me see."

Samia took the photo from Meral's hands and examined it more closely. "Yes, I'm sure," she said at last. "That's him."

Samia put the photo down and then looked up at Meral.

The policeman seemed preoccupied.

"Is this a very big deal?" she asked. "Who is he?"

"Someone lost who has been found."

Arms folded across her chest, the nurse watched as Meral slipped the photo back into the briefcase and then put his black beret on his head and adjusted it.

"So that's it?" she said. "I've been juiced, so back to work?"

"Can't be helped."

And yet for several moments the policeman did not move, both his gaze and a hand gently resting on the table. The only sound was the hissing of the burners' blue flames.

"So," he said at last.

"And so?"

Meral looked up at her in pleasant discovery.

"I never realized that your hair was so long and wavy."

"Yeah, you guys have those handsome little black caps while we've got to wear these ugly huge starched white bazongas. Why do Arabs need a great big Star of David on our caps? Why not a falafel or a piece of fried *kibbe*? All of that whiteness could be taken to be yogurt."

Meral looked at her with fondness for a moment.

Then abruptly he stood up.

"Well, I really must go," he said. "Much to do."

Both hands on the edge of the table, Samia pushed to her feet. "Me, too. I've got a whole bunch of stuff I've got to get to. Still I'm glad you came by."

"No problem."

"Right."

As they walked into the living room and headed toward the door, Meral stopped at the wall filled with painted blue irises. "Lovely work," he observed. "This must have cost you a great deal of money."

"Oh, well, that'll be the day. I did it myself."

Meral registered surprise.

"You paint? You've never mentioned this."

"No. With a talent this phenomenal you've got to lay low. Too much envy out there."

Again that glint of fondness came into Meral's eyes as for a moment he stood and read the nurse's face. Then abruptly he turned and, with Samia following behind him, he walked to the door, opened it, stepped into the hall, and turned around. The preoccupied look had returned.

"Thank you for the coffee," he said.

"Oh, for heaven's sakes, why can't you smile?" Samia blurted. "Would it kill you to smile, Meral? Would it? Would it kill you to smile just once?"

Meral lowered his head.

"Thank you for your help," he said.

And then he turned and walked away.

"Come again anytime," Samia called out to him. "Maybe next week?"

"So very busy, Samia. But thank you."

"The week after, then. Bring photos of Hungarian para-troopers!"

The nurse watched him begin to descend the staircase that would take him down to the street, and only when the policeman had vanished from her view did she slowly and quietly close the door. For a moment she stood in thought, staring down at the floor and shaking her head; then, looking up, she walked briskly back to the kitchen where she sat at the table, slid open the drawer, and extracted her diary. " 'Glad you came by.' 'No problem,' " she mimicked with a mocking face and tone. "No problem?" she expostulated. "No *problem*?" She lowered her forehead into a hand, then looked up, drew a breath, and picked up her pen. "He just came by and my heart began to shiver and dance all at once" she wrote in the place where she had left off. "He did seem somehow different in a way. Can't explain it though, really. Just something. But in the end his little visit turned out to be basically business as usual. And kind of creepy business at that. I'm so glad I'm just a weirdo and not a cop. Anyway, I guess I'm giving up. Yeah, it's back to Frank Sinatra records on the phono and a scotch every night for the romantic Samia, or even maybe, like Mayo's fond dream of Carmel, being happy with a now and then glimpse or conversation or maybe just a smile and a wave of hello."

Samia read it over and then crossed out the reference to a smile.

Down in the street below Samia's apartment, Meral sat in his police car alone for a time as he stared in consternation at the Teletyped photo in his hand of the Albanian military officer reported to be missing from his U.N. contingent on the Golan

Heights: the one Samia had just positively identified as the man who had lived with Wilson. In line with all previous descriptions of Temescu, but unlike the blurry image on his driver's license, this sharp new photo was of a man with a strong rugged face and a scar that bisected his lips into a snarl.

His name was Colonel Jeton Agim Vlora.

CHAPTER 28

Wilson moved slowly to a chair by the window of his little apartment in Jerusalem Hills. He was looking for light. Head bent, his expression unreadable, he slowly sank down into the chair and for very long moments stared fixedly at the envelope of a letter that minutes before he had taken from his mailbox: "Michael Wilson, 17 Rue Melee, Jerusalem Hills, Israel 90835." He angled the envelope a little to catch the sun's rays on the faintly inked postmark. It was local. He tilted it straight and continued to stare at the elegant and achingly familiar handwriting.

At last he slit open the envelope, slipped out the letter inside and read it. Then he lowered it slowly to his knee and for a time sat motionless, staring through the yellowing window glass as the fracture of afternoon sun and shadow mottled the building across the way in slow dull shifts of melancholy drabness, like a broken kaleidoscope with only two colors. He stood up and went to sit at a little square writing table where he opened a drawer, took out a pen and stationery, and began to compose a letter that in the end would be added to a purple-ribboned bundle of others that would never be delivered.

"Dearest Jean," he began.

And then he lowered his head and wept.

CHAPTER 29

Meral entered his room, removed his jacket, hung it up, and then sat on the edge of his bed. The day had been longer and more tiring than usual. He'd gone fruitlessly searching for Wilson both at Wilson's apartment and at Hadassah, and then later in the evening at the Casa Nova where Wilson had been scheduled to make a repair but unaccountably never showed up. Despondent, Meral lowered his head and shook it, and then lifted it to stare at the photos on his desk. He would have to buy a frame for one more.

A little later, while preparing for sleep, Meral thought he might read to coax slumber to his eyes and to a restless mind, but on opening a drawer of the bedside table where he kept all his paperback books, he found something on top of the stack that he couldn't remember ever seeing before. Where had it come from? he wondered. He lifted it out and sat again on the edge of his bed as the muted strains of a violin concerto started up in the room of some nun down the hall. Meral stared at his find. It was a sheaf of unmailed, handwritten letters held together by a band of purple ribbon.

All of them began with the words, "Dearest Jean."

He moved slowly and soundlessly as a specter through a series of vaulted, shadowy avenues flanked by arched portals and massive pillars until at last he stopped at the edge of an enormous room where the letter had told him they were to meet. He was in Solomon's Stables, a massive and cavernous hall of stone that was directly underneath the Temple Mount. A waiting silence almost deeper than God's was broken only by the quiet cooing of a dove in one of the apertures just above the level of the streets outside that were aglow with the promises of late morning sunlight sifting down at an angle to the shadowy floor. He took a step to the side to keep his back against a wall. He waited. Listened intensely. Then he heard the soft step he'd been waiting for, the step that he knew so well. He saw her moving toward him from behind a pillar until she was captured by a column of sun, where she stopped and stood silently staring at him with deep-sunken eyes in a drug-ravaged face that, like the world, held no more than a distant memory of its beauty.

"Hello, Paul," she said hollowly.

"Hello, Jean."

Paul Dimiter's gaze shifted quickly to the left as Stephen Riley stepped out from behind another pillar. Still in the priestly garb of Dennis Mooney, he was gripping a long-barreled pistol equipped with a silencer.

"Why good morning, old buddy and mentor."

"Why good morning to you, too. You look so different."

"Plastic surgery. You know the drill."

"Oh, a very nice job, Steve."

"Fuck you, too, pal! Just don't move! Don't move an inch!"

"I won't."

"Not an *inch*! And put your hands up in the air. Yeah, good. And just keep them there. You know, I can't believe you didn't see through this, that you actually came. Is there a net about to drop from the ceiling on top of me, Paul, or am I standing right over a trapdoor? Come on, tell me. What's the catch?"

"There's no catch."

"I can't believe it. And you came here unarmed!" Riley marveled.

"No, I'm armed," answered Dimiter quietly.

"I don't see it."

"No, you can't. But it's there."

"Oh, well now you've got me thinking all those rumors might be true, *mi amigo*: you know, that maybe you've lost a few marbles? Ah, well, hell. Just too bad this has to be. I mean, crazy or sane, we'll still miss you."

"You're going to kill me?"

"Now I *know* you're demented! Of *course*, I'm going to kill you!" Riley snarled. "Jean, step over to the side. You're in the way."

"Yeah, okay," she said, meekly repeating, "to the side."

But instead, she took a halting step toward Dimiter, her turned-up hand reaching out to him, imploring. "Oh, Paul, I'm so sorry," she said. There was a tremor in her voice. "I'm . . ."

"Shut up, Jean!" Riley ordered sharply with his eyes still pinned to Dimiter. "All right, Paul-o," he began. "So you came after us. How did you find out we were here?"

"I never came after you, Stephen."

"Bullshit!"

"No, it's true. Until I got here I thought you were dead."

" 'Until you got here'?"

"Yes, I recognized you."

"How?"

"From your step."

"From my? . . ."

"Steve! . . ."

"Jean, shut up!" Riley savagely commanded, his stare never

straying from Dimiter's. "This is borderline hilarious," he mocked. "I'm supposed to believe that your being here is just a coincidence?"

"There is no such thing," Dimiter answered him quietly.

"So you admit it, then! You *were* coming after us!"

"No. I was hunting someone else. That's the truth. It wasn't you. You're going to kill me now no matter what I say. Why would I lie?"

"Because—"

"You see? It's all for *nothing*, Steve! All for fucking *nothing*!" Jean Dimiter shrieked at Riley. "He wasn't after us at all!"

"I don't believe him," Riley answered her evenly. "Now get out of the way, Jean! *Move!*"

"I forgive you, Jean," Dimiter said to her. "Remember that. Remember that always. I forgive you."

"Sorry, Paul," Riley told him as he aimed his weapon. "We had some really good times. I mean it. Really good. Okay, now, Jeannie, love. Move, please! Move! Move right now!"

"It's alright, Stephen," Dimiter told him. "Here, I'll do it. I'll move into the clear. Come on, Stephen. Here's your clean shot."

And as Dimiter moved to the side with a fond stare settled upon the face of his wife, Jean Dimiter suddenly burst into tears and raced forward toward her husband with her arms outstretched to embrace him just as grace and a bullet exploded white fire into her brain.

"Jesus Christ!" Riley uttered in shock.

Dimiter looked down at his wife's crumpled body. And then back up at Riley. "And I forgive you, too."

"What the hell are you talking about, you fucking psycho?"

The next two bullets were unrepentant. Dimiter fell beside the body of his wife so that their posture, when they were discovered on the following day, could have easily been taken for that of lovers who were turned aside for sleep, an impression that would not have been very far wrong.

There was no parting.

PART THREE

FINAL REPORT

June 7, 1974

CHAPTER 31

FINAL INTERVIEWS AND DISPOSITION OF MATTERS
RELATING TO THE REMLE STREET INCIDENT,
PAUL DIMITER, JEAN DIMITER, STEPHEN RILEY,
AND COLONEL JETON AGIM VLORA

Present: Moshe Zui, I.I.; William Sandalls, Charles Bell, American
Embassy; Sgt. Major Peter V. Meral, Kishla Station; Shlomo Uris,
Jerusalem Sub-District. Recordist: Annette Assaf.

ZUI: Alright, this is mainly for Bell and Sandalls. Bill, you've got copies of everything, right?

SANDALLS: No, not everything. But fine. Go ahead. I mean, that's what this is for, not so?

ZUI: Okay. Shlomo Uris, will you start? Although, no. First I'll run through the basics. So now posing as a Catholic Franciscan priest named Dennis Mooney, Stephen Riley and Jean, Paul Dimiter's wife, were being blackmailed by the Russians into now and then killing certain people that the Russians wanted dead without it being traced back to them. They got them—

SANDALLS: Where are you getting this stuff?

ZUI: We have a source.

SANDALLS: Who?

ZUI: Later, Bill. Surprise. Meantime, we also sourced a stack of unmailed letters that Dimiter wrote to his wife.

SANDALLS: Where'd you get them?

ZUI: Sergeant Meral. He found them in his room.

SANDALLS: Dimiter's room?

ZUI: Meral's.

SANDALLS: Start over.

ZUI: No, you heard me correctly. Meral found them in his room at the Casa Nova and we don't know how they got there. Now can I do this, please, fellows?

SANDALLS: Go!

ZUI: Okay, Riley and Dimiter's wife were secret lovers. They grabbed the radar plans they were sent to get, faked their deaths, sold the plans to the Russians for a fortune, and Stephen Riley has surgery to change his appearance. After that, they come here to hide out. So far so evil. But then the Russians say, "Aha! A little blackmail is in order!" and they force them to agree to make a hit for them every now and then, first by putting salmonella in the target's food or in our sparkling "Drink This and Remember the Camps" bottled water so the target winds up in Hadassah where friend Riley the *goniff* and phony Catholic priest can off them with a fatal and untraceable injection. It's a great place to do it. People die there every day. Who's to notice? But then Dimiter shows up here as Wilson, and not really looking around for any trouble at all. So— Off the record for a second, Annette: Look at Sandalls and Bell, how they're smiling like they've won the Israeli Lotto!

SANDALLS: Drinks on us at the King David bar tonight!

ZUI: Good. We aim to please. Okay, back on. So now Riley spots Dimiter somewhere and immediately assumes that he's tracked them down and he's come here to kill them, so at first Riley hires some Yemeni gunman and part-time assassin to try to off Dimiter for him at the top of the Russian Church Tower where he knows he always goes on certain days around dawn, and he shows him how to set up the "wire," and the guy strings it up on a day Dimiter usually comes, and he hides in this closet at the top of the Tower. Now Dimiter comes that day right on schedule but he spots the "wire" and the guy winds up charging him—there must have been a few things about Dimiter that Riley left out when he was briefing this putz—and he misses, of course, and he trips and falls down all those stairs and breaks his neck. Rest in Peace and fuck him and his horse. And so now Riley decides he'll have to do the job himself and that the best way to do it is to get Dimiter's wife to lure him into a trap.

SANDALLS: And so where is all of *this* coming from? Another letter?

ZUI: Yes, partly. It's a letter that Dimiter gets from the wife that she writes to try to lure him to Solomon's Stables. It was with the ones Meral found in his room. She tells him she's so sorry for everything and even tells him about the hit with the "wire" just to make her contrition sound real. At least that's my guess. Plus, as I mentioned, our unimpeachable source.

SANDALLS: Moshe, come back a sec.

ZUI: What is it?

SANDALLS: The wife. She knows that Riley's set this up to make the hit on her ex?

ZUI: Yes, she knows it, Bill.

SANDALLS: Cold.

ZUI: I'm not so sure about that. Her body was a pincushion. Needle marks all over it. Heroin. A recent heavy dose of it showed up in the drug screen. She must have taken it—or maybe Riley injected her—just before they went to the Stables. It was how Riley was able to keep her in line.

BELL: You seem sure of that.

ZUI: Our source. Her last letter. And one other thing.

SANDALLS: What?

ZUI: Riley shot her in the back of the head.

SANDALLS: I scc. We'll be getting all these letters, by the way?

ZUI: Yes, you'll have them. Almost everything's in them. I just wanted you to have the big picture. We've even found out what his mission was.

SANDALLS: Whose? You mean Dimiter's?

ZUI: Yes.

SANDALLS: Oh, for crying out loud! Are we back to that now? You just told us that he came here for the waters, that he *had* no mission!

ZUI: I said the first but not the second.

SANDALLS: I think I just stepped through the looking glass.

ZUI: You haven't. Just wait, Bill. You'll see. Now we'll be moving along to the body that we found in Christ's Tomb, and then that Remle Street incident that Meral was into. We'll be getting into all of that. And Dimiter's mission.

SANDALLS: Yes, our mission to Andromeda.

ZUI: Can we try to move forward?

SANDALLS: I'm trying.

ZUI: Okay, first thing on the docket: I'd like Inspector Uris to recap the brilliant work he did on his end of things. Inspector?

URIS: I much prefcr Shlomo.

ZUI: Then Shlomo. Tell us how you caught Riley.

SANDALLS: What, you *got* him?

BELL: You got *Riley*?!

ZUI: Yes, we got him and I hope there'll be no fight over jurisdiction.

SANDALLS: This is wonderful! Great! How'd you get him?
URIS: Well, I take no credit. It just fell into my lap. My uncle, Moses Mayo, was a doctor at Hadassah Hospital and died for no reason that anyone could find. He just gradually wasted away. Sergeant Meral was the first to suspect it could be murder. That my uncle was on to something—or to someone. So I tried to find out where my uncle might have been just before he started going downhill. He told the med school he'd be missing a lecture one morning because he would be driving to someplace out of town. But he wouldn't tell them where. Suspicious. So I checked incoming calls leading up to the day that he drove out of town and one of them right away made me sit up straight. It had come from a public phone in Beit Sahour, where there's a chapel that's run by a Franciscan priest named Dennis Mooney who lived there in a couple of rooms that were attached and with a full-time housekeeper-cook who was living in some sort of guest hut beside it.
SANDALLS: And so why would Beit Sahour make you sit up straight?
ZUI: Here we go. The real Dennis Mooney had a mother in Brooklyn, New York. Father dead, the mother old, hard of hearing. She hasn't heard from her son in a couple of years. She writes letters and asks him to send her some pictures of him—pictures in the Chapel of the Angels, outside in Shepherd's Fields, all of that. But she never gets an answer. No photos. Nothing. So she writes to Franciscan headquarters, right? And they write back and say they had no

trouble at all getting in touch with her son and that they got back a letter from him saying he was fine and that he'd send his mother photos and also that he'd never gotten any of her letters.

Two months later, still no letter from Mooney to his mother. So she writes to the head Franciscans again, and it's the same old bullshit all over: they write back and say they wired her son and told him, "Write to your mother right away and send her pictures!" And then Riley, he calls his HQ this time and he swears he sent pictures, and he can't understand why she hasn't received all the letters and the photos that he's sent, and he was going to write to her again, right away. And then as usual, the mother gets nothing.

And so now she's getting worried and also annoyed as holy hell, and then somebody tells her to contact the State Department, and the upshot is that finally your ambassador here passed the inquiry on to us, it lands on my desk, when I see this priest is in Beit Sahour, I'm thinking, "Aha!" and I call up the head Franciscans myself and I ask them for a photo of Mooney, which they send, and with this in my hand I make a trip to Shepherd's Fields like a tourist, and then there I am a Jew singing Christmas Carols in this chapel full of *goyim* and paintings and statues of angels though, I promise you, with no disrespect in my heart—so I can see for myself that Dennis Mooney isn't really Dennis Mooney because the real one they killed and then buried before the poor guy even makes it as far from the airport as the Casa

Nova, so that no one would know what the real Mooney looked like.

So I see this and I go into the village to Beit Sahour and the local police post there and I call Tel Aviv for some serious backup and they come and we take him, this *momzer*, this Riley. We take him and he spills his guts. He tells us everything; even things we didn't ask him about.

BELL: Boy, that almost surprises me more than anything else.

ZUI: You have your methods. We have ours.

SANDALLS: Are yours legal?

URIS: Absolutely not. We threaten them with readings of Jewish haiku. Of course, meantime, you know, it turns out Riley's so-called housekeeper there in Beit Sahour was . . .

ZUI: Yes, we know. She was Dimiter's wife.

SANDALLS: What I don't get is how Riley killed your uncle. Did he really?

URIS: Yes, he did. He gave my uncle some figs that he'd injected with a deadly toxin that leaves no trace; it just starts the ball rolling downhill, and then it goes away.

ZUI: Many thanks, Inspector Uris.

URIS: Shlomo.

ZUI: Shlomo. Great work.

SANDALLS: Let's have a drink sometime, Shlomo.

URIS: My pleasure.

ZUI: Alright, on to Sergeant Meral.

BELL: And so what are we doing here? Homicide cops on parade?

ZUI: Just a moment. Let me look at this note that I've just been handed.

[Reads note] Okay, we'll break for fifteen.

SANDALLS: Really?

ZUI: Yes.

[BREAKS AT 0944 AND RESUMES AT 1002]

ZUI: Want to start out with Remle Street, Sergeant?

MERAL: No, with Vlora.

ZUI: Okay, Vlora.

SANDALLS: Who's Vlora?

MERAL: He's the man discovered dead in Christ's Tomb who at first we thought was someone named Joseph Temescu and then mistakenly, of course, Paul Dimiter, when in fact he was an Albanian Security officer who had gotten himself attached to the Albanian contingent on the Golan Heights.

SANDALLS: My head's spinning again. Why would Vlora want to do that?

MERAL: To be able to kill Dimiter.

SANDALLS: Why?

MERAL: Because Dimiter killed his son.

SANDALLS: Good reason.

MERAL: Quite. But not in the way you and I would understand it. Vlora despised his son. Vlora ordered men tortured in the name of what he thought was a greater good, whereas the son inflicted pain for the pleasure it gave him. Albanians have something called the "code of the *bessa*": Someone

307

murders your blood and you have to murder theirs. Any male. If he's the only one available it could even be a child. It's something like a moral imperative with them. There wasn't any passion in Vlora's hunt for Dimiter. It was all principle. Honor. Duty.

BELL: When did Dimiter kill his son?

MERAL: While on his mission to ordain the new priests in Albania. He was captured for a time and tortured and interrogated by Vlora, and then in making his escape he killed Vlora's son. Up to here are we clear?

SANDALLS: We'll see.

MERAL: Well, then, things took a strange and extraordinary turn. After rescuing Vlora from a car crash that without his intervention would most certainly have killed him, Dimiter had him treated at the Government Hospital in Jerusalem and then took him from there to his apartment in Jerusalem Heights where he slowly brought him back to some semblance of health: you know, feeding him, nursing him, reading to him, keeping up his spirits; at times, it seems, just by his presence alone, and that's something that I know about at first hand.

SANDALLS: What do you mean "first hand?"

MERAL: I mean that just being in his company changes you.

SANDALLS: Changes you how?

ZUI: That's not important. Back to Vlora, please, Sergeant. You were saying?

MERAL: Colonel Vlora was stunned. I mean, this from a

man that he'd ordered tortured for endless days and in the most unendurable and horrifying ways and whom he'd just tried to kill. It was the code of the *bessa* turned on its head! Vlora changed. He was overcome. Made new. In its way this was Vlora's own mystical experience. And then the truly amazing thing happened.

SANDALLS: We're talking letters again?

MERAL: Yes, that's right.

SANDALLS: Are we getting our hands on those letters?

ZUI: Yes, we're sending you the batch. You have my word.

SANDALLS: Moshe, thanks. And now what's this "amazing thing," Meral?

MERAL: It truly is! Vlora knew that someone else was targeting Dimiter. Dimiter had told him that. Then a few weeks later he asked Dimiter to walk with him to the Church of the Holy Sepulcher and when they were almost there he revealed his intention, telling Dimiter that if a staging of Dimiter's "death" were made known in some extremely dramatic and public way, it might cause the would-be killer to believe that he'd made a mistake, that Wilson wasn't Dimiter after all and that he had targeted the wrong man. Dimiter had so many different looks, after all. Vlora's plan was to die and to be taken for Dimiter, and so early on the morning he was to execute the plan he went over to the apartment he had rented, but in fact never occupied, and salted it with all of those documents that led us to think that Vlora was Dimiter. When Vlora told him his intention, Dimiter was appalled. He didn't want this. No. Not at first. Though of course it made no difference since the venom was already in Vlora's system. And that brings me to the second part of Vlora's thinking. Who could possibly think this was a suicide, he thought. Who would choose to end his life with the incredibly painful Deathstalker venom when a handful of sleeping pills would do the job as well? To a mind like Vlora's that had been trained to view the world with the remorseless squint of the *bessa*, it was this, he believed, that would likely persuade any would-be assailant that Dimiter had indeed been killed and by someone who had hated him intensely.

SANDALLS: Maybe yes, maybe no.

MERAL: Precisely. And that's what's even more remarkable about it: that there was no guarantee his plan would work and that Vlora chose extraordinary pain just on the chance of it.

SANDALLS: I think I get your point. So what came next?

MERAL: Well, there was nothing now that Dimiter could do and so he went into the Tomb with Vlora, who as soon as the others in the chamber had left took another massive dose of chloral hydrate, lay down on the burial slab, folded his arms across his chest, and then closed his eyes and waited to die.

BELL: The crossed arms? What was that? Some Albanian thing?

MERAL: No. It was just something that would add to the aura of mystery intended to capture the attention of the press and the public. Dimiter promised Vlora he would stay to the end, and when it came he slipped out of the Tomb and then the church. End of story.

SANDALLS: Who salted Vlora's apartment with Dimiter's I.D.? Was it Vlora?

MERAL: Yes, Vlora. All except the juggling balls and the clown things. Vlora didn't know their significance so Dimiter added them to the items that Vlora had salted. He didn't want his sacrifice to be in vain.

SANDALLS: Okay, thanks.

MERAL: You're very welcome. Inspector?

ZUI: Okay, let's get into Dimiter's mission.

SANDALLS: I'm going to say this until I'm blue in the face. He was here on his own.

ZUI: But he did have a mission.

SANDALLS: Oh, for Christ's sake, Moshe!

ZUI: I think you've just hit the nail on the head.

SANDALLS: What do you mean?

ZUI: If you'll listen for a minute you'll find out.

SANDALLS: Okay, I'm listening. I'm listening intently.

ZUI: Good. It has something to do with your St. Paul, who was originally our Saul and like Dimiter a legendary assassin. He hunted down Christians and killed them mercilessly. Then one day on the road to Damascus along with a number of companions all determined to annihilate the Christian community there, he had a mystical experience in which he was knocked to the ground by some force, by some brilliant white light in the sky, and he also heard a voice, and soon after our Saul became your St. Paul. Something similar happened to Dimiter. He had a mystical experience that stunned him, something to do with Jesus Christ. And like Saul, at first he didn't understand what had hit him. But being Dimiter, what does he do? Why of course! He comes to Jerusalem to find out what it was that just knocked him to the ground. Or off his horse, as some people seem to think.

BELL: I still don't get it. Why Jerusalem?

ZUI: He loved the sound of people constantly arguing. Sergeant Meral? Would you take it from here, please?

MERAL: Yes. Now you'll recall that Paul Dimiter's preparation whenever he was tasked with a high-level hit had him spending many weeks, sometimes months, researching personal data about the target he'd been assigned to hunt down and kill: what the target ate, how he walked, how he dressed, what he read, what made him laugh, what made him cry, what made him angry, and so on and so on—every possible fact that could be gathered about him, but above all else how the target thought, so that when he had finished with his preparation Dimiter virtually *was* the target.

SANDALLS: Listen, maybe I'm just thick, but what's this all got to do with his coming to Jerusalem? Why here? And didn't we agree he was hunting an *idea* here and not some person?

MERAL: No, there was a "Target X." It was a person.

SANDALLS: Are you kidding me, Sergeant? You're sure of that?

MERAL: Yes. Absolutely.
SANDALLS: And so who was he hunting?
MERAL: Christ.

[1055: INTERVIEW TERMINATED **ABRUPTLY**]

In the tense exchange that followed, Bell and Sandalls asked for copies of the "Dimiter Letters" and left hastily, edgy and somehow flustered, refusing Zui's request that they stay behind to discuss a "very new and unsettling development." When they and Sergeant Meral had left, Zui sighed, picked up the note he'd been handed much earlier and then slowly shook his head as he numbly reread it.

"Wait until they hear," he murmured. "Wait!"

CHAPTER 32

His large hands gripping the black iron railing at the top of the Russian Church Tower, Meral stood and looked eastward at the reddish brown twists of the forbidding and precipitous Mountains of Moab, with their salt sides bleached and sloping whitened in the sun, while before and below them sweeping fields of yellow dandelions bright in tall grass shone like promises of rain and redemption. When he'd arrived there were several other tourists at the top, but now they were leaving and Meral was grateful. He wanted to be here alone, as he had at dawn on many mornings before when he had come to hear the echo of Dimiter's footsteps, to inhale the last lingering traces of his presence. It was different at dawn when the world was hushed and the sun was slipping up from behind its rim like a shimmering benediction; but after the Final Report had concluded, some mysterious and irresistible impulse had drawn Meral here despite the less favorable time of day. And now he waited. But for what? Then something crossed his mind. Had he come here for a sign? he wondered. He thought of Dimiter's letter about seeing the "wire" and his "special thinking," his only letter about his visits here. Would something appear? Meral stayed and was alone for a while, and when he looked at his watch and was about to leave, from out of nowhere a sudden fierce wind sprang up that was so strong it pinned his back to the tower wall until, just as it had arisen, it abruptly died into absolute stillness. Meral started his descent still not knowing what had drawn him there in so unquiet a time of the day. He had remembered Dimiter's letter about his "special thinking."

But forgotten his mention of the sudden strong wind.

CHAPTER 33

Meral entered his room, slipped off his uniform jacket, hung it up, and then sat on the edge of his bed where, as he did every night of his life, he stared lovingly and long at each of the photos on the top of his desk, the last of them a new one. Mayo's. Then his gaze dropped down to the slim center drawer of the desk. He leaned forward and pulled it open, reached in a hand, and then lifted out a single sheet of paper on which the love that had created the beauty of things had now written a letter of its own. It was Dimiter's last letter to his wife.

Meral had withheld it.

He was certain it had been written for him.

Dearest Jean,

You're alive! Oh, my joy! You live! And you've confessed to me all that you have done, what you and Stephen have done, and still mean to do, which is to kill me. And now you want me to meet you in secret and away from Stephen. You now hate him, you say. You fear him. And you want me to help you escape him. You want to come back to me, you say, and that you are filled with remorse, which, if true, is surely the only thing you've told me that is, for you have sent me an invitation to my death. Although I think there's something else you said that's true. That you still love me. Oh, I know you don't think so. But in that part of your soul still untouched and unstained by this fallen place, the part that remains the Jean I've loved for so long, I believe that you do.

I am coming to your meeting. I'll be there. And I will make no resistance. I am coming to tell you and to show you I forgive you, for who knows then what blithe and unexpected grace might one day beckon your heart to where it's always belonged. And then finally allow you to forgive yourself.

I will love you forever, my Jean.

Your Paul

Head bent, Meral's gaze remained on the letter.

"Yes, 'Forgive yourself,' " he murmured softly.

Besides the fact it had been written for Meral, the letter differed from the others in another way as well.

This one had been delivered.

A dry sherry, please, Patience."

" 'If it were done when it were done.' "

"Yes, precisely. And kindly don't put anything in it."

Meral stood at the counter in the Casa Nova bar. It was the end of another day of work and he had changed into a blue linen jacket, khaki pants, white shirt, and a summery pale blue tie. It was the pre-dinner hour. Meral turned and looked around. There were only two other people in the bar and therefore many free chairs, all with camel-leather seats and backs and hollow shiny black metal legs. Meral turned one around so he could keep an eye on Patience, and then he sat down.

"Oh, well, hello there, old chap!" Meral turned his head. It was Scobie with a folded-up newspaper clutched in his hand. He looked over at the bar. "My usual, please!" he called out, and then he sat in a chair one away from Meral's.

"Don't mind if I sit with you, old chap?"

"No, not at all. You're quite welcome."

Scobie squinted at him dubiously. "I am?"

"Well, of course, you are, Scobie. Please sit."

Scobie continued to stare for a moment, then at last turned away and unfolded his paper. "Oh, well, you've heard about the latest bit of bloody tomfoolery at bloody Shin Bet, I suppose."

"No, I haven't."

"No? Misplaced the dead body of a secret agent and a bloody damned famous one at that. You know that Dimiter fellow? The twits! First they give me a pranging about misinforming them. And now this. This country is becoming unlivable."

Meral turned to him. Scobie was holding up the newspaper wide in both hands and with his nose only inches away from the text while his eyes scanned about for some item of interest.

"What are you talking about, Scobie?"

Scobie turned to him.

"You really mean you haven't heard?"

"They've lost his body?"

"Oh, well, they had him iced up in the morgue and all ready

to ship him to the States, and now they're saying that his body's disappeared! They can't find it!" He turned back to his paper. "Bloody prats. Can you imagine? What a bloody balls-up! Misplaced a body!"

Meral looked off in a reverie of thought and wonder while, as if from some minor and distant planet lost in the tumbling, silent swirl of the galaxies, he heard the voice of Scobie.

"Well, now, this Dimiter, you know. Ever meet him?"

"Yes. He gave me a sunflower once."

"Okay, I'm here."

Meral turned to look up at Samia.

"This okay?" she asked. "What I've got on?"

She was wearing a pale blue dress, pink sandals, and a red and white Beethoven T-shirt. "I mean, Beethoven wasn't Catholic," she went on, "he was Protestant. They're not snots about that kind of stuff here, are they, Meral?"

"No, they aren't," Meral told her.

He stood up.

"And your attire is lovely," he added. "First a drink and then dinner? The chef is doing Mexican tonight at my request. What's wrong? You're not pleased?"

Samia's eyes had been searching his face with concern.

"You look distracted," she said. "What are you thinking?"

"You wouldn't believe it."

"*Me?*"

Meral smiled.

A c k n o w l e d g m e n t s

Toward the end of the 1960s I attended a modest New Year's
Eve gathering at the home of my friend, the wonderful novelist and screenwriter, Burton Wohl, and it was there that I met
Marc Jaffe, then editorial director of Bantam Books. Familiar
with my work as a comic novelist, he asked me quite casually
what I was working on lately. My answer involved mention of
the State Unemployment Office but then, after debating
whether or not to risk losing Jaffe's respect, I talked for no more
than a minute or two about my idea for a serious novel, prudently withholding the fact that I had shopped it around to
various publishing entities and several Hollywood film studios,
all of whom eyed me with pity. But not Marc Jaffe. When I'd
finished talking, and without a moment's hesitation, he looked
me in the eye and said—his exact words—"*I'll* publish that!" And

he did. It was *The Exorcist*. Now, forty years later, a period of time during which we've had virtually no contact, Marc Jaffe has done it again, having made it a crusade to find the right publisher for this, the most personally important novel of my career.

I have no way of adequately thanking him.

The gift is too great.

My thanks also to Vivienne Jaffe who, along with Marc, gave invaluable help in the editing and preparation of the manuscript, as did also my wife, Julie.

Among others I would wish to thank—U.S. Army Colonel William R. Corson, personnel of Hadassah Hospital in Jerusalem, the Israeli National Police, and Isser Harel, the "father of Israeli Intelligence," who masterminded the capture of Adolph Eichmann and gave me invaluable research assistance—all have passed away, but I thank them here nevertheless, confident that their mortal deaths will not keep them from knowing that I have done it.

I would be most appreciative if readers of this novel in Jerusalem were to be so kind as to resist the impulse to write and inform me that there is not now, nor has there ever been, a "Remle Street." I know that. But only the name is fictitious, not the place, which is Hativat Jerushalayim, the usage of which utterly destroyed the rhythm of any sentence in which I attempted to use it. I didn't even try with Orthodox Armenian Patriarchate Road. *Shalom.*

EXTRACT

TERRY AND THE WEREWOLF

BY

W I L L I A M   P E T E R
B L A T T Y

Now maybe you'll think it strange that I should have been pouring coffee for the brown-eyed daughter of the New York City Police Commissioner just like I *was* a waiter or something, and it could be you'd be right except actually you'd be wrong inasmuch as at the time I was a waiter and everyone I waited on at this Catskill Mountains summer resort was either a New York policeman or somebody in his family. The resort was owned and managed by the New York City Police Department so I guess the whole thing was real proper and I'm sorry if I worked you up over nothing but I still get a little muddle-headed when I think of that time I first met Terry.

'You are somewhat late for breakfast, Miss,' I said to her really warm like.

'You're pouring black coffee into my Bran Flakes,' she answered me, possibly even *more* warm like. I mean, you'd expect she'd be ticked or something but when she looked up at me with that twinkly half-question, half-smile in her eyes, I felt something in my head go 'crunch,' although maybe that's how Bran Flakes react to hot coffee but that didn't occur to me at the time, I just felt that I'd fallen into like, which was good, but then we had the werewolf hunt, which was not.

And of course there was waiter Gregg Malloy.

Malloy had the looks of a young Greek god just finished with his junior year at Cambridge, and though there was indeed something otherworldly about the way he handled his section of the dining room he was unfortunately no myth. He also had an altogether earthly interest in the aforementioned eighteen-year-old Miss Harnedy.

'I have an interest in your new guest, a Miss Harnedy,' he said to me in the washroom of the waiters' bunkhouse the night of her arrival at the center. Cocking his head, he studied his Byronesque reflection in the wall-to-wall mirror above the washstand and then grabbed up a couple of bronze-backed hair brushes monogrammed 'G.E.M,' because wouldn't you know his middle name would be Edmund, the unregenerate, irredeemable creep, and began a fastidious slicking back of that shoulder-length, curly blond hair of his and so help me I was thinking of taking a scythe to it. 'Just a little research for my novel,' he added, leering and winking at me in the mirror. This did not please me. At all. You keep hearing people say that they enjoy competition. Well, I'm not one of them. I actually fear and detest competition, and while I don't have a face that looks like Camembert rinds, this Malloy was much more than good-looking – he was smooth, and like Leo Durocher, the old Brooklyn Dodgers baseball manager that people called 'Leo the Lip,' he had mastered the knack of dramatizing himself, so that when it came to women, he'd just pose against the backdrop of his graduate studies in journalism at Columbia University, always walking around looking deeply thoughtful and letting it be known that he was working on 'a very important novel,' a pipe-puffing, aura-of-mystery sort of gambit that made him the Lord Jim of the Catskills, his big killer weapon consisting of this penetrating, soulful look that seemed to say to every targeted woman, 'I alone understand you completely.' If the jerk had a chapter of his novel for every policeman's daughter he'd seduced, his novel would be longer than *War and Peace* and its just-discovered sequel.

And so, 'Listen, good buddy,' I said to him – I'd heard that's how truck drivers talk – 'don't you think that your "research" has carried you a little past the limits of art and into the dominion of the *Guinness Book of Records*? I speak specifically of Kinsey and his picturesque graphics and reports.' After spreading a little talcum powder over his disgustingly handsome face, Malloy grinned at me through the looking glass and, not being calm and unrufflable as Alice, when Byron Man taunted, 'Jealous, Lofler?', my right hand reflexively balled into a fist to administer 'Death Without the Sacraments,' but my hand was stayed by the music. It was the center dance combo, a group of high school seniors from Waterbury, Connecticut, who called themselves The Plainclothesmen, and even though they sounded like galaxies in collision, it meant a chance for the waiters and busboys to mingle with the guests (I was thinking of Miss Harnedy) on the dance floor of the center's huddle room. One anxious, seething stare into the mirror convinced me that Malloy, too, was thinking of Miss Harnedy, but more like a walrus thinking of flounder, so I assembled my shaving gear over a washstand and moved quicker than that cartoon hero The Flash, but almost half an hour later when I got to the huddle room I found Terry Harnedy dancing with Malloy. Still, they hadn't gotten cozy as yet because as usual The Plain- clothesmen were playing an Irish waltz, what most New York cops being Irish or Italian, with 'Arrivederci Roma' pretty sure to be next, so I sliced through the whirl of bodies on the dance floor like a Hoy Damascus blade through Unguentine.

'Cut!' I said, tapping Malloy's shoulder smartly, possibly a little more smartly than needed, and 'Of course!' he had to say, which is the downside of the polished college aesthete Ashley Wilkes gallantry gambit.

I had counted on this. I am cunning.

So 'Hello!' I said, smiling, and 'Hello!' she said back, and then brown-eyes and I twirled around at arm's length, an alto- gether unsatisfactory arrangement, but then, in their typically unpredictable way, The Plainclothesmen eased into 'Night and Day' and, overweeningly impetuous rascal that I am, I tried leaning my head against Terry Harnedy's, this sometimes being the prelude to intimate discussion, but at the touch she instantly pulled away her head and stared over my shoulder just like she was looking at Betelgeuse III, either that or the inside of an empty candy bag. I thought of her warmth at breakfast, the interested glances over the kidney pie at lunch, the smile that verged on adoration when at dinner I sneaked her a second caramel-custard.

And yet suddenly she was cooler than yesterday's pancakes.

'Will you be going to Mexico again do you think?' she asked in a distant, disinterested voice.

'Going *where*?' I said.

'To Mexico,' she repeated, a concept as likely as Mohandas K. Gandhi and Sitting Bull duetting on 'I'm an Indian Too'.

'Is this a joke?' I said, laughing a little. 'If I go anywhere soon it's back to Georgetown and my boys.'

She stopped dancing, her eyes widening as she pulled back to stare at me. '*Boys?* You mean you're *married*?'

'Oh no, no,' I said quickly. 'The "boys" are kids from poor families at the Georgetown Boys Club back in DC. I coach their basketball team and do some tutoring.'

'You live in Washington?' she asked with what looked like a frown of perplexity, and, 'Partly,' I answered. 'I'm a junior at Georgetown.'

'And Washington's your home?'

I said, 'Brooklyn.'

She stared blankly for a second, and then tilting back her head she started laughing in a richly husky, throaty way laced with Tinker Bell fairy dust, and then she closed with me again and just danced, still erupting in a giggle or two now and then – oh, sweetest, mysterious fandango of life! – her cheek was now warmly tight against mine, so as you doubtless understand, I didn't try pushing for explanations. Mexico, Schmecksico: I felt happily muddled and childlike again.

'May I cut in, please?'

Loath to pull my head away from Terry's, I swiveled an eye sideways and felt sick to my stomach at the sight of Malloy's perfect fiz, and on an unthinking impulse I threw aside couth and all it meant to Cole Porter as I growled, 'You may have the next waltz, Your Grace, but for now I suggest you get mercifully lost!' so that, trapped in his posture of courtliness with maybe a slight touch of heartburn in the mix, Malloy had to smile and tilt his head forward in a mini-bow and then turn with chin up and back straight and ooze away. I am a master of psychology.

Or not. Terry pulled her head away, her face pinking up.

'That wasn't very nice,' she said a wee bit coolly.

'This is true,' I intoned in the same way I would have said, 'Guilty with an explanation,' and then added, 'I just don't like that guy.'

'I don't see why,' Terry said. She leaned her cheek against mine again, and then after a spurty little giggle, she amended, 'On second thought, maybe I do.'

'You do?'

I felt her cheek getting warmer.

'Oh, honestly, I don't know how I could have been so stupid!'

she began; 'Your, ah – friend, is it? – Gregg Malloy—' Here she started to gaspingly chortle as she recounted, 'Well, he was telling me he's writing a novel and—'

'You mean the one that no one's ever seen a word of and when you ask what it's about, Malloy tilts up his chin and he shoots you this mystical stare and says, "Discussing it would fatally dissipate its energies"? I'm so sorry. You were saying?'

She went, 'Hmmm,' and, 'Well, I asked him some things about you and—'

'You asked about *me*?'

'Yes, you, and he said you were a migrant worker.'

'*What*?'

'And that summers you worked here as a waiter' – another giggle that continued in spurts through the rest of her statement – 'but for the rest of the year you were employed at a tuna cannery in Mexico!'

I said, 'I see,' as now a sudden intuition gripped my shoulders and shook me that although she seemed warm and down to earth and not a snob of any shape or dimension, still and all, being the Police Commissioner's daughter, Terry Harnedy's men had to have a certain dignity about them, which was bad, as this made her particularly susceptible to suave phony novelist types like Gregg Malloy, who was staring blue death rays at me from the sidelines, may his eyes become Medusa's and roll up and stare inward.

'Say, my dad's coming up here at the end of the week,' Terry told me as she snuggled in pleasingly close, 'and I'd really, really like you to meet him.' The second 'really' was significant. I slept well.

And woke up to a nightmare when at eight the next morning the thirty-eight guests at my tables came pouring through the dining-room doors like famished trout into a government-stocked pond. No other waiter's guests, mark you. No. Only mine. Most guests usually dribbled in for breakfast anywhere from half-past eight until ten and now where they were and all at once!

Well, I tried. First I went to the Mosers' table where they wanted two oatmeals, one Post Toasties, one Wheaties and two Shredded Wheats, one with whole milk and the other with skim.

'And what's for eggs today?' asked Mrs Moser.

'Only scrambled and boiled, ma'am.'

'Really? No basted?'

'I'm sorry.'

'Oh well, then, Mr Moser and I will have three-minute eggs. And you, Andy?' she asked the two-year-old in the high chair.

'I don't want none!' he bawled.

'Three-minute eggs for him also,' said his mother. 'The older children will have two-minute eggs and for little Chester, a ninety-second job, and he'll have it before his cereal.'

'Is he one of the oatmeals?'

'No, the Wheaties.'

Are you grasping this? We didn't write the orders down, we remembered them!

I saw them glaring at me from over at the Carey table so I went there right away for their orders. 'Mornin', Officer Carey!' I greeted with totally phony relish.

'Mornin' Lofler! Look, just coffee for me to start. And would you bring it right away? I can't see straight 'til I've had my first cup.'

Just then someone at the Kurtz table hollered out for me and seconds later *all* my guests had gotten into the mood and started joining the increasingly testy chorus while two little boys who were red-haired and freckled and no doubt alumni of the old *Howdy Doody Show* on TV started banging their forks and spoons against glasses and plates, at which, smiling reassuringly, I raised an arm and waved my hand all around at my tables as if to say I had everything under control, which was doubtless Custer did with his troops about a minute before the start of the Battle of the Little Bighorn, and then quick like I turned and made tracks toward the swinging doors that led into the kitchen, but as I made to enter I ran into the blistering gaze of Wild Willie Dolan, the center's head waiter, who was just coming out. Red-eyed and bald, except for two elfish tufts of white hair behind his ears and a few scattered single strands atop his head, Dolan folded his arms and gritted hoarsely and pretty much loud enough for everyone to hear, 'What in blue thunder's going on here?' and 'I don't know,' I told Dolan, answering softly like the good book says, but if it 'turned away wrath' I was unable to detect it inasmuch as Dolan now raised his voice even louder. 'If you find it *impossible* to handle your tables,' he threatened, 'we can *always* divert you to the dishwashing unit!' I heard laughter and I sneaked a look around and everyone was staring at us, bemused, and with their eyebrows lifted up. All except one person. Terry. She was staring through a floor to ceiling window at Indian Head Mountain in the near distance with a sort of funny look on her face and I speak not at all of funny *ha ha*.

Unkempt, unhaloed and unstrung, I shambled into my room right after the dinner serving and flopped face-down on my cot. Was I feeling despondent, you ask? Does Charlie Chan like egg foo yung?

From his bunk across from mine, Charlie Price, a seventeen-year-old busboy and my bunkmate, was appraising me from underneath droopy lids. Tall and lanky and about to be a high school senior, he had lusterless, whale-gray, beady eyes and a W. C. Fieldsish bulbous, red-tipped nose.

'So Wild Willie lowered the boom on you,' I heard the kid twanging in his colorless and adenoidal voice.

'Yup,' I answered dismally into my pillow.

'And all your guests came in for breakfast at the same time this morning?'

'I am running out of yups.'

'And of course you have no interest in hearing how come?'

I turned over, sat up, then swung my legs over the side of the cot and, clasping my hands together, I hunched over, head down, and with the whites of my eyes very strongly in evidence as I lifted a glowering stare up to Charlie, assured him, 'The level of my interest is deep.'

Charlie reached into a front flap pocket of his khaki For God and Empire shorts, and slipped out a slightly creased two-by-four inch card that he handed across to me with a quietly portentous, 'Read this.'

I took it and read it. It was one of the center's official announcement cards, with Police Recreation Center engraved in black lettering at the top, while below it was the following typed advisory: PLEASE TAKE NOTICE THAT BREAKFAST WILL BE SERVED TOMORROW MORNING, MONDAY, BETWEEN 8 AND 8:30 ONLY SO THAT NEEDED REPAIRS MAY BE MADE IN THE KITCHEN AND PRIOR TO THE DAY'S LUNCHEON SERVICE.

It was signed 'William Dolan, Director.'

I looked up at Charlie. 'But only *my* guests came in at eight!'

'Forsooth.' This was one of Charlie's two favorite expressions, the second being completely unknown to me, Charlie having explained that it was 'secret' and 'I only like to say it to myself.'

'Maybe only *your* guests got the cards,' Charlie uttered with portent.

'What do you mean?'

'I mean maybe I also saw a certain long-haired waiter slipping them under only certain guests' doors last night.'

I looked off and muttered dazedly, 'I've been juiced!'

'Indeed. And I have even *more* exhilarating news.'

I shifted wary eyes to him. 'Such as what?'

'Like where Terry's going to be at half-past eight, which is down at the spaghetti place with this waiter whose eye you are wishing the Grim Reaper would catch.'

'The spaghetti place?' I gaped at him in horror.

'The spaghetti place.'

Leaning over, I lowered my head into both my hands and quietly murmured, 'Disaster.'

The spaghetti place was a tiny woodframe home not far from the driveway leading up to the center. It was owned by a little old Italian couple who during summer nights turned their dining room into a makeshift Italian restaurant for workers at the center who wanted a break from a diet of Irish stew with 'sautéed shamrock drizzle.' Serving only spaghetti with red sauce, rolls and the cheapest available chianti, the old couple had so tiny a margin of profit that instead of plastic grapes hanging down in the dining room, there were *photos* of plastic grapes. The clear and present danger about the spaghetti place was the romantic walk back on that hibiscus-smelling, apple-tree-lined road, most especially if there happened to be moonlight, plus you heard the nearby splashing of little Bridal Veil Falls as well as songbirds outdoing themselves thinking one night St Francis of Assisi might come by, and even the crickets being discreet deliberately lowering the volume on their chirping. The walk was Creep Malloy's favorite and, by all accounts, sure-fire prelude to Close Encounters of the Most Desired Kind, and tonight, as it happened, the moon was to be full!

I grieved, 'Charlie, I *like* this girl!'

'Good for you. So when it's dark why don't you moose down the hill to the spaghetti place, wait outside, and when Terry and Malloy come out you just say to him, "Cut!" then take Terry by the hand and say you're walking her back.'

'Oh come on!'

'No, it will work, Master,' Charlie intoned with an accent meant to imitate the giant genie in the movie *The Thief of Baghdad*. 'Everyone is knowing this Malloy, he be—'

'Charlie, quit it. I'm just not in the mood.'

'Understood. Look, what I'm saying is Malloy is chicken and will fold like a fan in the hand of a ticked-off geisha.'

'And if he doesn't?'

'Then you bust him in the chops.'

'This is not the way of Zen,' I said. 'Bad. A very bad idea.'

'I give you goodies and you answer me with oriental farts.'

'Farts are morally neutral,' I primly riposted.

I could almost hear Charlie's big bushy eyebrows sickling up as he said to me, '*Why*, Pete? *Why* is it bad?'

'It isn't dignified, Charlie.'

'It isn't *what*?!'

Here I lifted my head and eyed him. 'Chazz, I have read the runes and for numerous reasons that are far too innumerable to enumerate, they are telling me Miss Harnedy feels about dignity in men the way Frank Lloyd Wright must have felt about Euclid,' I finished, omitting mention of how St Simeon Stylites felt about him, and with this I looked back down at my shoes and my woes.

'Me, I wonder how dignified Malloy would look stretched out on the road on his kisser,' I heard Charlie ruminating darkly. 'It wouldn't come to that, though,' he went on; 'Malloy's even scared of Willie Dolan's chihuahua. Hey, Pete, do you remember—'

And abruptly I heard only the sound of silence, and then bedsprings creaking sharply, and then running shoes thumping to the floor, and looking up I saw that Charlie was now sitting on the edge of his cot with his normally narrow slits for eyes that gave him the look of a drowsy cobra now wide and lit up like aurora borealis, as 'Pete!' he declared with excitement, 'You remember the night we walked home from the movies and you scared the living urine out of? You remember?'

Not only did I remember but, being possessed of oracular powers that, had word of them ever reached her, would have sent the storied Sybil at Cumae into deep depression and to reading books like *I'm OK, You're OK*, and almost anything else about self-esteem, I had an instant intuition of what Charlie had in mind, and 'Knock it off!' I very quickly and testily rumbled. 'You're a kid and that is definitely kid stuff out the kazoo!'

'But it'll work, Pete! Don't you see? You've got this gift!'

'I said forget it! It's too childish for words!'

Around a quarter to nine I was on my way down to the spaghetti place with Charlie, locked and loaded and ready to carry out his plan: for the love of Terry Harnedy I was ready to revert to infancy, and even mutter 'Rosebud' any number of times. With the moon obscured by clouds, the darkness was inky black so that Charlie stumbled up against me when the road took a sharp and sudden turn to the left, and there, up ahead and close by, we saw the brightly glowing entry lanterns on each side of the front door, which right away came open as a man and a woman and two little kids came out, and 'Come on!' I whispered huskily at Charlie as I tugged him by his blue and white Brooklyn Prep sweatshirt toward a clump of four-foot-high grass where we hid ourselves, and waited for whoever it was to pass by, which was fairly soon when the door to the spaghetti place opened and a group came out, a man and a woman and two kids. We instantly ducked down our heads, and when the people passed I thought I recognized the voice of the man as a cop named Kurtz, who was a guest at my tables, though I couldn't be absolutely sure inasmuch as when they passed us I was busy plucking thistles off the collar of my T-shirt that were stinging my neck. Then the family's voices faded and we stood up and bided our time as we awaited the main event and now with butterflies beginning to flutter around in my stomach.

'And so how did you come by your gift?' Charlie asked me with this earnest and concerned kind of social-worker interest in his voice like I was Jeanne Val Jean at the age of nineteen and he was building my case file so he could authorize trading in the silver that I'd stolen from a Catholic church for food stamps. 'You've never really told me,' he finished.

'Yes I did, but you've forgotten,' I answered him curtly, a little edgy about what was coming up, 'or is this going to be the sequel to *Of Mice and Men* where you keep asking me to tell you again about the rabbits?'

Charlie quietly said, 'No.'

I said, 'Okay then, for the second time: I first did it after seeing Lon Chaney in the movie *The Wolfman*. Are you happy?'

'It's just so freakily convincing,' Charlie uttered with a note of apprehensiveness in his voice wedged in there along with all the slobbering awe, and at the same time he was searching my face intently as if for signs of hairs sprouting from my ears and from my nose, and then we suddenly crouched lower down into the grass as a door-shaped slab of light was scooped out of the dimness and through it came the heartbeat I was constantly listening for, and behind her that creep, that fraud, that were some horrible misfortune to suddenly strike him I would feel more *Schadenfreude* than all of Germany, Austria, and Lower Saxony could ever hope to contain. The door closed and I couldn't see the hoax-crossed couple any more so I waited for their sauntering footsteps to approach and move past us, along with their warm and semi-intimate laughter and quiet chatter that was making me totally nuts, and when they'd passed clenched my jaw and was totally ready to do this thing that I had to do and that I'd done at the center only once before out of madcap exuberance and for Charlie's edification right after we'd seen *Frankenstein Meets the Wolf Man* at the movie house in nearby Tannersville Village. Yes, the very thing, as someone afterwards recounted, that once caused Baskerville, the center director's giant hound, to hunker down whimpering and trembling with fear, or at the least, most observers agreed, deep unease. Charlie's theory was it might cause a similar and – shall we say undignified? – response in a certain waiter-novelist whose name wasn't Dostoevsky and which I was hoping to turn to mud. So now I gulped down a lungful of cool night air mixed with equal parts brazenness, desperation, and the Red Queen's maddest, most impetuous whim, cupped my hands to my mouth, raised my head, and cut loose with a blood-chilling, ululating howl you would swear was Lon Chaney's movie werewolf cry. The sound of gasps and running feet blended nicely with the end of it, a forlorn and descending, weakening whine that died in my throat with a sorrowful whimper as if the werewolf were having regrets, and as I lowered my hands the full moon had momentarily slipped out from behind the clouds revealing Charlie standing petrified, his eyes wide and shiny and staring and his arms held stiffly at his sides like some acned, teenaged Bronxville zombie, a sight that was mercifully covered over when clouds obscured the moon again and there was darkness. 'Chazz, snap out of it!' I ordered him huskily. He came to and shook his head, and seemed about to make some comment but I shushed him as from somewhere up the road I heard rave reviews, though unfortunately not from Gregg Malloy. It was the Kurtz kids, whimpering and sobbing, and their mother trying to calm them down.

I turned a questioning, rueful look to Charlie.

'Collateral damage,' he said with a shrug.

I said, 'No. Friendly fire.'

'War is war.'

Settled back comfortably on reclining chairs on the center's second-floor patio and looking as loose as two giant boiled noodles, Charlie and I had to struggle not to grin and show the world we were eating our cookies as Malloy, slightly limping, and with Terry beside him, came breathlessly stumbling up the winding stone steps from below and flopped down into one of the chairs facing ours. Charlie and I had raced back to the center along a shortcut in the woods that I knew, where, at Charlie's insistence that we needed insurance, I'd paused to cut loose another call of the wild, before taking our positions barely a minute before.

'Oh man!' Malloy wheezed, still catching his breath.

'Hey, what happened? Sprain your ankle?' Charlie asked him.

'So flipping dark out there!' He reached a hand to the injured ankle, checking it tenderly for soreness and swelling, I suppose, as he added, 'Yeah, I fell. I fell running.'

'You were running? What for?' Charlie asked.

Malloy lifted his head in mild disbelief. '"What *for*"? Didn't you hear that wolf howling out there? It was loud enough to wake the dead!'

Charlie looked incredulous, his forte.

'In the Catskills? Are you serious?' he snorted. 'A *wolf*?'

'Oh well, I heard it too. It was a wolf. I grew up on a ranch in Montana and I know that sound quite well.'

We all turned to the source of the somehow chirpy yet cracked-leather voice. It was a little old lady who was seated with a bigger old lady about eight or ten feet away. 'Blood-curdling, it was. I heard it twice.'

'Oh, me too!' chimed in the bigger old lady, 'and it sounded like a wolf to me as well, a very angry and troubled one.'

I decided it was time for judicious intervention.

I said, 'Maybe it was someone *imitating* a wolf.'

Twisting around in her chair and fixing me gravely with a glittering eye, 'Young man,' the little old lady intoned, 'I assure you nothing human could have made that sound.'

'Yes, that's exactly how we felt about it too,' Gregg Malloy was quick to agree. 'I mean, Miss Harnedy here and I.' He turned to Terry, whose expression, while placid, was somehow strange, as he said, 'It was terrifying, Terry, right?' and turning back to the elderly women, Malloy told them, 'We ran back here as fast as we could!' And then, dear reader, dear patient, understanding heart, my cup, as they say, ranneth over as Terry turned an expressionless stare to Malloy, saying, 'Gregg, I didn't think it was scary at all. The only reason I ran was to try to catch up to you.'

Malloy's face turned the color of a psychedelic lark in a van Gogh wheat field. 'I could use a cold drink,' he said quietly to no one as he lifted his arm and started winding his Christina Rossetti wristwatch as he asked, 'What do you say we check the soda fountain, Terry? They're still open, I think.'

'You go ahead, Gregg, I'll join you in a minute,' she told him.

Suspicious, reluctant and apprehensive, Malloy looked me in the eye and, standing, held my gaze as he answered, 'Sure. Should I order for you?'

'A lemon Coke, please.'

'Okay.'

Malloy turned and, chin up and shoulders back, he walked stiffly and slowly toward the hotel lobby doors as if about to receive some high award, either that or that or a beating by

Turkish prison guards, and then Charlie too stood up with an obviously feigned big stretch and yawn and a muttered, 'Oh well, bedtime for Bonzo, you guys,' as with this he turned and, erratically lurching from side, beetled away toward the staircase that would lead him to the grounds and the waiters' and bus-boys' bunkhouse. 'Goodnight, Charlie!' Terry called after him, at which Charlie raised a languid hand into the air as, not turning, he answered, 'Yeah, yeah.'

Terry turned to appraise me the way Frankenstein must have first looked at his monster, which was doubtless with mixed emotions, especially if when it opened its eyes it looked unhappy.

'Haven't seen very much of you today,' I said blithely, imitating how I thought Cary Grant would have said it, but Terry wasn't buying it as her eyes seemed to narrow with suspicion as she asked me, 'Where were you when that animal cried out?' To which, parrying as skillfully as Scaramouche while his hand is groping frantically behind his back for the wall brick that, when pressed, will open up the secret door to escape, I put on my Max Beerbohm's Lord George Hell saintly mask and said innocently, 'Why?'

'Why?' Terry leaned her face close in to mine with a look of mock wonder and a sly and sardonic smile as, 'Why, Grandma,' she lilted in a Little Red Riding Hood piping, young voice, 'what great big eyes you have!' Then she reached a hand down to a cuff of my trousers, and, plucking something off it, straightened up and pressed it into my hand, which I can tell you really smarted because it was a thistle.

'I'll keep your demented secret, little boy,' Terry told me with an edge of cool contempt in her voice, and with that she stood and headed for the lobby entrance.

I jumped up and called out to her, 'Terry!' and she stopped and turned her head to me so quickly that for an unexpected moment of accidental grace a framing tress of her long, wavy, chestnut hair fell against her cheek. 'Yes?' she said, and in her voice I heard a softly rising note of expectation, or maybe it was hope, or maybe both, but being taken aback, almost stunned, by the moment's revelation, not merely of Terry's physical beauty but of something mysterious and almost otherworldly about her, like a momentary flash of something like remembrance, or even beyond that, recognition, and now there she was before me, standing and waiting for my answer, but in my brain-locked, dream-locked, cow-kicked-by-a-monkey daze, the only words to slip out from my lips were an almost unconscious, numbly murmured, 'Never mind,' and in the instant Terry's eyes lost their light and whatever had caused that light to shine and she turned a crisp heel, striding quickly and entering the hotel lobby, where through the glass façade I saw her heading for the soda fountain and Malloy and very soon she had vanished from my blundering sight.

The next day after breakfast service, I was resting on a patio recliner in a state of geometrically expanding funk. My attempt about an hour before to reignite the *status quo antewolfum* through a humorous appeal to sloppy sentimentality, by pouring a little coffee on Terry's dry cereal while at the same time attempting to evoke *Casablanca*, rasping in Humphrey Bogart's sandpaper voice, 'We'll always have the Bran Flakes and coffee,' which garnered me nothing but an incredulous glare. Bad enough. But now who comes up to me hefting a .22-caliber rifle along with maybe five other cops in a tight little semi-circle behind him who are likewise toting extended heat, but patrolman Herbie 'Depth Bomb' Kurtz, whose kids I might have terrorized the night before. 'You know how to use one of these?' Kurtz asked me, holding up the rifle lest his meaning evade my grasp, and when I nodded and told him that I did he turned and nodded in vindication at his comrades, saying quietly, 'See? I can always tell.' He then turned back to me and asked if I'd be willing to join 'a sort of ad hoc posse,' I believe is how he put it, formed to hunt down and kill 'the freaking goddamn wolf' that was 'scaring the living shit out of people,' citing mothers and wives and little children in particular. I felt a tingling up the back of my neck. Was this real or was it some kind of sting operation?

'Mr Dolan says you've been here lots of summers before,' Kurtz droned on in a monotone like Jack Webb as Sergeant Friday on *Dragnet*, and with a dead shark expression in his close-set eyes, 'and are exceedingly prone to have knowledge of the area and are therefore a valuable posse asset. So whaddya say,' he concluded, 'are you with us?'

I said, 'Sure, but are we doing this now, right this minute?'

'Yes, now,' Kurtz answered me grimly, the twin rotted rosary beads he had for eyes drilling into mine as he went on with a seething intensity, 'and after lunch and after dinner every day and every night until we nail this fucking noisy wolf bastard!'

I said, 'I'll have to be back in time to set up for lunch.'

'*Si, hombre*,' grunted Kurtz, whose precinct was in Little Puerto Rico in the Bronx.

'You know, I think my roommate Charlie would be a really good man to have along,' I suggested, and then mentioning that Charlie went to Xavier. 'It's a Jesuit military high school,' I said to them.

They gave me another rifle for Charlie.

I found him down at the horseshoe pits tossing lazily floating one-and-three-quarters, and after explaining about the posse and all I had to slap him around a little bit on account of he was laughing like a rummed-up kookaburra and I couldn't seem to get him to stop. Also, Sergeant Kurtz was waiting. Charlie sobered up in time for us to join the so-called Search Committee, with all these cops looking somber and frowning just like we were about to nail Dillinger, and I worked it so Charlie and I were paired up, and off we went, heads high, guns loaded and faces barely straight, and it only took to maybe about eleven-thirty as we were boringly feigning searching for the wolf in a field of chest-high wild grass not too far from that center's main building that Charlie dragged us headlong into madness and peril by suggesting that – how did he put it? – 'in all fairness,' I could give the other hunters a 'much keener sense of mission' if I were to cut loose with a werewolf howl!

'You mean *now*?'

'Yes, now.'

'Are you *crazy*?'

Charlie held up an index finger. 'Only one.'

'They might *shoot* us!' I squalled.

'Pete, none of these guys could hit the broad side of a barn with a banjo. They're traffic cops!'

'But *why*, Charlie? Why take the chance?'

Charlie shrugged and said laconically, 'Why not?'

Well, we traded level stares for about six seconds, and maybe we'd been tramping around bareheaded under August sunlight for a bit too long, but then I grinned and dropped my rifle as on a sudden and uncontrollable impulse I raised my head, cupped my hands around my mouth, gulped in a lungful of mischievous air and cut loose with a werewolf cry that would have made even Béla Lugosi blench, and when I'd finished and looked down with a smile at Charlie, he was giving me that same creepy mesmerized stare pretty much the same way that he'd done the night before. I said 'Charlie, relax! It's just me.'

Except it wasn't. Charlie was goggling at Wild Willie Dolan.

Like Dante's vision of hell, the center's dishwashing unit contained levels of wretched degradation and these were known as Scraper, Stacker, and Sorter. The Scraper used a rubber squeegee to push food scraps off the plates that the busboys brought in, while the Stacker arrange the squeegeed plates in wooden racks that were pushed into a steam-driven cleansing device called The Box, and when they came out in a burning-hot state, it was the Sorter's job to pluck them out of the racks and then to sort them and stack them on a broad metal apron that formed an entire side of the unit where the waiters would pick up clean dishes for their pre-meal set-ups. Have we got that? Good. You can't *believe* how good. So by the morning of the second day following the werewolf hunt, and at the end of breakfast service, the cast and crew of the morality play that was to come were in place. Charlie was the Scraper and I was the Sorter, while a teenaged local kid, Jim Clark, was kept in place as Stacker.

'So what's new on the Harnedy front?' Charlie asked me as he squeegeed pasty lima bean fragments from a plate with neither shame nor contrition for our present lowly state, and 'Oh, why hell, she just adores me since I got this new job,' I nearly snarled as I jerked a rack of dishes from The Box. 'My God, the girl can't keep her hands off me, Charlie.'

'Why don't you tell her you're doing research for a novel about dishwashers?'

I was about to make a churlish retort when fairest Fate made its entrance with its usual flair as the swinging doors between the kitchen and the dining room suddenly pushed open and into the kitchen came trooping not only Willie Dolan, flushed and beaming with pride, but also Terry Harnedy and her father, the New York Police Commissioner himself.

'The kitchen layout,' Wild Willie was burbling, his arm up and waving around surrealistically. 'It's all arranged for maximum serving speed. And the dishwashing unit' – he turned and I took a step back toward The Box as he pinned me with a withering glance – 'the dishwashing unit,' he repeated, 'is a mechanized and highly efficient assembly-line operation.' The Commissioner, a gray-haired, kindly looking elf of a guy, just sort of nodded and as Dolan went on with his spiel I thought I ought to look busy, so I picked up a stack of saucers, carried them over to the apron, set them down, and at last had the guts to lift my head and look at Terry, a bit of wasted derring-do, it turned out, since she studiously avoided looking back. Standing stiffly, both her hands in the pockets of a green silk jacket, her attention seeming fixed upon Wild Willie. In her face and in her posture I was reading confusion and uncertainty, even a struggle to keep looking away. Ah, but then came the good and the true part, the part about fate, which doesn't always necessarily have to be crummy, for now in through the swinging doors breezed Malloy, looking jaunty and slicker than snot, and sizing up the situation in a sweeping and condescending glance he swooped over to the apron, pounding on it hard with the flat of a hand you would have thought was meant exclusively for playing the clavichord, and with an air of authority and easy command he said, 'Step it up, Lofler! I need salad plates! Forty! In a hurry! Get cracking!'

Looking past him, I saw that Terry all of a sudden was watching as was everyone else in the kitchen, and, 'Oh, good! A chance to see our team in action now, Commissioner! Beautiful!' brayed Wild Willie as Jim Clark had already pushed a rack of salad plates through The Box, and as soon as they were out I made a show out of casually plucking them out of the rack, and after stacking up a pile of twenty of them, I picked up the darlings with both my hands and, ever eager to serve and please, slowly ambled to the apron humming 'My Way.' Are you with me? Ahead of me? Perhaps. You see, the first time you pick up a dish that's just come out of The Box, what you do is you wince, you yelp, and you drop it, there even being scattered reports of vivid cursing and spewing of profanities. But then after you've worked a day or two as a Sorter, the dishes will only feel lukewarm, even though to all others they will still feel hotter than a pizza oven in Cairo, most especially to a waiter with sensitive hands. Did that thought cross my mind as I casually set down the stack of salad plates on the apron in front of Malloy? Does Dracula have fangs? Oh, my dears, what a glorious, fantabulous, miraculous sight blessed my eyes as I watched Malloy pick up the stack and then drop them, yelping 'YOW!,' and then 'Holy *Freak*!' as every lettuce-loving, tomato-hugging sweetheart of a salad plate slipped from his hands and went crashing and smashing to the floor!

Terry's father looked slightly bemused, while two hairs on Willie Dolan's bald head stood up in shock screaming, 'What in thunderation was *that*?' a non-event since no one listens to inanimate objects. I of course turned a gauging look to Terry, and after a moment or two of uncertainty, she turned and caught my eye and I winked. For a second she looked startled, then a hand flew to her mouth to cover over a spouting giggle of realization and – so help me! – when she turned and saw Gregg Malloy's petrified expression she put a hand to her cheek and burst into that Mercedes Cambridge Tinker Bell laughter. Lads, I thought she'd never stop! And you know what? Now and then when I pick up a towel to help her dry the dishes, the missus gets this impish, twinkly smile in her eyes and starts laughing all over again, just remembering. Once she even leaned her lovely head on my shoulder, saying fondly as she wore a slight smile, 'Pete, I would have loved you even if you'd been the Scraper.'

But of course, that never was the case as Gregg Malloy turned out to be the center's speediest, most talented Scraper ever and I wouldn't have deprived him of his squeegee for the world. Nevertheless, as I am known in some quarters as Firm But Fair Lofler and ever ready to forgive once I've had my revenge, I'll admit that in one respect I had judged Gregg Malloy quite rashly, for as it turns out he really was working on a novel, which I know because it's going to be published this September. I've also had a chance to skim through a copy of the uncorrected bound galleys which came into my hands because of my work, which as it happens is for the *New York Times Sunday Book Review*. Of course, I'm recusing myself from this one, but I suspect Malloy's novel is in for a bit of a bumpy ride. The opening line of his Chapter One is, 'Last night, I dreamt I went to Manderley again.'